I0643054

The
Lagos
Flash Fiction Series

Tolulope Popoola

First published in 2025 in the United Kingdom by

Accomplish Press Ltd, Kemp House, 124 City Road
London EC1V 2NX
www.accomplishpress.com

Paperback Edition
ISBN 978-0-9931771-4-9

Scan the code to buy this book:

This book contains the six titles below:

Memoirs of a Lagos Wedding Planner

Memoirs of a Serial Best Man

Memoirs of a Lagos Baker

Memoirs of a Lagos Taxi Driver

Memoirs of a Lagos Junior Banker

More Adventures of a Lagos Wedding Planner

TABLE OF CONTENTS

Memoirs of a Lagos Junior Banker 305

Meet Onome 306

MEMOIRS OF A LAGOS WEDDING PLANNER

A Collection of Flash Fiction Stories

MEET BISI

I am Bisi, a wedding planner in Lagos. A fixer, a crisis manager, a last-minute problem solver, and sometimes, an emotional punching bag. I ensure that every wedding I plan is a flawless, picture-perfect affair. I handle demanding brides, controlling mothers, philandering grooms, and overzealous in-laws with the patience of a saint and the efficiency of a general leading an army.

But what they don't see, the part that never makes it into the glossy wedding albums is the chaos behind the scenes. The bride who fires her entire bridal train a week before the wedding. The mother-in-law who fakes a heart attack to stop the ceremony. The couple who cancels their wedding because of a scandal that unfolds just days before the big day.

Weddings in Lagos are never just about love. They are political, financial, and sometimes even scandalous affairs. Some are fairy tales, others are cautionary tales, and a few are absolute disasters in disguise.

Through it all, I remain composed, professional, and when necessary, ruthless. Because in my line of work, there's no room for mistakes. A wedding is not just a ceremony; it's a performance, and my job is to make sure the audience only sees the magic.

But behind the magic, there's always a story.

These are mine. Enjoy!

1. Besides The Bride

The wedding reception was going well, and all the guests seemed to be having a great time. Food and drinks were flowing, the hall was just the right temperature, and the lighting was perfect. There had been a minor hitch with the DJ just before the guests started arriving, but being an ever-efficient coordinator, I had it straightened out quickly. As I continued giving orders to the stewards who were going around with trays of desserts, I kept an eye on the proceedings of the reception programme.

The groom was now giving a beautiful speech, in which he thanked his bride for agreeing to marry him, and he professed his undying love and devotion to her. The bride was smiling and blushing as he spoke. As I scanned the hall, I saw the guests transfixed by the groom's words and I overhead a few signs and whispers from the table on my left. One of the young ladies seated was wishing she would find a man that loved her so much.

After the speech, it was time for the couple to have their first dance. The maid of honour carefully helped the bride to step down from the platform, and arranged her dress, so that it wasn't in the way. I paused from my activities and observed the couple as they smiled at each other and swayed to the music. It was so romantic, enough to melt anyone's cynical heart. I hurried into the kitchen to supervise the staff who would soon be serving pepper soup. I thought that if anything was to go wrong with this marriage, it wouldn't be through any fault of mine.

The florist had been late this morning. She had taken too long to get the church venue ready, and was stuck in traffic. My assistant and I had to rush to meet her where she was on, on hired motorbikes, collect the flowers, and take them to the hotel suites where the bride, groom and bridal party were getting ready. There was already a flurry of activity going on in the bride's suite by the time we arrived. The flower girls were getting dressed, the hair stylist was working on the bride's hair, and the make-up artist was working on one of the bridesmaids. The professional photographer was capturing some of the moments, and once in a while, there would be a knock on the door with room service delivering food or somebody else running an errand.

I gave each bridesmaid her bouquet and looked for the maid of honour. She wasn't in the suite with the other girls, so I assumed she was in the bathroom, probably the last to have a shower. I found another bridesmaid and handed over the floral arrangements for the flower girls, then I went across the hall to find the groom's suite.

I knocked on the door of Room 402 and waited for what seemed like an eternity. I was about to go and ask the bride if the groom had moved to a different suite, but then the door opened, and the groom peeped out, still looking a little worse for wear.

"You're not yet dressed!" That was the first thing I said. "Hurry up or you're going to be late to your own wedding."

He hung his head, looking like a little child being scolded for stealing a sweet. "Sorry, I overslept," he mumbled.

"How? Didn't you set your alarm? Here, I brought you the boutonnieres. Where's the best man? Is he not ready either...?"

I stepped into the room, and caught the reflection of a figure behind me in the mirror. I stopped my rant mid-way and turned around. There was the maid of honour in a tiny white towel, with a guilty look on her face.

2. Bridal Train Wreckage

U sually, I enlist the help of the chief bridesmaid and some of the bride's closest friends to help with planning the bridal shower. They are responsible for ensuring it's a surprise to the bride, and everything goes well. They usually know her personally, so they can add touches to the party that will really make the bride smile. Also, I rarely attend the bridal showers myself, but sometimes I send my assistant to make sure that everything goes smoothly.

My current bride was beautiful, fun-loving Caroline, who was based in the US, but had come to Nigeria just for three weeks before her wedding. We had been working together via Skype from the initial consultation, until she landed in Lagos. Although she seemed happy to be getting married, she wasn't keen on doing anything remotely bridal.

"I'm too unconventional," she said to me during one of our video calls.

She told me that she originally wanted to elope with her fiancé and get married with only two witnesses on a small island somewhere in the Caribbean. But her "very popular party-loving family" had dragged her into the whole huge wedding carnival. Her mum had actually called her on the phone crying that "her only daughter wanted to disgrace her in Lagos."

Eventually, her mum managed to convince her and they were happy to pay for everything. Caroline decided to have fun and spend as much as she wanted. She was having a wedding with over a thousand guests that she didn't know, so she decided to make all her old friends her bridesmaids so that she could have some familiar faces with her.

A week before the wedding was the bridal shower. I told my assistant to go and oversee everything, because I had to meet with a vendor.

Later that evening she called me from the venue, a nice restaurant in Victoria Island. As soon as I answered my phone, I could hear several female voices shouting in the background.

"Ma? We have a problem. The manager of the restaurant has kicked us out!"

"What's going on?" I asked. "Is everything alright?"

"No ma," she replied. "The ladies were drinking, and playing games, and it was all going well. Until they played a truth or dare game. And the bride confessed that she had slept with two of her friend's boyfriends!"

Great.

I tried not to laugh and feigned boredom. "Then what happened?" I asked.

"A huge fight broke out among the ladies here, and there's been ugly names and slaps thrown around. The staff and I tried to calm things down but things escalated and a couple of drinking glasses fell and got broken!"

Sigh.

"Okay, where is Caroline? What's happening now?"

"Three of her friends have left, but the others are still here and the fight is still going on."

"Can you give the phone to her now, please?"

"Yes ma."

I heard some more angry voices, and soon Caroline came on. I put on my firmest voice and said to her:

"Listen, I heard there's been an argument, I need you to leave that place now and go home. I will call you tomorrow morning. Is that okay?"

She put up a feeble protest, but eventually, she gave up and said "Yes."

I gave my assistant a few more instructions and hung up. Sigh. More mess for me to clean up so close to the wedding.

When I spoke to Caroline the next morning, she told me that she had basically ruined all her friendships with all the ladies on her bridal train except one.

"What a mess! My fiancé has eight groomsmen, and I have only one bridesmaid left! What are we going to do?" she wailed.

I thought quickly. "We're going to hire them."

"Huh? Hire bridesmaids?" She repeated.

"Yes. Leave it with me, and I will get back to you in a few hours."

"Okay, thank you." Caroline sniffed and hung up.

I started making calls.

A week later, no one could tell from the beautiful line-up smiling for the photographs that the bride was surrounded by strangers. Result!

3. Mummy Meltdown

The couple I was working with for this wedding had been away from Nigeria for a very long time. They both left Nigeria and moved to the US when they were teenagers, and they had been together since they met during their college years. When we started planning the wedding, they told me that neither of them had met their prospective in-laws. They didn't even remember some of their own extended family and other relatives.

As far as Kola and Vivian were concerned, they were already married, since they had gone to register at their local authority and signed their marriage certificate. But their parents had insisted that things won't be complete until the two families got together in Nigeria, so they decided to come home briefly. As soon as they arrived at Lagos airport, the bride called me, and we started the last minute plans in full swing.

The day after their traditional ceremony, which I was glad had gone without a hitch, the bride called me and asked to remove about thirty people from the guest list. I was surprised and asked what was going on.

"It's my fiancé's mother. She's unbearable."

"Hmmm. Tell me what's been going on."

She told me that her fiancé's mum had been getting on her nerves since their first meeting. The woman had complained that the bride didn't greet her properly and she looked "proud". Earlier that morning, the groom's mother insisted on taking her to their church for a pregnancy test, and approval of her wedding dress. Vivian said she felt insulted at the suggestion of the pregnancy test, and even more enraged when she was told that her wedding dress did not conform to the church's standards. The last straw was when the minister told her that they could not use their personalised wedding vows that she and her fiancé had written. Mother-in-law said they had to follow the rules, or she would not come to the wedding. To her shock, the couple had both said that was fine, her presence was optional.

I thought quickly. This could be tricky.

"But Vivian, are you sure? Is that how you want you and your husband to remember your wedding, with his mum absent?"

"I'm fed up with these nonsense rules and attitude she's been giving me!"

"I understand," I said. "It's two days to your wedding, you're feeling stressed and emotions are high. But try to stay calm and speak to your fiancé. Some things won't matter after the wedding, but I wouldn't want you to burn bridges because of small issues."

I spoke to her for a bit more and calmed things down. She promised to call me back with an update the next day. In the meantime, I called my back-up team to be ready, in case there was actually drama on the big day.

Thank God I was prepared.

On the wedding day, the mother of the groom behaved in a despicable manner. Half-way through the church ceremony, she tried to cause a scene by faking heart problems. When that didn't give her attention, she sulked and refused to participate in anything else. At the reception, just as the couple were having their first dance, she suddenly ran to the dance floor, wedged herself between them and clung to the groom and started crying. The bride was shocked and her jaw dropped, the groom froze and a few gasps were heard around the room.

I observed for a few seconds, and signalled to my assistant. We marched to the dance floor and pulled Mama off the groom and took her to a seat. My assistant gave her a drink and everything went smoothly for the rest of the night.

Later, the bride called to thank me as they were leaving for their hotel.

"What was in that drink you gave my mother-in-law?" she asked.

"Trade secret," I said with a big grin, "...for calming down drama queens."

She smiled. "You're a star!"

So I am.

4. No Intervention

Alot of my work relies on having excellent vendors. People that are professional, reliable and trustworthy. I've been working with Ogechi, my friend and make-up artist for three years. Whenever I take on a bride-to-be as a client, I always refer them to Ogechi because she is great at what she does, and she's a real people person. She goes out of her way to make sure the client is happy with her work, and she also helps me with making sure the wedding day activities go smoothly.

This weekend, we are working on a high society wedding. The bride is the daughter of a billionaire businessman and well-known philanthropist. Her mother is the owner of a very successful chain of restaurants, popular in Lagos and Abuja. The groom is the son of a governor, and fashion designer. Talk of the impending marriage has been in the lifestyle magazines, blog and social media for months. Everyone who is everyone in the society is coming to this wedding, so I know that my assistants and I, plus all our vendors have to be at the top of our game.

I'd met the bride and her mum during the planning stages and I thought they were both very lovely people. Even though they were wealthy, the bride has a sweetness and innocence about her that was very endearing. She was humble and polite, and a pleasure to work with. I hadn't met her fiancé but I sure hoped he realised what a beautiful person he was getting married to and he appreciated her.

On the day of the traditional engagement ceremony, Ogechi and I arrived at the bride's parent's house where the ceremony was being held. I went to coordinate the seating arrangements and serving points in the huge garden, while Ogechi went to start working on the bride. A few minutes later, my phone rang.

"Hello?" It was Ogechi.

"Please come upstairs. Come to the bride's room."

I went upstairs, and found my way to the bride's room where she was getting dressed.

"Ogechi, what's the matter?"

She turned to me and whispered. "The bride has bruises on her face. She said her fiancé hit her last night during an argument."

My heart sank. I went over to where the bride sat on her bed, crying.

"Ronke? Is this true?"

She nodded in-between her sobs.

I rarely get emotional, but I hugged the bride and got her to stop crying after a few minutes. I asked her if she still wanted to go ahead with the marriage, and she said yes. Ogechi and I exchanged a look, but we shrugged. I went to look for the bride's mother, while Ogechi said she would try to cover the bruises as well as she could with make-up.

I found the mother of the bride, she was already gorgeously dressed and was posing for photos with other members of the family. There was a photographer from one of the high society magazines there already, and I knew that those photos would be in the next magazine's edition. I excused myself and called the bride's mum aside to explain what happened. Her bright smile disappeared as I spoke to her.

She sighed slowly and shook her head.

"But he said he would stop hitting her after the last time," she said, avoiding looking at me directly. "Let me see what I can do."

She hurried off in the direction of the bride's room. I was torn between following her and returning to the garden. After a few minutes, I decided to return to work.

The next time I saw the bride, she had been transformed. She was dressed in gorgeous aso-oke, with beautiful jewellery and accessories. Ogechi had done a great job with her make-up, and there wasn't a hint of any sadness on her face. She was smiling for the photographers, and she looked happy, relaxed, even excited to be getting married. I saw her dance into the garden with her friends, join with the groom, and perform all the necessary rites of the engagement ceremony. I saw them kiss, and smile at each other. I saw them dance all evening and leave the house later, hand-in-hand in a brand new car, one of the gifts they had just been given.

On the morning of the white wedding ceremony, Ogechi called me again.

"This time, the bride's eye is swollen and half-shut. I don't think make-up can fix this."

5. Repeat Affair

Sometimes, when I work with a really cool, lovely couple, we end up becoming friends. After all, I'm communicating with them several times for months, leading up to their big, special day. I'm offering advice, support and maybe even a few relationship tips along the way.

I had a lovely rapport with Tade and Oyin, a couple I planned their wedding a while ago. During the planning process, they were great fun to work with. They didn't really argue, their ideas were in sync. They showed up on time for our meetings, they trusted my professional opinion on the things they asked advice on. Their wedding was amazing too, even if I say so myself. It was the talk of the town, for all the right reasons. Their photos were all over social media for months, and I was proud to know them, and make their wedding dreams come true. I even marked their wedding day in my calendar, as one of my success stories. After the big day, we kept in touch for a bit. Oyin wanted to plan an event for her office Christmas party, and she gave me the contract. I still saw them a few times after that, and they seemed to be settling well into married life.

This morning, I saw a notification on my phone that it was their wedding anniversary! I still had their phone numbers, so I decided to call them to wish them a happy one year anniversary.

I tried Oyin's number first. It wasn't going through. Something about the number not being recognised. I decided to try Tade instead. He could help me pass on my regards to his wife.

I called the number I had for him. Thankfully, it rang.

"Hey!" He picked up, sounding happy. "Great to hear from you. How are you doing?"

"I'm good," I replied. "I was looking at my calendar, remembered the date and decided to call you guys."

"Oh? What's the date?"

"Today is the 27th, don't tell me you forgot your anniversary?" I was shocked. Usually, couples make a big deal of their first year of marriage.

"Oh...er.. actually...er..." He paused.

"What's your excuse, hmmm?"

"Er, that marriage to Oyin is over..."

What?

"...she's even based in the US now."

I was stunned into silence for a few seconds. Why, how? Tade and Oyin, the hot couple, the beautiful marriage, over so soon? I was still trying to process the information when he continued:

"Actually, I was going to call you. I'm engaged now and I want you to plan my next wedding…"

I snapped out of my reverie. What was he asking?

"I'm sorry, the line is no longer clear. I'll call you back."

I hung up. Human beings will never cease to amaze me.

6. The Almost Wedding

My client and I had been planning this wedding for months. It was going to be a big affair, attended by the elite in society. Pearl had been dating her fiancé for five years, and she kept telling me how much he loved her. She told me the story of how they met and how he proposed to her on the most amazing trip in Thailand. The only problem they had was that some of her family members didn't really like him. So he was willing to spend a lot of money on the wedding ceremonies to impress her family.

When I told her my fees, she didn't even flinch. She paid my deposit straight away, and we got started with the planning. I was happy to oblige and indulge her, since she wanted no expense spared. So we ordered the biggest, most glamourous engagement and wedding cakes. Her jewellery was second to none. Her outfits were top-of-the line designers, right down to her accessories. We hired the best make-up artist, the best hair stylist, the best DJ, the best caterers, the best hotel and everything.

Today, we were meeting up for lunch, to have one of our last meetings before the big day. We were sitting in a lovely restaurant in Lekki, facing the waterside. It had a lovely atmosphere, a great menu and a lovely view of the lagoon. Normally, I would be relaxed in such a place, but today I'm not. The wedding is ten days away, and planning is at fever pitch. The reception is taking place at a very exclusive venue, and I have been asked to provide a final guest list for the table seating arrangements. I notice that Pearl is not her usual excited self today. She's distracted and barely listening to me. She keeps checking her phone every two minutes. I'm curious and also slightly annoyed but I don't want to pry. Instead, I continue with our business discussions.

"So please email me a final guest list, with the names of everybody who has sent in their RSVP," I said. "We should also provide for at least thirty extra guests, knowing how our people are…"

"Hmmm, okay." She sighed, and picked up her phone again.

I ticked off a few items off my notepad, and moved on to the next thing.

"You have your spa appointment next Monday, and your final dress fitting the day after."

She's frowning at her phone screen, ignoring me.

"Pearl? Are you listening?"

Finally, she looks up. "My sisters are up to something."

I paused to let her continue.

"They said I should expect a phone call soon." She looks at me, and snaps back into the present. "Sorry, you were saying?"

"We're finalising your itinerary for next week," I said, trying not to lose patience.

"Oh right, yes. My hair appointment is when?"

I was about to reply when her phone rang, and she jumped.

"Hang on, let me take this."

She moved away from the table and picked up the call. I could hear small bits of her side of the conversation:

"Hello? Yes... this is Pearl...yes... who is this?.... no... really?...alright...I'll meet you there in twenty minutes."

She hurried back to the table, grabbed her bag and her things, and said, "I have to go. I'll call you tonight."

I shrugged, paid for lunch and left the restaurant.

Later that evening, I got a text message: "My fiancé has impregnated someone. The wedding is cancelled."

And this is why I always ask for a seventy percent deposit upfront.

7. The Appointment

I had received a referral from a friend, which is a great endorsement of my work. With all businesses like mine, referrals are a life blood. When a client likes your work enough to refer you to their friends and family, you have to make sure you meet and surpass their expectations.

So it was to my annoyance and embarrassment that I was running late to my first meeting with the new couple I was going to be working with. A previous client had introduced me to her best friend, who, from all indications, was a high net worth client. She didn't want to have our first meeting at her house or in my office, but at an expensive classy hotel, in Victoria Island, instead. If I was going to make a good first impression, I needed to start by getting to our appointment on time.

However, Lagos traffic was not letting that happen. There had been an accident on Third Mainland Bridge, and there was a long line of cars stretching back the whole length of the bridge, as far as my eyes could see, crawling. I looked at my watch and cursed under my breath. If I didn't get out of this traffic in the next thirty minutes, I was going to be late.

As I was muttering under my breath, a space opened up in front of my car, and just as I was inching forward, another driver cut into my lane. I stepped on my brake and honked my horn fiercely. I was not in the mood for the crazy Lagos driving today.

Slowly, the traffic began to ease up. I switched lanes, went past the driver that had cut into my lane moment before and yelled something rude to him, before moving on. He scowled at me, but he was on the phone, and I didn't wait for him to react.

I arrived at my appointment fifteen minutes late. My prospective bride was already waiting at the hotel's restaurant. She had ordered juice and cocktails. I rushed inside with my folder, trying to sound confident, not as flustered as I felt.

"Hello Toke," I said, offering my hand. "Sorry I'm late."

She rose up to meet me, and we shook hands. "It's okay. I was speaking with my fiancé not too long ago, he said there's a lot of traffic. He's also on his way here."

"Okay that's great. Should we wait for him?" I asked.

"Yes, he said he's less than five minutes away..." she looked up and smiled. "There he is now..."

I turned around to say hello, and froze.

The groom was the guy I had been rude to in traffic!

8. The Second Almost Wedding

I rarely attend the church part of the weddings I work on. There's usually so much to do at the reception venue, so I'm needed there. I usually have my trusted assistant cover the proceedings at the church, while I supervise the setting up at the reception. There are an endless number of things that could go wrong at the last minute, with the décor, sound, lighting, seating arrangements and so on. And anyway, as long as the couple say "I do" at the right time, almost everything else can be overlooked in church.

I had been extra prepared for this wedding reception. My team and I started putting the hall together since the night before, and we were nearly ready, with a couple of hours to spare before guests were due to start arriving. The only thing we were waiting for, was the lady who was still setting up the cake. It was a complicated affair, being a 9-tier cake with floral arrangements, lights, and a small fountain. I decided that since the church ceremony was only a short drive away, maybe I should go and see that things were alright.

These clients of mine were really cool, and I had enjoyed working with them. It was one of those rare situations where I could honestly say that the groom adored his bride. He would do anything for her. He was a poet, and a romantic at heart. Throughout the planning process, he had done many thoughtful things, and added little gestures to their day, like the beautiful presentation he had put together to show during the reception. I looked at my watch. Maybe if I hurried, I could catch them saying their vows. The groom had decided he wanted to write personalised vows and I wanted to hear them.

As I got near the church, I noticed there was a huge crowd outside. That was odd, I thought. The service should have started already. There was a small commotion going on. One woman was shouting, it appeared a couple of other ladies were trying to calm her down. The rest of the crowd were huddled in little groups whispering. I parked my car and quickly scanned the crowd for my assistant. I saw her talking to two people who I guessed were relatives of the groom, from the colour of their attire. She spotted me, and looked relieved, then she excused herself.

"What's going on, Tinu?" I asked.

"I was just about to call you. The bride just left."

"Left? What do you mean?"

She looked around and spoke in a low tone: "The bride's ex-boyfriend showed up just before the service was about to start, and declared that he wanted her back. She said sorry to her husband-to-be and took off!"

"What! Where is the groom?"

"He is over there," she pointed. I looked in the direction she was pointing. The groom sat on a chair, frozen, staring into space. He didn't seem to notice that the priest was talking to him.

"I think he's still in shock," Tinu said.

I nodded. My attention was drawn to the hysterical woman. She was the mother of the bride. She kept saying, "This girl has disgraced me!"

Tinu said, "What happens now?"

My question exactly. What happens when the bride absconds from her own wedding?

Well, the mother of the bride wept. The guests went to the reception, ate, drank and gossiped all the way home.

And I got paid. Again, this is why I always ask for a seventy percent deposit upfront.

9. The Sponsors

I was meeting my prospective client for the first time. Usually, I meet brides-to-be with a friend, a sister or their mum. So this meeting was unusual because the bride came to my office with her uncle.

We talked about the dates they were looking at, what kind of wedding she wanted, locations, their budget, the guest list and so on. After she explained what her vision for her wedding was, the bride seemed happy to go with all my suggestions for vendors. Her uncle didn't have any objections either. This was looking good. At the end of the meeting, I was happy to take her on as a client, and we set a date for our next meeting.

But as time went on, and we started planning the wedding, I noticed something. She was asking me to split the payments for the vendors into different amounts, and send them to different people. One uncle was paying for food. One man who was her dad's friend was paying for the DJ and live band. Another older cousin was paying for drinks. Within two weeks, I was having to deal with several men paying for different things.

One day, I met with her and her fiancé. They were talking about paying for their hotel accommodation, when she mentioned that one of her uncles had given her money to pay for a hotel for eight nights. Her fiancé was surprised.

"Which uncle is that?" He asked.

"Uncle Shola, you don't know him," she replied. "He's based in Abuja."

"I thought it was Uncle Mike that was based in Abuja. The one who got you a new car two months ago."

"Nooo, Uncle Mike is in Lagos here, but he travels a lot. He's out of the country now but he said he'll try to be back for the wedding."

"You have many generous uncles," he said. "How come I've never met them?"

"Sweetie, they're happy for me that I'm getting married. Don't worry you'll meet them on the wedding day," she responded.

I was watching with interest, but I didn't say anything and we carried on talking about the plans.

On the day of the traditional engagement, just before the ceremony was about to start, I was running around coordinating, when one of the ushers came to me.

"The bride says she needs to talk to you urgently!"

I turned around. "Why?"

"I don't know ma."

I sighed and went to look for the bride. She was in a separate room from the main hall, where she was supposed to wait until she was called to dance in with her train.

I met her frowning and looking worried.

"Hello Bimbo, what's the matter?"

"Sorry, I should have told you this before now. Look at this man." She showed me a photo on her phone. "Please don't let him sit with my side of the family."

"But that's your uncle." I said. The photo was of the man she came to my office with, on our first meeting.

She looked at me, and rolled her eyes. "He's not my uncle. He's just sponsoring my wedding."

"Hmmm?"

"He's my *sugar daddy*. All the other uncles paying for the wedding are his friends. He just called me now and said he wants to sit down with my family, but I trust that you won't let that happen."

"I see. So you want me to stop him from coming to the wedding he's paying for?"

"No, just quickly create another table for him and his crew, not my side or the groom's side. You know, somewhere neutral."

I shook my head and did as I was told.

Later, I watched as the bride and groom danced the night away, surrounded by her "uncles" spraying them lots of money.

10. When In-Laws Misbehave

This wedding was turning out to be more work than I had envisaged. After the first two meetings with the bride and her mother, when they were prospective clients, I had assumed they wanted a simple, straight-forward ceremony. But as the wedding day drew closer, the bride became more and more demanding, and started to change everything.

First, she wanted a different venue, something grander than the one we had agreed on, and I had paid a non-refundable deposit. Then she wanted to change the menu for the reception. Then she changed her mind about the décor and the flowers, among many other things. Even her mother called me several times, asking why I did something, which we had previously agreed on. By the time the day finally arrived, I was tired, and I couldn't wait for it to be over.

Thankfully, the day had gone without a hitch. It was evening now, and the formal part of reception would soon be coming to an end. I called my assistant and told her that it was time for us to start distributing souvenirs and gifts for the guests to take home. She nodded and went off to the storage room

A few minutes later, she came back to me.

"Ma, the door is locked. Please give me the key."

"Which door?" I asked.

"The door of the storage room."

"I didn't lock it, and I don't have the key," I said. "Let's go and ask at the hotel's customer service desk."

We got to the desk and I told the lady that I needed to open the storage room.

"We've got boxes of gifts and souvenirs in there, and we need to get them out urgently," I explained. "I don't know who locked the door, but we need to get in."

"Right away ma."

She fished out a set of spare keys from one of the drawers and we went back to the storage room, where she tried to open the door.

"I can't open it," she said after trying a few times. "It's locked from the inside!"

Worried about the safety of our goods, my assistant and I started knocking the door loudly.

"Who is in there? Open up! We need to get in!"

We heard a scramble and a scuffle, and the sound of boxes being turned over. I was getting frantic. I shouted again:

"Open this door right now! Otherwise we will break in!"

I was about to ask the receptionist to go and get someone to break down the door, when it opened up, and we saw the mother of the bride and the father of the groom half-dressed and looking very guilty indeed.

"Oh!" My assistant gasped.

I stifled a smile. "Sorry ma, sorry sir. We want to take the souvenirs. Let's give you a few minutes."

At the end of the night, I got a notification from my bank. I had been paid very handsomely by the mother of the bride. More than enough to compensate me for the extra hassle.

MEMOIRS OF A SERIAL BEST MAN

A Collection of Flash Fiction Stories

MEET CJ

My name is Chijioke Obi, but everyone calls me CJ. I'm thirty-four and single, and no, I don't know when I'm getting married, so please stop asking. What I do know is that I'm damn good at weddings. Not my own, obviously, but everyone else's.

In the last seven years, I've been a groomsman more times than I can count and the best man at twelve weddings. If there's a wedding crisis, from missing rings to runaway brides, chances are I've seen it, fixed it, or noted it down in my memoir: *Memoirs of a Serial Best Man*.

Don't let the tux fool you, I'm not here for the free jollof rice or the champagne. I'm here to make sure the groom makes it to the altar, the bride doesn't cry (unless it's happy tears), and no one gets punched by a drunk uncle. Weddings are messy, unpredictable, and full of drama, and I wouldn't have it any other way.

Now, let me tell you how it all goes wrong…and how I make it right.

1. The Best Man's Kit

When my friend Tunde asked me to be his best man, I wasn't surprised. After all, I've been a groomsman more times than I can count. I could tie a bow tie while blindfolded and handle an overzealous mother-in-law with my eyes closed. What I didn't expect at Tunde's wedding was to become the hero of the day because of something as random as a tube of superglue.

The day started calmly enough. We were getting ready at the groom's house in Victoria Island. From there, we would transition to the venue for the traditional wedding ceremony. Tunde was a bundle of nerves. He paced the room while the groomsmen sipped cognac. I was putting on my shoes when the messenger from the tailor burst in, sweating profusely.

"There's a problem," he stammered, holding up Tunde's agbada. The intricate embroidery along the shoulder had come loose, dangling awkwardly like a broken wing.

Tunde's eyes widened. "What do you mean *problem*? I'm getting married in two hours!"

"Sorry sir," he said, with fear in his eyes. "The fabric hooked a nail…"

I sighed. In my years of being a best man, I've learned that weddings are never without chaos. I reached into my emergency kit (yes, I carry one, don't judge me) and pulled out a small tube of super glue.

"Hold still," I said, taking the agbada from the driver. I inspected the damage, and within minutes, I had the embroidery glued back into place.

When Tunde saw himself in the mirror, he exhaled with relief. "CJ, you're a lifesaver."

The ceremony went smoothly. We all danced in with Tunde and joined him to *dobale* (prostrate on the floor to beg the bride's parents to give us their daughter). Then the reception began, and Tunde gave his speech, thanking everyone for attending. His new wife leaned over to whisper something in his ear. He paled, turned to me, and mouthed, "The embroidery is coming undone again!"

I signalled the DJ to play a high-energy song and rushed Tunde backstage, where I worked my magic again. As the music covered our disappearance, I reminded myself why I carry that emergency kit: weddings are unpredictable, but a serial best man like me always stays ready.

2. The Bridesmaid Confession

Some weddings are chaos because of the vendors. Others are chaos because of the bridal party. This wedding was chaotic because of both.

My friend Ebuka begged me to be his best man, promising that everything would be smooth. He lied. By the time I arrived at the hotel for the morning prep, the bride was in tears. Why? Her makeup artist was MIA, and the caterer had also called to say they were running late.

But the real trouble didn't start until I ran into a bridesmaid named Tinuola.

I was standing outside the church with the other groomsmen, waiting for the bride's grand arrival, when Tinuola approached me with a sheepish smile on her face. "CJ, can I tell you something?"

"Sure," I said, adjusting my tie.

She hesitated, then blurted out, "I used to date Ebuka."

I nearly choked on the gum I was chewing. "Wait, *what?*"

"Yeah, for two years. We broke up, but I didn't expect to see him again until I found out he was marrying my cousin."

I glanced at Ebuka, who was standing near the entrance of the church. "Does your cousin know she is marrying your ex?"

She shook her head. "I didn't tell her."

"Did Ebuka tell her?"

"I don't think so."

"Why are you telling me now?" I asked, trying to remain calm.

"I just thought you should know... in case something happens."

I felt like I was standing on a ticking time bomb. I wanted to scream, but I knew better. Weddings have a way of amplifying emotions, and the last thing we needed was a blow-up during the ceremony.

"Nothing will happen," I said firmly. "Today isn't about you or the past. Let's focus on making this wedding a success."

She nodded, and to her credit, she stayed out of trouble. But later, when I caught her making heart eyes at Ebuka during the first dance, I knew this wouldn't be the last I'd hear of it.

3. The Runaway Groom

There are certain red flags you learn to spot when you've been a best man as often as I have. The groom sweating through his suit before the ceremony is one. Pacing around the hotel suite while checking his phone every five minutes is another. But when Kunle locked himself in the bathroom and refused to come out, I knew we had crossed into full-blown panic mode.

"Kunle! Bro, open the door," I said, knocking gently.

"No." His voice was muffled. "I'm not coming out."

Behind me, the groomsmen exchanged worried glances. One of them, Jide, leaned in. "Is he crying?"

I gestured for silence by placing a finger to my lips. "Kunle, you're getting married in two hours. Adesuwa is already on her way to the church."

"I know!" His voice cracked. "That's the problem. I can't do this."

Ah, cold feet, the enemy of every groom. I took a deep breath and dismissed the other groomsmen.

"Go downstairs and keep the guests entertained. I've got this."

They shuffled out reluctantly, leaving me alone with the crisis.

"Kunle, it's CJ," I said softly. "I get it. Weddings are stressful."

He sniffled. "You don't understand."

"Try me."

Silence. Then, the door creaked open slightly, and Kunle's tear-streaked face peeked out. I pushed the door fully open and stepped inside, sitting on the edge of the bathtub while Kunle slumped against the sink.

"I'm scared, CJ," he admitted, his voice barely above a whisper. "What if I'm not good enough for her? What if I mess this up?"

I looked at him, this 6-foot-3 tall man who could negotiate million-dollar deals for his company but was currently reduced to a nervous wreck over saying "I do."

"Kunle, let me tell you a secret." I leaned in. "I had cold feet once."

He blinked, surprised. "You did?"

"Yep. Three years ago. I was the groom, and I locked myself in the bathroom just like you." I chuckled at the memory, though it wasn't funny at the time. "I thought marrying Nneka would be the biggest mistake of my life. Spoiler alert: I didn't go through with it."

Kunle's eyes widened. "You called off your wedding?"

"Yep. But that's not the point. The point is, I was scared because I knew deep down that she wasn't the one. You? You're scared because you love Adesuwa so much that you don't want to mess it up. There's a difference."

He wiped his face with a towel. "What if I do mess it up, though? Marriage is forever."

"No one's perfect, Kunle. You'll mess up sometimes, and so will she. But you'll work through it, together. That's what matters."

For a moment, he said nothing. Then he let out a shaky laugh. "CJ, you're supposed to be the reckless guy, not the one giving deep advice."

"Even reckless guys have wisdom," I said with a wink. "Now, are you ready to marry the love of your life, or should I tell Adesuwa to find a new groom?"

He chuckled and stood up straighter. "I'm ready."

"Good. Let's get you cleaned up before someone declares you missing."

We got Kunle into his tailored suit, adjusted his tie, and sprayed him with enough cologne to mask any remaining stress. By the time we arrived at the church, the guests had no idea anything had gone wrong.

Later, Kunle stood across from Adesuwa, his voice unwavering. When he said, "I promise to love you forever," I knew he meant it.

Later, at the reception, Kunle pulled me aside. "Thanks for saving me today."

"That's what best men do," I said, patting him on the back. "But if you ever lock yourself in a bathroom again, I'm charging you by the hour."

We both laughed, and I thought about how close he had been to walking away from this moment. Weddings are unpredictable, but sometimes, all it takes is a little push from the right person to get things back on track.

As the party kicked off and the DJ blasted Burna Boy's latest hit, I grabbed a drink and watched Kunle and Adesuwa twirl across the dance floor. I couldn't help but smile.

Another wedding saved.

4. The Difficult Mother of the Bride

The wedding was supposed to be smooth. Everything had been rehearsed, the bride looked stunning, and even the notoriously picky caterer was ahead of schedule. I was convinced I'd make it through this one without any drama.

Then the mother of the bride happened.

I should've known there was trouble brewing when she showed up wearing a red and gold *gele* the size of a satellite dish. You don't wear something like that unless you're planning to steal the show. Her aura was that of a woman who always got her way, and unfortunately for me, her target was the wedding program.

I was standing near the music booth, finalizing the entrance music, when she appeared beside me, clutching a program pamphlet as though it had personally offended her.

"CJ," she said sweetly, the type of sweetness that comes before a storm. "There's a mistake in the schedule."

I glanced at the pamphlet. "What kind of mistake, Ma?"

Her smile tightened. "The couple's first dance is listed before my surprise presentation."

Ah. There it was. The dreaded surprise presentation was something I had been specifically warned against during the planning stage.

"With all due respect, Ma, the first dance is very important to the bride and groom," I said, maintaining my polite tone. "It's what they're most looking forward to."

She waved her hand dismissively. "This is their day, yes, but they wouldn't be here without me, abi? My presentation must come first. I have videos prepared, and my sisters are waiting too."

I sighed internally. "What kind of presentation is it?"

"A 30-minute tribute to their family legacy. Very important."

I nearly choked. "Thirty minutes? Madam, please, that's too long."

She narrowed her eyes. "Are you trying to say my family history isn't important?"

"Of course not, Ma." I was sweating. "But this timing..."

"Change it," she interrupted firmly.

I had to think fast. If I gave in, the entire flow of the wedding would collapse. I could already imagine the bride's face if I delayed her first dance.

"Ma, let me propose a compromise," I said, trying to sound confident. "We'll keep the first dance, but we'll reduce your presentation to 10 minutes and play highlights. The full version can be shown during dinner on a large screen."

She looked at me, contemplating my offer. "You're sure everyone will see the full video?"

"Yes, Ma. They won't miss a single moment."

Her eyes softened. "Okay, CJ. You're lucky I like you."

I exhaled, grateful for the small miracle.

The first dance went off beautifully. As the couple swayed to their song, the bride beamed, completely unaware of the battle I had just fought to preserve her dream moment. During dinner, the mother-in-law's presentation played as promised, and she received all the applause she could ever want.

Afterward, she found me by the dessert table. "You handled that well," she said, handing me a plate of puff-puff. "Next time, don't argue with me."

"Noted, Ma," I said with a grin, but in my head, I was already drafting a new rule for my memoir: *Beware of surprise presentations.*

5. Speech Gone Wrong

I had given so many best-man speeches that I could practically deliver them in my sleep. But this one? This one would haunt me forever.

It was my friend Dipo's wedding. The vibe was perfect. The décor was luxurious, champagne was flowing, and there was a highlife band that had the guests dancing even before the main course was served. As I walked to the stage for my speech, I was confident. Too confident.

"Good evening, everyone," I began, grinning at the sea of expectant faces. "I'm CJ, and I've known Dipo since our university days, which means I have enough embarrassing stories to write a book."

Laughter rippled through the crowd, and I smiled, encouraged. I launched into the story of how Dipo accidentally proposed to a waitress while drunk one night—a safe, funny anecdote that wouldn't get me in trouble.

But then I made the fatal mistake of going off-script.

"Of course, that wasn't the first time Dipo got into trouble over a woman," I said, chuckling. "Remember that time in Abuja when you spent the night on the balcony after your girlfriend found you texting someone else?"

The room fell silent.

I blinked, confused. What had I said wrong? Then I saw the bride's face—frozen in shock, her fork clutched mid-air. Oh no.

Dipo's current wife had never heard this story, and judging by the murderous look she was now giving him, she wasn't taking it well.

Dipo tried to salvage the situation. "Babe, it was before I met you—"

But she wasn't having it. She stood up, knocking over her chair, and stormed out of the hall.

I wanted to crawl under the table. The groom's mother glared at me, and the groomsmen stared at their plates, pretending not to exist.

Later, as Dipo passed by me backstage, he whispered, "Thanks for ruining my wedding, CJ."

"Sorry," I muttered. "Want me to give a second speech to fix it?"

"Don't you dare," he said.

The marriage survived, but I didn't get invited to their first anniversary dinner. Fair enough.

6. The Ex-Girlfriend

I didn't expect to run into Nneka at the wedding. But that's the thing about Lagos, everyone knows everyone, and it's only a matter of time before you cross paths with someone you've been trying to avoid.

I spotted her by the cocktail bar during the wedding reception, sipping a glass of champagne and looking as effortlessly stunning as ever. Her fitted green dress hugged her curves perfectly, and her signature smirk hadn't changed a bit.

I had two options: pretend I didn't see her or face the storm head-on. My ego chose the second option.

"Nneka," I said, forcing a casual tone.

She turned, her smirk widening into a full smile. "CJ. Long time."

"Didn't think I'd see you here," I replied, trying to sound unaffected.

"The groom is my distant cousin," she said, taking a sip of champagne. "Small world, right?"

Too small, I thought, but I nodded politely.

She typed something on her phone. Before I could say anything else, my phone buzzed. It was a text from her.

You look good, CJ. Miss me?

I nearly dropped my phone. I glanced up, and she was still smirking.

This wasn't good.

I was about to excuse myself when the MC announced that one of the groom's friends had a "special announcement."

I watched in horror as Nneka's date walked toward the stage, microphone in hand.

"Ladies and gentlemen," he said, his voice echoing through the hall. "I have something important to say."

The crowd fell silent. I could feel my pulse racing. Nneka's eyes met mine, and she mouthed, "Oops."

Please don't tell me what I think is about to happen, I prayed silently.

"I'd like to propose to the love of my life," the young man continued.

He walked toward Nneka and got down on one knee. The room erupted in gasps and murmurs, with phones popping out to capture the moment.

Nneka's face froze, her smirk disappearing.

I didn't know whether to laugh or feel sorry for her. She looked trapped, her eyes darting around for an exit. She wasn't the type to be cornered, especially not like this. I considered walking away, but something about the panic in her eyes made me stay.

"CJ," she whispered, barely moving her lips.

"You want me to save you?" I whispered back, half-amused, half-sympathetic.

"Please," she pleaded.

It was risky, but what the heck, I'm a serial best man. I thrive on wedding chaos.

I grabbed the nearest tray of drinks and "accidentally" bumped into the guy, spilling champagne all over his tuxedo.

"Oh no! My bad!" I exclaimed, making a big scene.

The distraction worked. He stood up, trying to wipe off the mess, while Nneka quickly slipped away toward the exit. I followed her outside, where she was pacing, heels clicking against the pavement.

"You're welcome," I said.

She stopped and faced me. "That was insane."

"You're the one dating him. Why didn't you tell him you weren't ready for this?"

She sighed, running her fingers through her hair. "We've only been dating for a few months. I didn't think he'd propose at someone else's wedding!"

"Classic rookie mistake," I said with a smirk.

We stood in silence for a moment before she spoke again. "You didn't have to help me."

"I know," I replied. "But you looked like you needed a hero."

She laughed softly. "Maybe I did."

Just then, her date stormed out of the hall, still wet and fuming. "Nneka! Where are you going?"

I took that as my cue to leave.

"Good luck," I said, giving her a wink before disappearing into the crowd.

Back inside, the reception had resumed as if nothing had happened. I grabbed a drink and watched the couple on the dance floor, wondering how many other hidden dramas were unfolding behind the scenes.

The next morning, Nneka texted me: *Thanks for saving me. Let's meet for drinks soon.*

I chuckled and replied: *Only if you promise not to bring a fiancé.*

7. The Missing Wedding Rings

"**Y**ou're joking," I said, staring at the ring bearer's empty pillow. "Tell me you're joking."

The seven-year-old shook his head, tears forming in his eyes. "I put them here! I don't know where they went!"

It was twenty minutes before the ceremony, and both the bride and groom were blissfully unaware that their wedding rings had gone missing. The boy had been playing with the pillow when they "disappeared."

I took a deep breath, resisting the urge to scream. "Okay. Don't panic. We'll find them."

"What's wrong?" the wedding planner's assistant asked me when I ran into her in the hall.

"The rings are missing," I whispered. "Start checking the entire venue."

We split up, searching under tables, behind chairs, and even in the flower arrangements. Time was ticking, the bride was due to walk down the aisle, and the officiant had already taken his place at the altar.

"Nothing," the assistant said, panting.

I pulled out my phone and called a jeweller I knew in Ikoyi. "I need emergency wedding rings. Can you quickly send something?"

"Ah! Emergency wedding rings ke? You just want to borrow rings? How will I get them back?"

I quickly explained the situation.

"Please, I need them urgently. I promise I will return them."

"Okay CJ. I can send you something, but they won't be personalized," the jeweller warned.

"Doesn't matter," I said, wiping sweat from my brow. "Just get here."

"It's because it's you o. I will send dispatch, so he can dodge traffic."

By some miracle, the delivery arrived just as the bride was about to walk down the aisle. I slipped the replacement rings onto the pillow and gave the ring bearer a stern look. "Don't lose these."

The ceremony went on without a hitch, and no one knew the chaos that had happened behind the scenes.

Later, during the reception, a waiter handed me a small box. "We found these in the garden."

The original rings. The kid had dropped them while playing outside.

I laughed, tucking the box into my pocket. Just another day in the life of a serial best man.

8. The Uninvited Guest

I knew something was off the moment I saw him. The wedding was exclusive, only 250 guests, hand-picked by the bride and groom. This guy, with his flashy agbada and overconfident grin, didn't fit in.

"Who is he?" I whispered to the wedding planner, pointing at the man laughing a little too loudly at the champagne table.

She checked the guest list on her tablet and shook her head. "No idea. He's not on the list."

I sighed. "Alright, let's handle this quietly."

The trick with uninvited guests is not to make a scene. Lagos weddings are breeding grounds for gossip, and the last thing the couple needed was the gossip blogs carrying a headline like *Gatecrasher Disrupts High-Society Wedding*.

I approached the man with my best fake smile. "Hello, sir. I don't believe we've met. I'm CJ, the best man."

He extended his hand confidently. "I'm Lanre. Cousin to the groom."

I raised an eyebrow. "Cousin, you say? Funny, I've known the groom since we were kids, and I don't remember you."

He chuckled, unfazed. "It's complicated. Distant family."

I leaned in, lowering my voice. "Lanre, you're not on the guest list. I'm going to have to ask you to leave."

His grin faded. "I came all the way here. You expect me to leave before the food is served?"

"Yes," I said firmly. "I do."

But Lanre had other plans. He brushed past me and joined a group of guests dancing near the DJ booth. My blood pressure spiked as I watched him spin one of the bridesmaids around, laughing like he owned the place.

I signalled the security team, who moved in discreetly. One of the guards tapped Lanre on the shoulder. "Sir, please come with us."

Lanre sighed dramatically. "Ah ah, you people are treating me like a criminal!"

He turned to the bridesmaid, who looked confused. "Tell them I'm family."

She blinked. "But…I don't know you."

Security began escorting him toward the exit, but Lanre wasn't done causing trouble. He stopped near the buffet table and grabbed a plate of small chops, stuffing a spring roll into his mouth. "You can kick me out, but you can't take my small chops!"

The guests nearby laughed, thinking it was part of some planned comedy skit.

I wasn't amused.

"Out," I said firmly, pushing him toward the door.

As security dragged him away, he yelled, "CJ, you'll hear from me! I'll be at your wedding, uninvited!"

"Good luck finding it," I muttered.

Later, the groom came up to me, laughing. "I heard we had a gatecrasher. Did you handle it?"

"Of course," I said. "He won't be back."

But in my head, I made a mental note: *Next time, hire stricter security.*

9. The Outdoor Reception

Outdoor weddings in Lagos are always a gamble. The weather can go from sunshine to chaos in minutes, and on this particular day, the weather decided to be unforgiving.

The wedding was being held at a beachfront property in Lekki, with an ocean view that looked like something out of a Nollywood romance movie.

I and the other groomsmen had just finished setting up a few extra chairs, per the instructions of the wedding planner.

I looked up at the sky to see dark clouds rolling in fast. I made eye contact with the wedding planner who rushed over.

"CJ, we have a problem," she said.

"No kidding," I muttered. "How long until the rain hits?"

"Ten minutes, tops."

I cursed under my breath. We didn't have time to move the entire reception indoors, but we weren't about to let the couple's dream wedding drown in a downpour.

"Let's start reorganising things," the wedding planner said. "And make some sort of announcement."

I nodded.

"Start covering the sound equipment," I said, turning to the other groomsmen. "Get the caterers to move the food under the tents and tell the band to hold off on setting up outside."

Guests had begun to arrive and were mingling, blissfully unaware of the impending downpour. I grabbed the mic and made an announcement.

"Ladies and gentlemen, we'll be relocating some activities indoors to ensure you remain comfortable. Please follow the usher's directions."

A few guests groaned, especially the aunties who had spent hours perfecting their makeup. But I wasn't about to let their *geles* suffer from water damage on my watch.

We were all huddled under the small porch in front of the reception hall when the rain arrived with a vengeance, pelting down as if the heavens were punishing us for something. I watched as the wedding planner's team scrambled to protect the cake, the DJ's equipment, and the buffet from the torrential downpour. Some of the guests abandoned the crowded porch and took shelter under tents, while others rushed indoors.

By the time the rain eased up, I was soaked to the bone. My shoes squished when I walked, but I didn't care, we had saved most of the setup. The bride's bouquet was a little wet, but she was too busy laughing with her new husband to even notice.

The reception was held inside, and despite the chaos, the guests were soon back to dancing and enjoying themselves. I even spotted a few guests dancing barefoot on the dance floor, embracing the spontaneous vibe.

"CJ, you're a miracle worker," the groom said, clapping me on my back.

"Just another day in the life," I replied, wringing water from my tie.

Later that night, as I collapsed onto my bed, my phone buzzed. It was a text from the bride: *Thank you for everything. Even the rain couldn't ruin today.*

I smiled, making a mental note: *Always expect rain, even in the dry season.*

10. Groom Gets Drunk

I always warn grooms not to drink too much before the wedding. Nerves are normal, but there's a fine line between being "relaxed" and being "drunk." Dele crossed that line with a cannonball.

It started in the hotel suite where the groomsmen were taking celebratory shots of tequila. I was finalising the boutonniere arrangements when I heard someone say, "Dele, slow down."

I turned around just in time to see him downing his third shot.

"Dele, easy," I said, snatching the bottle away.

"I'm fine," he said, slurring his words and grinning like a fool.

"You're not fine," I replied, my voice stern. "You're getting married in an hour."

But Dele was already stumbling toward the couch, laughing at a joke no one else heard. The groomsmen exchanged nervous glances.

"What do we do?" one of them asked.

"Coffee," I said. "Lots of coffee."

I dragged Dele to the bathroom, splashed cold water on his face, and forced him to drink three cups of black coffee. Slowly, he started to regain some composure.

By the time we arrived at the church, he was walking straight, but his eyes still had that glassy, "I've had one too many" look. I stood by his side, praying he wouldn't embarrass himself during the vows.

When the officiant asked him to say, "I do," there was a terrifying pause before he finally mumbled, "I do."

Crisis averted.

Later, at the reception, Dele hugged me. "You saved me, bro."

"Next time, no tequila before the wedding," I said, rolling my eyes.

"There won't be a next time," he laughed, already reaching for another glass of champagne.

11. The Wedding Hookup

It was supposed to be a harmless fling. Just one night, no strings attached. But I should have known better.

The wedding had been a success; there were no fights, family drama, or gatecrashers. The after-party had just kicked off, and I found myself dancing with Bidemi, one of the bridesmaids. She was funny, flirty, and exactly the distraction I needed.

"You've been working too hard," she teased when she pulled me toward the dance floor.

"I'm always working hard," I said with a grin. "But you're right, I deserve a break."

One drink led to another, and before I knew it, we were sneaking off to a private corner of the hotel. I'll spare you the details, but let's just say the night was...memorable.

The problem started the next morning. I was in the middle of counting the cash gifts the couple had received when Bidemi approached me, looking as fresh as ever, while I struggled to hide my hangover.

"Morning, CJ," she said with a sly smile.

"Morning."

"I hope you're not planning to sneak off without saying goodbye."

I chuckled awkwardly. "Of course not."

"Good," she said, leaning in. "Because I told my cousin all about us."

"Your cousin? Who's your cousin?" I asked her.

"The bride. I thought you knew."

"Wait, what?"

She shrugged. "We're close. She thinks it's cute."

I stared at her, horrified. "Bidemi, this was supposed to be…"

"Relax," she said, laughing. "I'm not trying to marry you. But if you ever need company at another wedding, call me."

She walked away, leaving me speechless.

The bride found me later, giggling. "So, CJ, I heard you had a fun night."

I groaned. This was going to haunt me for a while.

12. The Budget Wedding Twist

When my friend Seyi told me he was planning a small, intimate wedding, I supported him. The venue was simple, the guest list was capped at one hundred people, and the couple insisted on using minimal décor.

Everything was going smoothly until Seyi's rich uncle, Chief Olayemi, arrived.

Chief Olayemi was known for his extravagant lifestyle. He showed up wearing an agbada that cost more than the entire wedding budget and brought a whole entourage of more than twenty people with him.

"I can't believe he actually came," Seyi whispered, looking nervous.

I patted his shoulder. "Relax. What's the worst that could happen?"

Five minutes later, I had my answer.

Chief Olayemi pulled me aside and said, "This wedding is too plain. I'll fix it."

"Fix it how?" I asked, dreading his answer.

"Leave it to me," he said, pulling out his phone. Within an hour, trucks arrived carrying elaborate floral arrangements, a 10-piece live band, more canapes and drinks, and enough fireworks to rival New Year's Eve.

Seyi panicked. "CJ, I can't afford this."

"You're not paying for it," I assured him. "Your uncle's covering everything."

"But this isn't what we wanted," his bride added, looking distraught.

I nodded. "I'll talk to him."

I found Chief Olayemi directing workers as if he were producing a Nollywood film. "Chief, the couple wants a simple wedding," I said carefully.

"Nonsense! Simple is boring," he replied, waving me off.

I sighed and returned to Seyi. "Here's the deal," I said. "Let him add the extras, but you and your bride control the program. I won't let him hijack the ceremony."

Seyi agreed, and despite the over-the-top décor, the wedding retained its intimate charm. The couple had their quiet moments, and the guests enjoyed the unexpected luxury.

After the wedding, Seyi laughed. "You saved the day again, CJ."

"That's what I do," I replied, adding *billionaire uncles* to my list of unpredictable wedding hazards.

13. The Tailor Tales

Weddings are like storms. The calm at the beginning is deceptive, and if you're not careful, you'll get swept into the chaos without an umbrella.

I arrived at the groom's suite that morning with a box of emergency supplies. Cufflinks, shoe polish, spare bow ties, you name it. I'd been through enough weddings to know something *always* goes wrong. But even I wasn't ready for this.

Deji, the groom, was standing in the middle of the room in what could only be described as a disaster disguised as a tux. The fabric was beautiful, cream silk with gold embroidery, but that was where the compliments ended. The fit was problematic. The sleeves were too long, the trousers were overly tight, and the jacket hung loosely around his shoulders. He looked like a kid wearing his father's hand-me-downs.

"Bro," I said, trying to suppress a laugh. "What happened?"

Deji's best man, Tunji, was pacing the room like a madman. "The tailor happened! This is not what we ordered! These Instagram designers!"

I could see the panic in Deji's eyes. The ceremony was less than three hours away.

"Okay, don't panic," I said, slipping into problem-solving mode. "We'll figure it out."

We helped Deji out of the clothes and he sat on the bed, his head in his hands.

"Adanna is going to kill me. This wedding cost a fortune, and my clothes don't even fit."

I pulled out my phone and started calling every tailor I knew in Lagos. The first few calls went like this:

"CJ, I'm fully booked today."

"Sorry, bro. I'm out of town."

"Ha! Last-minute adjustments on a wedding day? God be with you."

Finally, I got a hold of someone who could help, a tailor named Uncle Joe, known for his lightning-fast alterations. But there was a catch. "You have to bring the suit and the groom to my shop in Surulere," he said.

I glanced at the clock. Surulere traffic on a Saturday morning? We were doomed. But we didn't have a choice.

"Deji, you're coming with me," I said, grabbing the suit and practically dragging him out of the room. "You guys, Tunji, Boye, stay here. Everyone, stay calm o. Don't stress out the bride."

We raced down the hotel lobby, jumped into my car, and sped off like our lives depended on it.

"Do you think we'll make it?" Deji asked as I swerved past a slow-moving truck.

"We have to," I said, weaving through traffic like I was auditioning for *Fast & Furious: Lagos Drift.*

Uncle Joe's shop was a small, cluttered space that smelled like fabric dye and hard work. The man himself was waiting for us, needle in hand.

"Where's the disaster?" he asked.

I handed him the outfit.

"We need a miracle, Uncle Joe. Can you do it in an hour?"

He examined the outfit like a doctor diagnosing a terminal patient.

"Hmmm. It's bad, but not hopeless. Sit down and pray."

He quickly measured Deji and got to work. We watched in awe as Uncle Joe worked his magic, loosening here, cutting there, stitching, and muttering Yoruba proverbs under his breath. At one point, his assistant brought him a bowl of peanuts, which he ate while hemming the trousers.

"Uncle Joe, time is ticking," I reminded him.

"Calm down, my boy. Good work takes time."

An hour later, he handed me the modified clothes with a proud smile.

"It should fit perfectly now."

Deji tried on the suit. It fitted him like a glove.

"Ah, thank you, thank you, Uncle Joe! We owe you big time!"

We paid him and bolted out of the shop. We made it back to the hotel with only minutes to spare.

"Where have you guys been?" the other groomsmen demanded.

"Saving the wedding," I said. "Deji, *oya* quickly get changed."

"Thank you, CJ, you're a lifesaver," Deji said, visibly relieved.

"Now, let's get you married before something else happens," I joked.

The ceremony went off without a hitch, and no one suspected that hours earlier, Deji had been a fashion disaster waiting to happen. As we celebrated at the reception, he pulled me aside.

"CJ, I owe you one."

"Don't worry," I said, raising my glass. "Just don't invite those fake designers to any future events."

We clinked glasses and laughed.

14. The Last-Minute Date

I didn't plan to bring a date to this wedding. As a serial best man, I've learned that flying solo means less drama. No awkward introductions to the bride's family, no one tugging on my arm while I'm running damage control, and definitely no complaints when I disappear for an hour to fix a crisis. But fate had other plans.

It all started the night before the wedding, during the rehearsal dinner. I was going over the speech with the groom when the bride's sister, Nkem, walked up to me, smiling like she knew something I didn't know.

"CJ, you're not bringing anyone to the wedding, are you?" she asked, batting her lashes.

"Nope," I said, popping a piece of puff-puff into my mouth. "Just me, myself, and the chaos I'm about to control."

She giggled. "Well, I have a friend. She's single and gorgeous, and you two would look good on the dance floor together. What do you say?"

I should have said no. My instincts screamed, *Run, CJ! Run!* But then Nkem showed me a photo of her friend, Tola, on Instagram. Tola was slim and dark-skinned, with the kind of smile that could melt concrete.

I swallowed my hesitation and said, "Alright, fine. Set it up."

The next day, Tola arrived at the church wearing a beautiful yellow dress that hugged her figure perfectly. I wasn't sure if I was supposed to escort her down the aisle or thank her for turning up and turning heads.

"You clean up nicely," she said, flashing me a dazzling smile.

"You're not too bad yourself," I replied, offering her my arm.

Things started great. We sat together during the ceremony, and she laughed at my jokes during the reception dinner. By the time the dance floor opened, I was beginning to think Nkem had done me a favour. But that's when things took a turn.

"CJ," she said, leaning in close as the band played Davido's *Kante.* "Let's get some photos together. You know, memories."

"Sure," I said, thinking she meant a couple of selfies.

She didn't.

She dragged me to the photo booth, where she proceeded to pose like we were a couple celebrating our first anniversary. She leaned on my shoulder, cupped my face, and even planted a kiss on my cheek for the camera. By the time the photographer handed us the prints, I looked like a man caught in a romantic ambush.

"Isn't this cute?" she cooed, showing the photos to Nkem and some of the bridesmaids. They all squealed in delight, while I forced a smile and prayed for the floor to open up and swallow me.

"I think we've got enough photos," I said, gently trying to pry the prints from her fingers.

"But we haven't taken one with the bride and groom yet!" she insisted.

Before I could protest, she dragged me across the hall toward the happy couple, who were cutting their cake. She positioned us right beside them and whispered to the photographer, "Make sure we're centred."

At this point, I was sweating. Tola was acting like this was her wedding, and I was the unsuspecting groom. The bride shot me a curious glance, and the groom mouthed, "What's going on?"

I mouthed back, *I don't know.*

After the photos, Tola looped her arm through mine and led me to the bar. "Let's get drinks to celebrate," she said.

"Celebrate what?"

"Us," she replied with a wink.

I stared at her, trying to figure out if she was joking. She wasn't.

"Tola," I said cautiously, "this is just a wedding. We barely know each other."

"I know," she said, tilting her head. "But I feel something special, don't you?"

Panic set in. I needed to escape before she started planning our honeymoon. "I just remembered, I need to check on the DJ," I said, pulling away. "Be right back."

I dashed to the DJ booth and hid behind a speaker, frantically texting Nkem.

Me: *Why didn't you warn me that your friend thinks we're soulmates?*

Nkem: *LOL. She's a romantic. Just play along for tonight.*

Me: *She's planning our future.*

Nkem: *You're welcome.*

I groaned. This was a disaster. I spent the rest of the evening dodging Tola, pretending to be busy with best-man duties. But she was persistent. When I wasn't fixing the microphone or checking on the caterers, she was popping up beside me, asking if I wanted to dance or take more photos.

Later that evening, I was helping the newlyweds into their getaway car when I felt a tap on my shoulder. Completely exhausted by then, I cautiously looked over my shoulder.

It was Tola. "I had a great time," she said, handing me one of the photo prints. "We look good together, don't you think?"

I nodded weakly. "Yeah, sure."

She winked. "Call me."

As she walked away, I slumped against the car and sighed. Another day, another wedding. Next time, I was flying solo, no exceptions.

Or so I thought.

15. Dance Battle Disaster

Every wedding has at least one wildcard, the unpredictable guest who turns a simple evening into a spectacle. At this wedding, that wildcard was Uncle Femi. The man was known for his legendary dance moves at family functions, but no one warned me he had a competitive streak.

It started innocently enough. The live band had just finished a set, and the DJ was heating up the floor with King Promise's *Terminator.* I had just handed the bride a glass of water when Uncle Femi appeared out of nowhere, dabbing sweat off his forehead.

"CJ! You're the best man, abi?" he asked, already swaying to the beat.

"Yes, sir."

"Good. Let's see if you can dance like a proper best man," he said, cracking his knuckles like we were about to wrestle.

I chuckled. "Uncle, I'm just here to make sure everything goes smoothly."

He wasn't having it.

"What's a Lagos wedding without a dance battle? Come on, don't embarrass the groom's side."

His voice was loud enough to attract a small crowd, who started chanting, "Best man! Best man!"

Before I could escape, Uncle Femi pulled me onto the dance floor, and the DJ switched to Kizz Daniel's *Cough (Odo)*. The crowd circled us, phones recording as the dance-off began.

I started simple, with a two-step, hip sway, hand clap. Easy. Uncle Femi mirrored my moves, grinning like a man with something to prove.

Then he took it up a notch, breaking into an energetic *shaku shaku* that had the crowd cheering. Not to be outdone, I followed with some *zanku* legwork, my shoes sliding across the marble floor with precision. The energy was electric.

But Uncle Femi wasn't finished.

"Watch this!" he shouted, leaping into a move that looked like a cross between a breakdance spin and a backflip. The crowd went wild, chanting his name.

I had two options: admit defeat or go all in. My competitive side won.

I dropped into a squat, did a quick leg sweep, and transitioned into a clean spin. The crowd roared. Uncle Femi clapped, acknowledging the challenge, and launched into another round of flashy moves. I was keeping up, but barely. Sweat dripped down my face, and my breath came in gasps.

That's when it happened.

He attempted a jump-and-split combo. His agbada flared dramatically, and for a second, it looked like he'd nailed the move. But then his landing went wrong. His right foot slipped, his legs buckled, and the next thing I knew, he crashed directly into the cake table.

The massive, five-tier cake, decorated with gold ribbons and delicate sugar flowers, wobbled precariously. Time seemed to slow down as the top tier tilted, then toppled. The entire cake collapsed in a sugary avalanche, covering Uncle Femi in sponge and buttercream.

Gasps filled the room, followed by a stunned silence.

"Oh no," I whispered, rushing to the stand. The bride stood frozen near the stage, her eyes wide in horror. The groom looked like he was debating whether to laugh or cry.

Uncle Femi sat up, dazed and covered in frosting. "What just happened?"

"The cake happened, Uncle," I said, pulling him to his feet. "Are you okay?"

"I think so." He wiped buttercream from his face and looked around sheepishly. "Maybe I overdid it."

Understatement of the year.

The wedding planner and her team went to work with the hotel staff. They quickly carried the cake away and were able to salvage the bottom two tiers and decorate it with leftover flowers. Meanwhile, I pulled the DJ aside and told him to play something upbeat to distract the guests.

"Ladies and gentlemen," I announced, grabbing the mic. "Let's give a round of applause to Uncle Femi for...spicing things up tonight."

Laughter rippled through the room, breaking the tension. Even the bride chuckled, though I could tell she was fuming. She and the groom cut the salvaged cake while the guests clapped and cheered.

Later, Uncle Femi found me by the bar.

"CJ, you're a good sport," he said, handing me a glass of champagne. "I didn't mean to ruin the cake."

"I know, Uncle," I replied, clinking my glass with his. "But next time, maybe stick to two-step."

He laughed. "Deal."

Another chaotic wedding, another day saved. Just the way I like it.

16. The Crying Bridesmaid

It's always the quiet ones. The bridesmaid you think will be the easiest to manage, who smiles politely and stays out of trouble, is always the one who surprises you.

Her name was Aisha, and she was one of the bride's closest friends. Throughout the ceremony, she had been a picture of grace, dabbing her eyes delicately during the vows and standing perfectly composed during the group photos. I should have known that all that restraint was building up to something catastrophic.

It all started after the reception dinner. The DJ had just transitioned the music from a sweet melody to a dancing tune. I was mentally patting myself on the back for another job well done when I saw it: the unmistakable sight of someone sobbing.

I turned toward the sound and found Aisha sitting at the edge of the dance floor, mascara streaking down her cheeks like rivers of regret. She was clutching a glass of champagne in one hand and a tissue in the other.

Oh no.

I approached cautiously. "Aisha, everything okay?"

She looked up, her eyes glassy from either tears or alcohol or both.

"No," she sniffed. "Everything is *not* okay."

I sighed. I had seen this before. Weddings have a way of bringing out buried emotions, especially in single friends watching their loved ones tie the knot. But Aisha wasn't just tearing up, she was having a full emotional breakdown.

"What's wrong?" I asked, gently taking the champagne glass from her hand.

She hiccupped and blew her nose. "It's my ex."

Of course, it was.

"I thought I was over him," she continued, her words slurring slightly. "But seeing the bride and groom so happy...ugh, it just reminded me that I'm alone and miserable and probably going to die surrounded by cats."

"You don't have any cats," I said, trying to lighten the mood.

"Not yet," she wailed dramatically. "But I will if I don't get my life together."

I scanned the room, hoping no one was recording this. The last thing the bride needed was a viral video of her bridesmaid crying about cats at her wedding.

"Okay," I said, pulling her to her feet. "Let's get some air."

I led her out to the balcony, where the cool night breeze worked wonders on her flushed face. She took in a few deep breaths, and the sobbing slowed to a sniffle.

"Better?" I asked.

"A little," she mumbled, leaning against the railing. "I'm sorry. I'm ruining the wedding, aren't I?"

"No," I lied. "But you do need to pull yourself together before the bride sees you."

She groaned. "She's going to think I'm pathetic."

"No, she's going to think you're human," I said. "But let's keep this between us, okay?"

She nodded, wiping her face with the tissue. "You're a good, best man, CJ."

"Thanks. It's part of the job," I said and handed her a bottle of water. "Now, drink this and stay here for a bit. I'll check on you later."

I thought that was the end of it, but I was wrong.

A few minutes later, when I returned to the ballroom, Aisha was on the dance floor, twirling barefoot like a child discovering freedom for the first time. The guests around her clapped and cheered, oblivious to the fact that she was still emotionally unstable.

I rushed over just as she collapsed into my arms, giggling. "CJ, I feel great now!"

"You feel drunk," I muttered, trying to hold her steady.

She grabbed my tie and leaned in. "You're cute."

I froze. "Aisha, let's not do this."

"But you're single, and I'm single, and..."

"Nope. Nope, nope, nope," I said, gently peeling her hands off me. "We're not doing this at your friend's wedding."

Thankfully, one of the other bridesmaids noticed the situation and helped me escort Aisha to a quiet corner. "We'll take it from here," she said, giving me a sympathetic smile.

"Thank you," I replied, relieved.

As I returned to the dance floor, the bride approached me, looking concerned. "What's going on with Aisha?"

"She's fine," I said quickly. "Just needed a break."

The bride sighed. "I was worried something like this would happen. She's been struggling since her breakup."

"She'll be okay," I assured her. "She just needed to let it out."

The bride smiled. "You *really* are the best man."

"Don't remind me," I said, chuckling.

By the end of the night, Aisha was back to being her composed self, thanks to a combination of water, fresh air, and some stern advice from her fellow bridesmaids. As she left the venue, she gave me a small wave and mouthed, "Thank you."

Another night where I earned my title as the serial best man. I made a mental note: *Always keep tissues and water handy at weddings.* You never know when the tears will start.

17. Replacement Wedding Officiant

Everything had started smoothly, too smoothly. I should've known trouble was lurking around the corner. Lagos weddings don't allow you the luxury of peace for long.

We were at a beautiful hotel with an outdoor space for the ceremony. I was sipping on a bottle of water and mentally reviewing my best man speech when Mike, one of the groomsmen tapped me on the shoulder.

"CJ, we have a situation."

I sighed. "What now?"

"It's the officiant. He's lost his voice."

"What do you mean he's lost his voice?" I asked, following him to the side of the stage that had been set up as the altar, where the officiant, a distinguished elderly man with a perfectly pressed cassock, was sitting. His face was calm, but when he tried to speak, all that came out was a scratchy whisper.

"Did he eat pepper soup or something?" I asked.

The groomsman shrugged. "He said it started this morning."

"We can't do the wedding without him!" I muttered. "What about the backup officiant?"

"There is no backup," the groomsman replied. "This isn't a concert."

Panic started to bubble under my skin. Sade, the bride was already waiting in the wings, and guests were starting to fill the rows. If we didn't figure this out quickly, I'd be explaining to the bride why her big day had turned into a silent movie.

"Okay," I said, thinking fast. "We need someone to fill in."

The groomsman blinked. "You're not suggesting..."

"Yes. Me. I'll do it."

"But you're not a priest, CJ."

"Obviously," I said, pulling out my phone. "But I've attended enough weddings to fake it. I just need the script."

I found an online wedding ceremony guide, quickly skimmed through it, and made a few notes on my phone. The officiant gave me his blessing with a nod and a thumbs-up before being whisked away by an usher to drink hot tea in the hotel's restaurant. I told Mike to brief Kola, the groom on the slight change of plans.

Then I took a deep breath, put on my most serene expression, and approached the altar. The guests had no idea anything was wrong. They thought this was all part of the plan. I just had to get through this without accidentally marrying myself to the couple.

The violinist began playing the processional music. The groom's eyes lit up as Sade started walking down the aisle, and for a moment, I forgot about the chaos. Weddings have that effect; they remind you why you're willing to put up with the madness.

When the couple finally stood before me, I cleared my throat and began. "Dearly beloved, we are gathered here today..."

Kola, the groom, looked amused, but Sade looked uncertain.

"Why is CJ officiating?" she whispered.

Kola smiled and mouthed, "Just go with it."

As for me, I was nailing it. My voice was steady, my delivery on point. I even threw in a gentle smile to make it seem more authentic.

Things were going great until we got to the vows.

"In sickness and in health, for richer or poorer," I said, nodding to the groom. "Now repeat after me."

The groom did fine.

Sade seemed distracted and stuttered on her words.

I repeated the line she was supposed to say.

She blinked, then nodded, and repeated the vows like a pro.

The ceremony was back on track until we got to the part where the rings were exchanged. I had skipped a line. "Uh, please hand the rings over to the groom," I improvised, hoping no one would notice the mix-up.

Guiding the couple through the rest of the ceremony like a magician covering up a failed trick, by some miracle, we made it to the final blessing.

"With the power vested in me," I said, pausing dramatically for effect, "I now pronounce you husband and wife. You may kiss the bride."

The crowd erupted in applause, and I let out a breath I didn't know I was holding.

As the couple kissed and the organist played the recessional, I quietly slipped away from the altar and collapsed onto a chair.

One of the groomsmen handed me a bottle of water. "That was insane."

"Tell me about it," I said, gulping down the water.

Later, at the reception, the couple found me.

"I can't believe you pulled that off," Sade said, with a smile.

"Neither can I," I admitted.

Kola laughed, clapping me on the back. "You *really* are the best man."

The officiant who was now recovered and sipping water, walked over. "I heard you did a good job," he said, his voice still raspy.

"I wouldn't recommend hiring me permanently," I joked.

By the time the night ended, I had added another chaotic but memorable adventure to my list.

18. Switched Phones

If you think Lagos weddings are chaotic, try adding a phone mix-up to the equation. Trust me, nothing good comes out of it.

I was standing near the cocktail bar, enjoying a rare moment of calm, when the drama began. The couple had made their grand entrance into the reception hall and taken their seats. The food was being served, everyone was enjoying the lively music, and I was thinking I might get through this wedding without any major incidents.

Then I saw my phone screen light up.

New message: *Did anyone else see you there that night?*

I froze.

That message wasn't meant for me. My heart started pounding as I checked the phone's wallpaper. Instead of the photo of my car, there was a picture of a lady, smiling sweetly.

Oh no.

I had someone else's phone.

I retraced my steps. Earlier, I had placed my phone on the bar while ordering a drink, and I must have picked up the wrong one. Now I was holding a lady's phone, and she was holding mine. Somewhere in this venue, someone had access to my entire message history, including the bachelor party details that could sink this entire wedding.

I scanned the room, searching for the lady in the photo. There she was, sitting at a table, scrolling through *my* phone.

I rushed over, trying to remain calm.

"Hi! You have my phone."

She looked up. "What?"

"Phones got switched. That one's mine."

She checked the screen, her eyebrows furrowing. "Wait. You are CJ, the best man?"

"Yes," I said, praying she hadn't seen anything incriminating.

Her face lit up with excitement. "Oh my God, I've been reading your texts. You're hilarious! Who is Ogechi, and why does she keep texting you about palm wine?"

I groaned internally and sat down next to her. I leaned in so we could hear each other over the music.

"Long story. Can I have my phone back now?"

But instead of handing it over, she scrolled further. "Oh, what's this? Bachelor party in Ghana?"

My stomach flipped. "It's not what you think," I said, trying to grab the phone.

She pulled it away, laughing. "I'm joking. Relax. But seriously, what happened in Ghana?"

"Nothing happened," I said quickly. "It's just groomsmen stuff. Please give me the phone."

Before she could reply, her phone buzzed in my hand. I glanced down and saw a message pop up: *I'm still in love with you.* The sender? The groom.

I blinked. "Um, what's this?"

Her face fell. "Oh no."

"So, *you're* the groom's side chick!"

"CJ, I can explain—"

"What are you both up to?" I whispered, trying to keep my voice down. "Does the bride know?"

"No," she said, panicking. "It's not like that; I'm not trying to mess things up!"

"Doesn't matter," I said, checking the time. We had exactly 20 minutes before the couple's first dance. "Come with me *now.*"

I pulled her aside and dialled the groom's number from my phone. He answered after two rings. "CJ, what's up?"

"We have a problem," I said. "You texted your side chick."

Silence.

"I-I didn't mean to," he stammered. "I was nervous, and…"

93

"No time for excuses. Where are you?"

"I'm upstairs, changing for the first dance."

"Stay there," I ordered. "I'm coming."

I dragged the lady with me, weaving through tables and dodging photographers and got the lift to the 10th floor. Dele opened the door to the suite. His face was pale, and his bow tie was slightly crooked. He looked like a man on the verge of fainting.

"You better have a good explanation," I said.

"It was an accident!" he said, running his hands through his hair. "I was scrolling through my old texts, and I panicked and…hit send by mistake."

"Does your bride know about this?"

"No!" He looked horrified at the thought.

I turned to the babe. "You haven't replied, right?"

She shook her head. "No, I swear."

I exhaled, relieved. "Okay, here's what we're going to do. Delete the message on both phones, and we pretend this never happened."

They both nodded furiously like school kids agreeing to keep a secret from their teacher.

"Actually, why don't we delete your entire message history?" I said.

I grabbed both phones, deleted the messages, and handed them back.

"Now," I said, straightening the groom's bow tie, "get your act together. You're about to dance with your wife."

The babe slipped away.

"Thank you, CJ," he whispered, looking like he owed me his life.

"Don't thank me. Just don't mess up again."

As I watched them take the dance floor to Timi Dakolo's *Iyawo Mi,* I finally relaxed. The bride was glowing, oblivious to the situation we had just avoided.

Later, the babe found me by the bar. "Thanks for not making it a big deal."

"Just doing my job," I said, sipping my drink.

"Maybe one day, you'll need my help covering up your secret," she teased.

I laughed. "Let's hope it doesn't come to that."

But in Lagos, you never know.

19. The Stalker Ex

The day had been surprisingly calm, and that should've been my first clue. Lagos weddings don't stay calm for long. As the best man, I'd handled my fair share of disasters. Missing rings, emotional breakdowns, drunk uncles, you name it, but nothing could have prepared me for the nuclear bomb that was about to drop.

It started when the groom's ex, Felicia, waltzed into the reception like she had an invitation. She didn't.

She was wearing a dangerously short red dress that hugged her curves, and the heels she wore could've been classified as a weapon. Heads turned as she strutted through the crowd, a glass of champagne in hand and a confident smirk on her face. I nearly dropped my plate of *jollof rice* when I saw her.

"No, no, no," I muttered, setting down my plate and rushing over to the groom. "We have a problem."

"What now?" the groom, Tobi, asked, mid-conversation with the bride's parents.

"Felicia. She's here."

His face went pale. "Felicia? *My* Felicia?"

"No, the one from *The Real Housewives of Lagos.* Of course, your Felicia!"

He groaned, rubbing his temples. "How did she even get in?"

I had no idea, but that was a problem for later. For now, we needed her out before she did something that would end up on every Nigerian gossip blog by morning.

"Keep the bride occupied," I said. "I'll handle it."

I approached Felicia at the bar, where she was helping herself to a glass of champagne. She smiled when I walked up.

"CJ. Long time."

"Not long enough," I replied. "What are you doing here?"

She shrugged, taking a sip of her drink. "Just paying my respects."

"You weren't invited."

"Well, that's a shame, considering how well Tobi and I know each other."

I clenched my jaw. "You need to leave."

"Oh, don't be so dramatic," she said, swirling her glass. "I'm just here for the cake."

"And what happens when the bride sees you?"

Felicia laughed. "Relax, CJ. I'm not here to cause trouble."

I didn't believe her for a second. I motioned to security, who approached discreetly. "Escort her out," I whispered to them.

She sighed dramatically. "Fine, I'm leaving. But tell Tobi I said congratulations. I'm sure he'll need a good honeymoon to recover from all this."

My heart skipped a beat. "What do you know about the honeymoon?"

She smiled wickedly. "Oh, I overheard someone mention it while I was mingling. Bora Bora, right? Great choice. I've been dying to visit."

Panic set in. If she showed up at their honeymoon destination, this wedding would go down as the most scandalous event of the year.

"Felicia, please don't do this," I said, following her as security led her toward the exit.

She stopped and turned to face me. "Why not? Wouldn't it be fun to run into each other on the beach?"

"No," I said firmly. "It wouldn't. The bride doesn't deserve this, and neither does Tobi."

For the first time, her playful smirk faltered. "So, you're defending him now?"

"This isn't about him," I said. "It's about doing the right thing. You're better than this, Felicia."

She hesitated, her fingers tightening around her purse. For a moment, I thought I had lost her, but then she sighed and leaned in closer.

"I'm not going to Bora Bora," she whispered. "I just wanted to scare you."

I exhaled, relieved. "You almost gave me a heart attack."

"Good. That's what you get for siding with Tobi," she teased. "But don't worry. I'll find my own vacation spot, one that doesn't involve newlyweds."

Security resumed escorting her out, and I followed to make sure she didn't change her mind at the last second. I watched as she got to her car and opened the door. Before she stepped in, she turned back to me.

"CJ, you *are* the best man. I almost feel bad."

"Almost?"

She winked. "Almost."

I watched as she drove out of the venue's parking lot and disappeared into Lagos traffic before heading back inside. The DJ was playing Asake's *Joha,* and the dance floor was packed. Tobi caught my eye and mouthed, "Is she gone?"

I gave him a thumbs-up and headed toward the bar, finally allowing myself to breathe.

Later, as I sipped my drink, the bride approached me, glowing with happiness.

"Thank you for everything today, CJ. I didn't see you much, but I know you were busy."

"You have no idea," I replied with a chuckle.

20. Eru Iyawo Drama

The day started with promise: blue skies, perfectly aligned chairs, and the smell of *jollof rice* wafting through the air. The traditional Yoruba engagement ceremony was supposed to be the calm before the storm of tomorrow's wedding. But knowing Nigerian families, I had prepared myself for any eventualities.

I was chatting with the caterers and wedding planner about the order of serving food when one of the bride's aunts sprinted toward me, her *gele* slightly tilted as she waved a fan frantically.

"CJ! Come now. We have a big problem!"

The words "*big problem*" are kryptonite for any wedding planner or best man, and my stomach immediately tightened. "What happened?"

"It's the *eru iyawo*. The groom's family brought the wrong items."

Wrong items? I followed her into the bride's family compound, where a beautifully decorated area had been set up for the traditional gift presentation. The groom's family, dressed in matching attires, sat on one side, looking confused and slightly nervous. The bride's family sat on the opposite side, with scowls that could scare a lion.

In the middle of the chaos sat the *eru iyawo,* the traditional gifts for the bride's family. These gifts are crucial. They symbolise respect, goodwill, and the groom's ability to provide for his new wife. They typically include items like yam tubers, baskets of fruits, crates of soft drinks, bottles of schnapps, and fabrics.

Except this time, the fruits and crates of soft drinks were nowhere to be seen. Instead, someone had placed bottles of sparkling water on the display table, along with random snacks like plantain chips and packaged *chin-chin*.

One of the bride's uncles folded his arms and glared. "What is this insult? Plantain chips? Is this a joke?"

The groom's father, looking bewildered, stepped forward. "We were told to bring some refreshments. Is sparkling water not acceptable?"

"No, sir," the bride's aunt hissed. "This is not a business meeting. You were supposed to bring crates of *Fanta*, *Coke*, and *Maltina*. And why is there no alligator pepper for the prayers?"

Another Aunty spoke up. "Did you not collect the full engagement list?"

I ran a hand through my hair, trying to think of a way to diffuse the situation. Alligator pepper was essential for the traditional blessing. Without it, the bride's family could call off the ceremony or demand a fine.

"We also didn't see the correct number of yams," another relative added. "Where are the tubers we requested?"

The groom's family glanced nervously at the smaller pile of yams, about fifteen at best. Someone whispered that their supplier had delivered the wrong number, but that explanation wasn't going to cut it with the bride's side.

I needed to act fast. "Please give me a moment," I said, excusing myself. I pulled the groom aside, away from the judgmental stares of both families.

"Bro," I said urgently, "who was in charge of the *eru iyawo*?"

"My cousins, Shalewa and Banke," he muttered, rubbing his temples. "These GenZ people are always messing things up."

"Well, your Gen Zs have potentially ruined your marriage before it even starts. We need to fix this, *now.*"

I called the wedding planner and told her about the situation.

She quickly contacted a local vendor to deliver crates of soft drinks and additional yams immediately. She got her assistant to rush out to buy fruits.

"And find someone selling alligator pepper on the street if you have to," I added.

"Got it," she replied, already sprinting toward the car.

While she handled the logistics, I returned to the families and did what I did best: stall and sweet talk.

"Ladies and gentlemen," I said with a confident smile, "these minor delays are simply a result of some logistics problems and traffic. We all know how Lagos can be on weekends. But everything you requested is on the way."

The bride's mother gave me a sceptical look. "And what about the disrespect of bringing plantain chips?"

"Think of them as a bonus snack," I said, improvising. "A gesture of hospitality. I'm sure the elders can enjoy some refreshments while we wait."

She didn't look convinced, but the groom's uncle quickly chimed in. "Yes, yes! Snacks are good. Let's not make a mountain out of a molehill."

By some miracle, my stalling worked, which bought us enough time. Thirty minutes later, the vendor arrived with crates of *Fanta*, *Coke*, and *Maltina*, stacked neatly on a wheelbarrow. Behind her was another assistant carrying alligator pepper, a bundle of extra yams, plantains and fruits.

I breathed a sigh of relief as the gifts were rearranged, and the bride's family finally looked satisfied. The drummers gathered round, the ceremonial presentation began, and the mood shifted back to festive. I could feel the tension melting away.

As the bride's family accepted the items and blessed the couple, the bride's mother pulled me aside and whispered, "You saved the day, CJ."

I smiled. "Just doing my job."

MEMOIRS OF A LAGOS BAKER

A Collection of Flash Fiction Stories

MEET DAYO

People think running a bakery is easy. They imagine soft music playing in the background, flour-dusted countertops, and the gentle hum of the oven as golden cakes rise to perfection. What they don't imagine is chaos like:

Last-minute wedding cake orders. Clients who price my work like I'm selling tomatoes in Mile 12. Delivery drivers who think potholes are part of a rally race. And of course, the occasional cake thief.

Welcome to my world.

My name is Dayo, and I own Sweet Cravings Pastries, a cake and pastries business in Lagos. I operate the business with the help of Cynthia, my friend and pastry expert, Morayo, our shop assistant and social media manager, and Mohammed, our dependable delivery driver. Baking isn't just my job, it's my life. I left a career in IT five years ago to follow my passion, thinking it would be smooth sailing.

Instead, I walked straight into the madness that is Lagos events.

I've baked cakes for brides who almost didn't get married. I've chased delivery vans down Third Mainland Bridge. And once, I even had to convince a five-year-old that eating her cake wouldn't hurt the princesses inside.

Every order has a story. Some are hilarious. Some are frustrating. And some remind me why I love what I do.

These are the stories from my bakery. The sugar-coated chaos. The buttercream betrayals. The fondant-fuelled madness that comes with being a Lagos baker.

So, if you ever think cake is just cake, sit back, grab a slice, and let me prove you wrong.

1. The Best Friend's Cake

The first red flag was the client's name on the booking form.

Teniola Banjo.

I squinted at it like maybe my screen had glitched. Teni? As in my Teni? Teni from Ojodu? Teni, who used to sneak out of school with me to buy puff-puff? Teni, who held my hand the night I found out Akin had cheated on me with the choir leader?

I blinked. Maybe it was a different Teniola Banjo. Lagos is big. Life is random. People share names.

Then she sent a follow-up message:

"Dayo! Long time! I'm getting married o, can't believe it! You're the only one I trust to bake my cake!"

My heart slid into my stomach. I typed back a safe reply.

"Teni!! Wow! Congratulations babe! Of course I'll do it. Send me the brief and we'll fix a consultation."

My hands shook as I pressed send.

Ten minutes later, Cynthia strolled into the kitchen holding a cup of tea and eyeing the swirl I was piping.

"Who got you looking like say NEPA just took your destiny?"

I forced a smile. "Old friend. Big wedding."

She raised a brow. "Trouble?"

"Not yet," I said. "Let's see."

Three days later, Teni came for her consultation. She breezed into the shop in a pink jumpsuit and huge sunglasses, looking like someone who now got facials twice a week and did yoga in Ikoyi.

I hugged her tightly, partly from habit, partly to steady myself.

"You look amazing, babe!" she said.

"You too!" I managed. "You've always been fine, sha."

We laughed. It felt normal…for about five seconds.

"Let me call my fiancé," she said, taking out her phone. "He's parking. You remember Folarin?"

I froze.

"Folarin…?"

She smiled like someone dropping gist. "Folarin Adeniyi. He said you guys met a while back, but it didn't work out. Small world, abi?"

Small world? It was microscopic.

Folarin was *the* Folarin. The one I dated for a year and a half. The one who ghosted me three weeks before Valentine's. The one I cried over while baking vanilla cupcakes in my first flat in Yaba. That Folarin.

And he was marrying Teni. My childhood best friend. And I, I, was about to bake their wedding cake.

You see how Lagos likes to humble people?

Before I could respond, the door chimed. He walked in.

Tall. Beard still sharp. Polo shirt tucked into expensive jeans like all Lagos finance bros.

He paused when he saw me. That split-second pause where his smile faltered, and our shared history hovered in the air like too much icing sugar.

"Hi Dayo," he said.

"Folarin. Long time."

Teni beamed, oblivious. "You see? Lagos is small-small."

I swallowed my pride. I swallowed my ego. I swallowed the ghost of all the vanilla cupcakes I baked to get over this man.

Then I brought out my iPad and said, "So, three-tier or five-tier?"

We went with five.

Champagne velvet sponge with white chocolate ganache, covered in ivory fondant, and gold leaf details. Clean. Classic. Elegant.

I put my feelings aside and smiled sweetly as we discussed payment and delivery venue.

The day I started baking, I decided I was doing this for closure. Every time I piped a rose, I imagined it curling into the memory of our breakup. Every time I smoothed fondant; I smoothed over the conversations I would never have.

Cynthia clocked it by the second day.

"You're baking like a woman trying to prove something."

I gave her a look.

She raised her hands. "Oya, sorry. But this cake is fighting all your demons."

On the wedding day, we delivered the cake to the venue in Lekki. Cynthia and Morayo set up the table while I hovered by the back like a reluctant ghost.

Guests flowed in, all dressed in glitter and Gucci sunglasses. A saxophonist played Tiwa Savage instrumentals near the entrance.

I watched from a distance as they unveiled the cake. I saw Teni gasp and Folarin nod in approval.

People clapped. Cameras flashed. No one knew the cake was laced with closure.

As I turned to leave, someone tapped my shoulder.

Teni.

She pulled me into a hug. "Thank you, Dayo. This cake is perfect."

I smiled. "I'm happy you're happy."

She hesitated. "I know... you and Folarin had history. I wasn't sure if you'd be okay."

I blinked. So she knew.

"We weren't close when it started," she said quickly. "And he told me the truth."

I nodded.

"No hard feelings?" she asked.

I paused. Then I said the only honest thing I could think of.

"No. Just layers."

Layers of sponge. Layers of silence. Layers of old things, baked fresh and sweet, because life had to go on.

She squeezed my hand, then ran back to her reception like the queen of her fairytale.

I walked back to the car, opened my cooler box, and pulled out a cupcake I had saved for myself.

Red velvet with cream cheese frosting.

I took a bite, exhaled, and smiled. Bittersweet.

But mostly sweet.

2. Last-Minute Order

Some clients plan their weddings twelve months in advance. Others give you a spreadsheet, a Pinterest board, and a three-person committee. And some, like Yvonne, call you on Thursday night, sounding as though she has just survived a minor plane crash.

"Hi, is this Dayo of Sweet Cravings?"

"Yes," I said, already wary. Her tone had that urgent *wahala* pitch.

"My wedding is on Saturday. I need a five-tier cake. Something classy, nothing too dramatic. But elegant."

I blinked. "As in two days from now?"

"Yes," came the reply.

"Ma'am, with all due respect..."

She cut me off. "I'll pay double."

That silenced me.

She continued, "Bisi, the planner recommended you. She said you're the best."

Now, I couldn't even argue. *That* woman again. Bisi always had a way of dragging me into last-minute miracles, like I was the Jesus of fondant.

"Do you have a design?" I asked, resigned.

"I trust your judgment. Just make it unforgettable."

And she hung up.

Cynthia looked at me from across the room where she was boxing mini cupcakes.

"What was that?"

I blinked again. "A bride. Saturday wedding. Wants a five-tier luxury cake. Hasn't paid a deposit. And I think I just agreed."

Morayo clutched her chest. "You want to kill us."

"I didn't say yes," I lied.

I'd said yes. I called Bisi to confirm that the booking was legitimate and to ensure I would receive payment.

By Friday morning, I was elbow-deep in cake batter and stress.

Cynthia drafted the stencil, while Morayo handled logistics. I called my fondant supplier twice and begged him to deliver before 2.00 pm. I even pulled out my special gold dust, the one I reserved for my premium brides and corporate clients with deep pockets and low emotional stability.

By evening, my kitchen smelled like a combination of victory and sleep deprivation.

I stepped back to admire the progress. Four tiers baked, filled, and crumb-coated. The fifth was in the oven. My Spotify playlist was playing Asa. For a second, I felt peace.

Then Cynthia's voice shattered it.

"Dayo! There's a problem!"

I turned sharply. "What again?"

"Power just went out. The generator isn't coming on."

I stared at her like she had just announced the end of the world. NEPA had struck. My generator, a grumpy beast of a thing, was refusing to cooperate.

"Did you check the fuel?"

"Yes!"

"Oil?"

"Yes!"

"Did you sweet-talk it?"

"No, I'll try that next."

While she whispered sweet nothings to the generator, I stood in my dark kitchen, arms folded, praying over my unfinished cake.

That fifth tier was crucial. You can't serve a four-tier cake when your bride is expecting a five-tier cake. That's how wars start in Lagos.

Ten minutes later, the generator coughed, sputtered, and roared to life.

Relieved, I nearly cried.

Saturday morning arrived, and the cake was ready.

It was a thing of beauty: tall, sleek, and fondant so smooth you'd think it had been photoshopped. It had a white base with gold trim, hand-painted floral details, and a touch of edible pearls. Even I was impressed with myself.

The only problem? We didn't know where to deliver it.

Yvonne hadn't sent the venue address.

I called. No answer.

Texted. Nothing.

By 10.00 am, I was pacing. Cynthia was already in her "let me call Bisi" mode.

Thirty minutes later, Bisi replied, cool as ever:

"Eko Atlantic, white tent by the fountain. 1.00 pm sharp."

Of course.

Because where else would a bride with five-tier cake dreams and no time management skills be getting married?

We got there by 12.30 pm. The sun was blazing like it was fighting for its life. Our carefully laid edges were sweating. The tent was surrounded by luxury cars, floral arches, and human statues painted in metallic colours.

We wheeled the cake in carefully, and I almost hissed when someone tried to pose beside it for a selfie.

"Please, the cake is not a backdrop," Morayo warned.

At 2.45 pm, forty-five minutes late, naturally, the bride arrived.

She stepped out of a Rolls-Royce, dressed in a dazzling lace mermaid gown with a veil long enough to cover the whole of Oshodi bridge.

She didn't notice me, of course. She was busy being a bridal goddess.

But as the guests gasped at the cake, I stood at the back and smiled.

Later, just before we left, she walked past and paused. Her eyes locked with mine. For a second, recognition flickered.

She smiled. "You must be Dayo."

"I am."

She nodded at the cake. "You outdid yourself."

I nodded back. "Thank you."

Then she walked away.

Back in the car, Morayo passed me a cold drink and asked, "Would you do that again?"

I took a long sip.

"For double the money?" I said. "I'd do it in heels."

3. The Birthday Mix-Up

It was one of those chaotic Thursdays where the mixer was acting like it wanted to resign, the AC was not cooling enough, and Cynthia was chewing gum passionately, as if it was a form of stress therapy. I had just iced a batch of lemon drizzle cupcakes when Morayo came into the kitchen, holding the printed order sheet like it was an exam script.

"Ma," she said carefully. "There's a small problem."

I froze. That sentence never ended well.

"What happened?"

She placed the sheet in front of me. Two cake orders. Two clients. Both named Ronke. Both ordered birthday cakes. Same pick-up date. Different destinations.

"Ronke Balogun ordered a pink-and-purple unicorn cake for her daughter, turning five."

"Okay," I nodded.

"Ronke Oladapo ordered a navy-blue Louis Vuitton-themed cake for her boss, turning fifty-five."

I looked at her. She looked at me.

"Cynthia," we called in unison.

Cynthia came into the room, still chewing, icing sugar on her shirt.

"Yes?"

"Did you mix up the Ronke orders?" I asked.

She blinked. "Ehn?"

"You sent the unicorn cake to the office in Ikoyi?"

"Yes! I gave it to Mohammed to deliver to the customer an hour ago."

"And the Louis Vuitton cake?"

"The girl's dad picked it up."

Morayo slapped her forehead. I closed my eyes.

So now, somewhere in Ikoyi, a fifty-five-year-old executive was opening a cake box to discover a pink unicorn smiling at him with edible glitter.

And somewhere in Gbagada, a five-year-old girl was probably sobbing in front of a navy-blue cake with gold LV patterns and the inscription: "Happy Birthday Sir. More Wins."

Jesus wept.

Cynthia gasped. "Wait, maybe they haven't opened it yet!"

I snatched my phone and called the Ikoyi number. A calm voice answered.

"Hello, good morning. This is Dayo from Sweet Cravings Bakery."

"Yes," the woman said coolly. "This is Bimbo, PA to Mr Femi Bamidele. I was just about to call you."

I winced. "I'm so sorry. There's been a mix-up…"

"Yes," she said. "I assumed the unicorn cake was a joke. Mr Femi is allergic to strawberries."

I mouthed "strawberry flavour" at Morayo. She winced.

"Please," I said. "Allow us to fix this by bringing the correct cake."

There was a pause.

"Bring it before lunchtime."

Done.

Next call: the Gbagada Ronke. She was less calm.

"Excuse me, what kind of nonsense is this?! My daughter is crying! My husband is shouting! LV cake?! For what?!"

I apologised, begged, and explained.

She finally sighed and said, "Just bring the correct cake. And please add cupcakes. Extra."

I looked at Cynthia. "Oya, quickly go and bring the LV cake from Gbagada."

She nodded, her face a picture of guilt, and quickly called a taxi.

I paced the shop nervously while she was away. The lunchtime deadline for the LV cake was close.

Cynthia came back within an hour with the LV cake. Morayo and I carried it into the van and raced to Ikoyi.

Of course, traffic was waiting for us at Obalende.

We reached the office, where the receptionist waved us up. Bimbo met us at the door, straight-faced.

"Mr Femi is in a meeting. But I'll pass this on."

We handed over the LV cake. She opened it and nodded.

"This one is better."

Then she handed me the unicorn cake box.

"Please remove this temptation from my sight."

As soon as we brought back the unicorn cake, Cynthia got into a taxi and raced back to Gbagada.

Ronke Balogun later sent me a voice note:

"Thank you for fixing it. My daughter is happy again. She's eating the ears off the unicorn. Please tell the delivery girl that her eyelashes are beautiful."

I forwarded the message to Cynthia. She responded with "*LOL, I was crying when I arrived, but okay.*"

Later, we all collapsed on the couch in the back office, eating leftover cupcakes.

"You know what's funny," Cynthia said, licking frosting off her finger. "The two Ronkes ordered within five minutes of each other."

I blinked. "You're joking."

She pulled up the order timestamps on the system.

"Ronke Balogun at 11:07am. Ronke Oladapo at 11:12am."

"Same first name, same delivery day..."

"Same chaos," Morayo added.

I sighed. "From now on, we collect surnames, phone numbers, and BVN."

We all laughed until our stomachs hurt.

4. When the Consultation Went Left

Some consultations start with mood boards and end with champagne. Some start with champagne and end in tears. This one? It started with matching outfits and ended with a table nearly breaking.

The couple walked into the shop on a sunny Wednesday afternoon, holding hands and wearing his-and-hers t-shirts. I remember because Cynthia nudged me from the till and cooed, "Aww. Lovebirds."

"Hi!" the bride chirped. "We're here for our cake consultation. I'm Nengi, and this is my fiancé, David."

David nodded, eyes scanning the shop like he was assessing if we had potential.

I led them to our consultation table, offered cold drinks, and pulled out my tablet.

"So," I began, "tell me your dream wedding cake."

Nengi leaned forward excitedly. "Five tiers. Maybe something with coral patterns."

David raised a brow. "Five tiers? You didn't say five before."

She laughed. "Babe, it's a big wedding now."

I smiled politely. "How many guests are you expecting?"

Nengi said, "About 500. But I want the cake to look taller. You know, for the photos."

David frowned. "But we agreed on three tiers."

I paused.

Nengi waved a hand. "It's just two extra dummy tiers. It's not a big deal."

David muttered, "Everything's always 'not a big deal' until the invoice comes."

I cleared my throat. "We can do a mix of real and faux tiers to stay within budget. Let's talk flavours?"

Nengi lit up again. "Oooh, yes! Red velvet, coconut sponge, lemon drizzle…"

David cut in. "That's a lot of flavours."

She blinked. "It's just three."

"You know I don't like lemon."

Nengi rolled her eyes. "It's not for you. It's for my cousin who's allergic to dairy."

David scoffed. "So now we're tailoring our cake to suit Tega's allergies?"

The air changed. Even Cynthia peeked over the counter like she was watching a Netflix drama.

I tried to steer us back. "Maybe we should go with red velvet and coconut?"

Nengi nodded. David grunted.

I clicked through designs. "What about this style?"

"Wait," David interrupted. "Why is the groom's figurine kneeling?"

I blinked. "Sorry?"

"The cake topper. Why is the groom kneeling while the bride is standing?"

Nengi snorted. "Because it's cute?"

He folded his arms. "So I should be kneeling on our cake? In front of our parents?"

She rolled her eyes. "David, it's a figurine. Not real life."

"I'm not doing that."

"Fine," she snapped. "Let's just make the bride kneel. Since that's your idea of romance."

I sat frozen, watching my consultation spiral into an ugly couple's spat.

David pushed his chair back slightly. "You know what, let's just get a plain cake. No designs. No figurines. Just 'Happy Married Life' and move on."

Nengi stared at him. "Are you serious?"

He shrugged. "You're turning this into a battle. It's just cake."

"Just cake?" She folded her arms. "You can cancel it then. Since I'm so difficult."

I coughed. "We don't have to decide everything today. We can pause and…"

"No," David said, standing. "I'm not spending half a million on sugar."

"Correction," Nengi said, standing too, "you're not spending anything. My parents are paying for this wedding."

He laughed dryly. "Exactly. So I'm just decoration."

And then he stormed out.

The door slammed behind him. A little too hard. The glass rattled. Cynthia gasped. I nearly dropped my tablet.

Nengi remained standing, arms crossed, lips trembling, staring at the door

"I'm sorry," I said gently.

She sighed. "It's not you. He's just… been like this lately. We've fought about the band, the hall, even the colour of his suit."

I offered her a tissue. "You don't have to decide today."

She sat back down, wiped her face, and said, "Can I just see one more design?"

So I showed her one.

She stared at it and whispered, "If I go ahead with this wedding, that's the cake I want."

126

The "if" was loud.

She looked at me and added, "I'll call you next week."

Then she left quietly.

Two weeks later, I got a text:

Hi Dayo. Just wanted to say thank you. There's no wedding anymore. But I'm ordering a birthday cake for myself. Red velvet. Same design. Just one tier. With the words: 'To New Beginnings.'

And that was the real cake consultation.

5. Fake Money and Fresh Puff-Puff

If you've ever run a bakery in Lagos, you'll know two things are certain:

Someone will ask for an "urgent birthday cake" at 7.30 pm.

One day, somebody will try to pay you with fake money.

It happened on a Monday. The kind of Monday where the weather cooperated, the ovens worked, and everyone was in a good mood. Cynthia and I were piping frosting onto red velvet mini cakes when two young men strolled into the shop.

They were dressed in oversized designer shirts, chains glinting like those of overachievers, and sneakers too white for the streets of Lagos.

"Good afternoon," the shorter one said, smiling too hard.

"Welcome," Morayo replied sweetly. "How can we help you?"

They pointed at the display.

"We want four of those chocolate mini cakes," said the taller one.

"And five puff-puff packs," added his friend. "Extra sugar on top."

While Morayo packed the order, they made small talk. Who's the owner? Do we make cakes for celebrities? Can we do cakes shaped like a Benz? Normal Lagos cruise.

The total came to ₦13,500.

They pulled out a bundle of ₦1,000 notes and counted the cash, then fanned it like they were hosting a giveaway.

"₦20k," one of them said. "Keep the change."

Morayo raised a brow. "You people are feeling generous today."

I collected the notes and glanced at them.

Something felt... off.

I turned one under the light. The colour was dull. The watermark looked like it had stage fright. No shimmer. No texture. It felt too smooth, too clean, like a note that had never seen the inside of a Lagos wallet.

Cynthia saw my expression.

"You suspect?"

I nodded slowly.

"Morayo," she called, "bring the fake money pen."

Morayo fetched it from the drawer. We use it sometimes for large transactions, rub it on the note. If it turns black, it's fake.

I marked one of the ₦1,000 notes.

It went dark immediately. Black as sin.

I looked up.

"Oga, please, where did you get this money?"

They both froze.

"Ah! What do you mean?" the taller one said. "That's clean money o!"

Cynthia crossed her arms. "This note is fake."

The shorter one scoffed. "How can it be fake? I just got it from POS!"

I tapped the counter. "POS that doubles as a printing press?"

They looked at each other. The taller one tried again. "Maybe your pen is faulty."

We tried it on our own ₦1,000 note. No colour change.

Silence.

Morayo started packing the cakes back into the display. Cynthia put her hands on her hips.

"Please, we're not Central Bank of Nigeria. Collect your paper and leave."

The shorter one leaned in, suddenly defensive. "But we don't have any other cash!"

Cynthia laughed. "So you people planned to scam us out of our cakes and puff-puff with monopoly money?"

I raised a brow. "Should we call police? Or just security from the next compound?"

Their attitude shifted fast.

"Abeg no vex," the taller one muttered. "We didn't know. Somebody gave us the money."

"Abi ghost gave it to you?" Morayo said, already wiping down the counter.

They mumbled apologies and shuffled out, avoiding eye contact.

We watched from the window as they crossed the road and disappeared into the street like escaped criminals.

Cynthia exhaled. "Lagos will not kill me."

Later that day, one of our regulars, Aunty Rose, came in to pick up her carrot loaf. She ran a food canteen nearby and knew every gossip on the street.

We told her the story.

She nodded knowingly. "Those boys? Ah, they've been trying that scam around this area for weeks. They used to target *keke* drivers. Now they've graduated to bakeries."

"God saved you," she added, putting the cake into her bag.

I smiled. "Or our fake money pen."

At closing time, Cynthia brought out the leftover puff-puff and dropped it on the staff table.

Cynthia raised her puff-puff like a toast. "To real money and fresh dough."

We all laughed.

6. The School Pastry Chaos

When the receptionist from *Little Ivy International School* first called, I thought it was a prank.

"Good afternoon," she said in that perfect Lekki-posh voice. "We'd like to place a large order for our school's 10th anniversary. Pastries only. A variety, for 350 children and 120 parents. Nothing too sugary. Also: gluten-free options, nut-free options, dairy-free options… and we'd like them colour-coded by class."

I stared at the phone.

"Sorry, you said…colour-coded?"

"Yes, pink boxes for Nursery, yellow for Year 1, green for Year 2, and so on."

"And you want all this by…?"

"Friday morning. Assembly starts at 9.00 am."

It was Tuesday afternoon.

I laughed. The kind of laugh that starts polite and ends in prayer.

But then she added, "Our headteacher's cousin is Bisi. The wedding planner. She says you're excellent."

Of course. Bisi.

Cynthia heard the order and said, "Ah. These school people want to kill us."

Morayo pulled out a whiteboard and wrote: Operation No Sugar, No Gluten, No Wahala.

We started brainstorming and researching recipes that night.

Coconut madeleines, banana oat muffins, vanilla-almond sponge bites, dairy-free brownies, and something Cynthia called "oat-choco energy bars" that tasted like regret but ticked all the allergy boxes.

By Thursday night, our shop looked like a science lab.

Cynthia was sticking colour-coded labels like her life depended on it. Morayo was layering cupcakes into boxes with surgical precision. I was double-checking the nut-free list, silently begging God that no child with a food blogger for a mother would find fault.

Friday morning. 6.00 am.

We loaded the van like we were carrying gold.

The school was in Ikate. Traffic was decent until we hit a roadblock near a construction site. I nearly wept.

However, we made it by 8.15 am.

A woman with a Bluetooth headset met us at the gate, her eyes sharp, as if she was born to supervise.

"You must be Dayo."

"I am."

"Fantastic. The food table is that way. Please be discreet. The children are meditating."

Ah. Lagos children?

I nodded and followed her through a courtyard where kids were doing yoga to soft afrobeats.

The setup was beautiful with bunting everywhere, floral arches, and balloon pillars in gold and navy blue. A table had been arranged with cake stands for the pastries. We began unloading carefully.

Everything was going smoothly until the mums arrived.

You know them.

Face beat by 8.00 am. Wedges. Waist trainers tighter than the nation's budget. And war in their eyes.

One of them spotted a pink box.

"What's that?"

"Nursery set," I explained. "Coconut muffins and oat banana cookies."

She frowned. "No fruit tarts?"

"No. Those were for Year 3 and above."

She raised a brow. "But my son is allergic to bananas."

Before I could reply, another mum chimed in.

"Is the chocolate *dairy-free*? Or Nigerian dairy-free?"

Cynthia gave her the smile we reserve for troublemakers.

"Imported cocoa, oat milk. Certified by two health stores in Ikoyi."

"Hmph," came the sceptical reply.

Meanwhile, another mother snuck behind the table and opened a yellow box.

"My daughter doesn't like raisins. Can I swap?"

Before I could answer, the woman with the Bluetooth headset reappeared.

"Please, ladies, do not touch the boxes. We're setting up."

The mothers backed off temporarily. But I could feel it. They were circling like sharks around a buffet.

At 9:15 am., the children filed in, led by prefects in blazers that were two sizes too big. They sat cross-legged on the lawn, legs swinging, eyes wide with sugar-free anticipation.

Then the headteacher gave her speech.

And then, it happened.

She invited the "parents' committee" to help "distribute snacks."

God help me.

The boxes I had labelled meticulously got rearranged and mixed up.

The nut-free, dairy-free, no-banana sets? Swapped.

I watched in horror as a Nursery child chewed a brownie meant for Year 6 while a Year 2 boy wailed that his cupcake was "not blue."

A mother handed me a box.

"This one says 'Free from eggs'. But Jaden is gluten-free. Do you have anything else?"

Cynthia snorted loudly. I pinched her.

Chaos. Pure, educational chaos.

At 10.00 am, the PA system crackled.

"Can we have the baker report to the front, please?"

I froze.

Was this how it would end?

But when I walked up, the headteacher smiled.

"Please come forward. We'd like to say thank you to *Sweet Cravings Bakery* for making today extra special."

Applause.

Children waved at me. Some still had the remnants of brownies smeared on their cheeks.

The headteacher leaned in and whispered, "I don't know how you did it. But this was perfect. Thank you."

I exhaled, smiled and curtsied. We packed up our boxes and the leftovers and trooped into our van.

Back at the shop, Cynthia collapsed onto a chair. I brought out the leftover oat-choco bars.

No one had touched them. I shrugged and took a bite.

They still tasted like regret.

7. The Yacht Cake

When the request came in, the tone alone told me it wasn't your regular Lagos party.

"Good afternoon," the voice said. Male. Calm. Expensive.

"We need a bespoke cake. Luxurious. Masculine. Discreet. Delivery must be on water."

I blinked. "I'm sorry, did you say…water?"

"Yes. It's for a private birthday dinner. On a yacht."

Ah. One of those.

The client didn't want a consultation. He didn't want options. He sent a design reference via email: *a sleek, two-tiered black-and-gold cake with edible cigar toppers and gold fondant coins, plus a subtle oil rig silhouette pressed into the side.*

No names. No writing. Just a card: "To the Chairman."

Paid in full.

No questions asked.

Cynthia was immediately suspicious.

"You know Lagos. Next thing we'll end up baking for a cartel boss."

Morayo added, "Or a senator's side chick's birthday."

I shrugged. "Whoever he is, he likes his fondant classy and his delivery quiet."

We named the order "Project Chairman" and got to work.

Dark chocolate sponge, filled with brandy buttercream. Black fondant so smooth it looked like patent leather. Gold-dusted decor, no shimmer, no noise. Just power in cake form.

When it was done, even I stood back and whistled.

"This is the kind of cake that doesn't do TikTok dances," I said.

Cynthia nodded. "It just steps out of a G-Wagon and says, 'How's the crude selling today?'"

Delivery day came.

We were told to meet a boatman named Kelvin at the VI jetty by 7.00 pm. He'd ferry us and the cake to the yacht anchored somewhere between Banana Island and a location Google Maps refused to acknowledge.

Cynthia and I arrived early, cake box in hand. Morayo stayed behind to run the shop.

Kelvin turned out to be a lean man in dark shades who said very little except: "We move in five minutes."

We strapped the cake carefully into a cooler. I climbed into the boat, heart pounding.

"You okay?" Cynthia asked.

"I've never delivered a cake on water before," I whispered. "What if it tips over?"

"Then we jump in and swim with it like Titanic," she replied. "Hold the Chairman till the end."

The boat cut across the lagoon like it had secrets to keep. Lagos skyline shimmered behind us. Soon, we saw it.

The yacht.

White, elegant, absurdly large. The kind of boat that doesn't host "parties" but "gatherings."

We climbed aboard, the cooler between us.

A steward met us. He wore white gloves.

"This way," he said, leading us into the dining area. There were about ten people inside, all men, all dressed like they were about to vote on who would run Nigeria next.

We placed the cake gently on a mirrored table already lined with cigars, whiskey bottles, and designer watches as decor.

No balloons. No noise. Just low music and political tension in the air.

One of the men, in a navy kaftan and heavy gold wristwatch, walked over. He said nothing. Just stared at the cake. Then nodded once.

I took that as the review.

He turned to me. "You're Dayo?"

"Yes, sir."

"Nice work."

"Thank you, sir."

He turned back and walked away.

That was it.

No photos. No "Happy Birthday" song. No fireworks. Just a nod.

On the boat ride back, Cynthia burst out laughing.

"What?"

"That man looked at the cake like it was a stock portfolio. So much gravitas."

"I'll take it," I said.

The next morning, we got an anonymous email:

Thank you. Elegant, flawless, and quiet. Just like him.

P.S. He asked for your card. Discreet bakers are rare.

Cynthia printed the message and taped it to our fridge beside a sticky note that says, "Remember to buy flour."

Above it, she scribbled: Cake fit for the Chairman.

8. Symbols and Sentiments

The email subject line read: *Traditional wedding cake – Yoruba symbols required.*

I sighed and opened it, half-expecting drama. It didn't disappoint.

"We are requesting a traditional-themed cake for our son's engagement. It should reflect our culture. Cowrie shells, talking drum, gourd, cowries, etc. Please include an image of *ileke idi* (waist beads). And the bride's family insists on a dove."

I blinked.

Morayo, reading over my shoulder, said, "A dove? On a traditional cake?"

Cynthia snorted. "This one looks like it'll be sweet and spiritual."

The groom's mum, Mummy Olayiwola, came in first for the consultation.

She arrived wearing royal blue iro and buba with gele with lines sharp enough to slice fondant. Her handbag was designer. Her tone was not for the weak.

"I want something regal," she said, flipping through our portfolio. "Yam tuber symbols for fertility. Cowries for wealth. And please, no kolanut. That one is for elders."

I nodded and took notes.

"What about the bride's family?" I asked.

She scoffed. "They're the ones saying they want dove and beads. I said what has dove got to do with Yoruba marriage?"

I smiled professionally. "We'll harmonise both sides."

That was a lie.

The next day, the bride's mother, Mummy Adepoju, arrived wearing a peach-coloured lace dress and large gold earrings. From the way she strutted into the shop, you'd think she was here to inspect property she intended to purchase.

"Good afternoon," she said, eyeing our cakes like they were undercooked.

She sat down, crossed her legs. "I hope you understand symbolism."

"We do, ma."

She pulled out a folder containing actual printed images. Mummy Adepoju clearly meant business.

"This is what we want. The dove means peace. The beads mean femininity. Gourd means union. No talking drums, please, they are too loud in nature."

I swallowed.

"No cowries?"

She hissed. "Cowries bring argument. Let's focus on purity and fruitfulness."

Cynthia peeped in and whispered, "This is not a cake. It's a thesis."

I sent both mothers a mock-up design via WhatsApp.

Tier 1: Talking drum and cowries.

Tier 2: Dove and gourd.

Tier 3: Adire pattern with fondant beads.

Simple. Balanced. Peaceful.

One hour later, two messages came in. Simultaneously.

Mummy Olayiwola: Why is dove on the cake? It looks like burial symbol.

Mummy Adepoju: Why is cowry shell on the cake? Are we dedicating the marriage to Sango?

I closed my laptop and went to lie down.

Three days before the wedding, they both stormed into the shop unannounced.

I was in the kitchen. Cynthia came to warn me: "Two lionesses outside. And they're not here for cupcakes."

I walked in smiling. "Good afternoon, madams…"

"No!" Mummy Olayiwola snapped. "No more fondant dove!"

"This is a Yoruba engagement, not wildlife documentary," said Mummy Adepoju.

They both turned to each other.

"I told you", one said.

"No, I told you!" said the other.

Voices rose.

It escalated fast.

Something about bride price. Family pride. One called the other "too modern." The other hissed and said, "At least my daughter is not marrying into thunder!"

Morayo quietly pressed play on gospel music. Cynthia made tea.

I just stood there, watching my cake design dissolve like poorly set gelatin.

Eventually, I raised a hand.

"Ladies, may I?"

They both paused, blinking.

I cleared my throat. "We can do this", I began in placating tones. "Let's do beads and calabash for the first tier, to symbolise the bride. For the second tier, it'll be cowries and a drum, for the groom's heritage." Encouraged by their rapt attention, I continued. "Finally, we'll have a small fondant dove inside a gourd, signifying peace within union, not outside."

Silence.

Then, slowly, two reluctant nods.

One muttered, "Let the dove hide, then."

The other said, "No feathers. I don't want feathers."

"No feathers," I promised.

On the day of the wedding, the cake stood tall and proud.

Ivory fondant. Everything perfectly placed.

Both mothers posed beside it.

They didn't smile at each other, but they smiled for the camera.

And when the MC said, "This cake represents unity in diversity," everyone clapped.

Especially me.

9. Valentine's Day Madness

If you think Lagos traffic is bad, try running a bakery on Valentine's Day.

The orders start trickling in early in January. Orders for small cakes, cupcakes, and heart-shaped cookies. Cute, harmless.

But by the second week of February, chaos sets in.

By the 13th? Madness.

By the 14th? Mayhem.

This year, I swore we'd be prepared. I even made a Valentine's Survival Checklist:

Pre-bake as much as possible.

Triple-check deliveries.

Expect last-minute orders, but set a strict cut-off time.

I wrote it down. I laminated it. I made everyone recite it like a national pledge.

None of it helped.

At 6.30 am on Valentine's Day, I was in battle mode.

I arrived at the shop early, wearing my game face. The kitchen was already warm with the scent of red velvet, strawberry buttercream, and baked promises.

Morayo was boxing up pre-orders. Cynthia was decorating mini heart cakes, humming Love Nwantiti like a woman about to witness relationship drama.

The first problem occurred at 8:45 a.m.

A text came from a customer:

"Hi. My girlfriend is allergic to chocolate. I forgot. Can I swap for vanilla?"

The client's order? Triple-layer chocolate overload cake. Already boxed. Already in the van.

I called. "Sir, we can't swap at this point..."

"Please, I'll pay extra! My relationship is on the line."

Cynthia muttered, "Let the line cut small. It builds character."

We repacked vanilla cupcakes. Crisis averted.

The next dose of drama arrived at 11:00 a.m.

Cynthia was at the counter when two men walked in, one after the other, with no awareness of each other.

The first man wore a black kaftan, sported a gold wristwatch, and gave off big man energy. He collected his order:

"For My Queen, My Life. Love you forever."

The next man wore a navy blue agbada and stank of perfume strong enough to slap you. He collected his order:

"For My Baby Girl. Love you always."

Both cakes? The same design. Red and white fondant, gold lettering, same damn bakery box.

Cynthia had just handed over the second cake when the first man turned back.

"Wait," he frowned. "That cake looks exactly like mine."

The second man glanced at his box. "So?"

Morayo and I froze.

The first man opened his cake box. His face changed.

He turned to the other man. "Who are you giving that cake to?"

"Why do you care?"

"Wait, WAIT!"

It clicked.

Husband. Wife's cake.

Boyfriend. Wife's side cake.

Both ordered from my bakery.

Cynthia had dived into the kitchen like a soldier dodging gunfire. Morayo started rearranging display cupcakes like she wasn't hearing anything.

I cleared my throat. "Sir, let's..."

But before I could finish, the first man dropped his box, turned, and stormed out.

The other man adjusted his agbada.

"Let me make sure the writing is correct," he muttered, and left like nothing happened.

Cynthia peeked out. "Are we dead?"

I exhaled. "Not yet."

At 2.00 pm, another episode ensued. A corporate client had placed a huge order for mini cakes for their staff, plus one large red heart cake with the words:

"To our most special employee."

Seemed sweet, until the PA called in panic.

"Please, remove 'Most Special Employee.'"

"Why?" I asked.

She sighed. "Oga's wife just saw the cake invoice, and now they're fighting. If he carries that cake to work, it's war."

Cynthia cackled. "Oga is finished."

We re-piped it. "Happy Valentine's, Team." Bland. Safe. Marriage intact.

By the time we closed, we were battle-worn but standing.

Cynthia and Morayo collapsed onto the couch. I grabbed a leftover cupcake and raised it in the air.

"A toast. To surviving Lagos Valentine's."

Morayo added, "And to men who know their main chick's allergies."

Cynthia finished, "And to wives who deserve cakes from both husband and side boo."

We clinked cupcakes like champagne and cackled like witches.

Outside, couples held hands, cake boxes in tow, walking into the night.

And me?

I went home, curled up with a mug of tea, and ate my own damn cake in peace.

Because love is sweet, but cake is sweeter.

10. The Groomzilla

Brides get a bad reputation for being dramatic. But let me tell you, sometimes, the real problem is the groom.

Meet Chuka. Thirty-six, a financial analyst, a perfectionist, and the most exhausting client I have ever had.

His fiancée, Ifunanya, had booked the wedding cake. Sweet girl, polite and easy-going. She'd sent a mood board, picked classic ivory fondant with pink and red roses, paid the deposit, and said, "I trust you."

I should have known peace wasn't my portion.

Because one week later, Chuka called.

Call #1 – The Spreadsheet

"Hi, Dayo. Just checking in. I sent a spreadsheet with cake specifications. Did you see it?"

I checked.

This man had sent a nine-page Google Doc.

Breakdown of cake tiers.

Measurements down to millimetres.

Font options for lettering.

Edible gold vs non-toxic shimmer.

I blinked.

"Mr Chuka," I said carefully, "we usually finalise details during the tasting."

"Oh," he said. "I assumed you'd appreciate the structure."

I did not.

The couple came in for a tasting. Ifunanya loved everything. She smiled and looked through our pictures. She happily tasted the samples. Excited bride energy.

Chuka? He sat there composed and analytical, like an investor evaluating a business pitch.

"This vanilla sponge," he said, chewing slowly. "What's your flour-to-liquid ratio?"

I frowned. "It's...balanced?"

He nodded like a professor. "And this red velvet? Can you guarantee it won't dry out by hour three of the reception?"

Cynthia muttered, "Does he want a wedding cake or is he here doing a research paper?"

I fought the urge to throw my pen at her.

Meanwhile, Ifunanya was already picking her favourite: vanilla and coconut.

But Chuka? No. He needed a risk analysis.

Call #3 – The PowerPoint presentation

Yes.

This man emailed me a PowerPoint deck.

SUBJECT: Cake colour simulation and guest interaction

I opened it.

Slide 1: Ivory fondant shade variations.

Slide 2: Cake angle options for best guest views.

Slide 3: Potential guest reactions to the cake (he had actual stick figure illustrations).

I dropped my phone.

Cynthia saw my face and burst out laughing. "I swear, you attract premium Lagos madness."

Call #4 – The panic call

One week to the wedding. 10.00 pm. My phone rang.

Chuka.

"Dayo," he breathed, like a man with bad news. "I have a concern."

I sat up. "What happened?"

"The cake topper."

"What about it?"

"I changed my mind. I don't like figurines. It feels... unserious."

I rubbed my temples, mildly frustrated. "So what do you want instead?"

Silence.

Then: "Do you think we can get a small crystal ball?"

I nearly choked. "Crystal *what?*"

"A glass orb. Symbolising clarity and vision."

"Sir, this is a cake. I can't promise that."

Finally, the wedding day came. I was relieved because my patience had been tested to the limit.

We delivered the cake, perfect ivory fondant, pink and red roses, zero figurines, zero crystal balls, and all. It was stunning.

But guess what?

Chuka, the human spreadsheet, was late to his own wedding. One full hour.

His bride, Ifunanya, was fuming.

When he finally showed up, he was all smiles, full of apologies and something about a "minor delay." Later, after the cutting of the cake, the servers wheeled it back, where my team and I set about reducing it to slices for the guests. Ifunanya dropped by and tapped me on the back.

"Thank you for everything, Dayo. I told you; he overthinks everything."

Then she smiled at her new husband.

"Lucky for him, I have patience."

I believed her.

10. The Influencer Bride

When Tara first walked into the shop, I recognised her immediately.

Not because I knew her personally, but because everyone in Lagos Instagram did.

Tara The Trendsetter. The one with 500,000 followers and luxury brand deals. Signature long blonde wig.

And now, a high-profile Lagos wedding.

I already knew how this would go. She wasn't here for a cake. She was here for *content*.

She entered wearing oversized sunglasses, a crop top, and ripped jeans that probably cost somebody's annual rent. Her three-man media team streamed in behind her. Photographer. Videographer. A personal assistant holding a ring light like she was cradling destiny.

I smiled. "Welcome to Sweet Cravings."

Tara barely looked up from her phone. "Hi, babe. Are you recording?"

The camera handler nodded.

Finally turning to acknowledge me, Tara smiled and suddenly became the warmest bride in Lagos.

"Oh my God, Dayo! I LOVE your cakes! Guys, meet my cake bestieeee!"

She threw an arm around me. Flash. Click. Boomerang.

Cynthia snickered.

Tara wanted a statement cake.

"Forget basic tiers," she said excitedly. "I want drama. I want levels. I want something that says, 'This is the wedding of the year!'"

I nodded. "What design are you thinking?"

She gestured wildly. "Something huge. Maybe like... a floating cake?"

Morayo's head snapped up.

Tara scrolled through Pinterest. "Or maybe a chandelier cake?"

I rubbed my temples. "You mean upside down?"

"Yes!" She gasped. "Or a levitating cake. Is that possible?"

I inhaled deeply. "We'll see."

After two hours of debating non-realistic cake ideas, Tara finally settled on:

7 tiers.

Pearl-studded fondant.

LED lights inside the cake.

Before I could draft an invoice, she paused.

"Wait," she frowned. "What if my followers don't like it?"

Cynthia muttered, barely audible. "Maybe they should pay for it."

Tara sighed. "Lagos people can be mean. If my cake is not giving soft life, they'll drag me on Twitter."

I forced a smile. "Let's finalise, so we can start sketching and baking."

She gasped. "Oh my God, baking! Babe, let's film me pretending to bake!"

Before I could say no, there she was, taking position beside an empty mixing bowl. Her crew obediently clicked and filmed everything as she posed and pouted. She even borrowed an apron from Cynthia.

She left with promises of immediate payment.

One day passed.

Two.

A week.

No payment.

Then, on Instagram, I saw her story:

"Cake hunting is so hard! Thinking of flying in a baker from Paris 😩 😩 "

I almost threw my phone.

Cynthia burst into laughter.

Morayo was furious. "Does she think she can pay the Paris baker in exposure?"

I just hissed and blocked her number.

On the wedding day, I got curious.

I checked her IG live.

And there it was, her wedding cake.

Guess what? It was a simple three-tier cake. No chandelier. No LED lights. No floating magic.

She had just hyped air.

Cynthia smirked. "Her followers won't like it."

I smiled. "Neither will the Paris baker."

11. The Power Outage

In Lagos, it's a known fact that when your need for power is greatest, NEPA will betray you. It doesn't matter if you've paid your light bill, prayed against suffering, or even sacrificed a bottle of Fanta to the gods of steady electricity. When you need light the most, it will disappear. And that's exactly what happened on the hottest day of the year, with five cakes in the oven.

It started beautifully. The sun was shining, the buttercream was fluffy and light, and it was at just the perfect temperature. The mixer was behaving itself.

The team was in flow mode, Cynthia rolling fondant, Morayo piping frosting, and I supervising a batch of wedding cakes while humming to Burna Boy.

Then, at 11.46 am, the lights flickered. Then the lights went off.

I looked up. This was unusual.

"Don't panic," Cynthia said. "It might just be a flicker."

We waited. Nothing. No hum from the AC. No beeping from the oven. No sign of resurrection.

I sprinted outside and yanked the generator's cord like I was starting a generator Olympics.

Nothing.

Cynthia joined me, chanting motivational words. "Come on, baby. Just turn for us."

But the generator was unbothered. Meanwhile, inside, my cakes were still inside the oven.

The heat was trapped, but only for a short time. If I didn't restart the oven soon, they'd sink in the middle and be as useless as a bad WhatsApp broadcast.

I dialled my fuel guy.

"Where are you?"

"Ah, aunty, wahala dey now o. Fuel scarcity."

Chai.

We started to brainstorm ideas.

Option 1: Find another bakery and beg to use their oven.

(But which baker will allow you to enter their kitchen and finish your cake?)

Option 2: Start over.

(Buy more eggs, mix more batter, pretend my blood pressure isn't rising.)

Option 3: Use the neighbour's gen.

(Madam Bose's tailoring shop, but she once caught Cynthia insulting her overpriced zips.)

We had no choice. I sent Cynthia. She returned two minutes later, looking humbled.

"She said…we can use it."

I exhaled. "God is good."

"She also said I should buy her Fanta and dash her a free cake."

Three cakes were no trouble at all. We hurriedly went to collect her generator and carried it to our shop.

Madam Bose's generator was small, but mighty. We plugged it in, pulled the cord, and hallelujah! The ovens came back on.

Fifteen minutes later, the cakes had risen beautifully.

I patted the cakes. "We passed."

Just as we finished decorating, guess what?

NEPA returned.

Bright, bold, flashing lights everywhere.

Cynthia wagged her spatula threateningly at the switch. "These people just wanted to play with us today."

Morayo kissed her teeth. "So NEPA just wanted to test our faith."

I took a deep breath, shook my head, and picked up my phone.

Later that night, after all the orders were delivered, Morayo turned to me.

"Aunty, we survived."

I raised a brownie. "Indeed. To emergency generators."

12. Mummy's 70th Surprise

If you've ever planned a surprise party for a Nigerian mother, you already know it's impossible. They sense it. They see it coming from a mile off. And somehow, no matter how careful you are, they will find out.

So when Kunle, an old friend, called on a Wednesday afternoon, I should have known where this was headed.

Kunle's voice was too calm.

"Hi, Dayo. My mum's 70th is on Sunday. I need a cake."

I checked the calendar. "This Sunday?"

"Yes."

I pinched the bridge of my nose. "Mr. Kunle, why are we just discussing this now?"

He chuckled. "It's a surprise party. We didn't want her to suspect."

I sighed. "What design?"

"Three tiers. Maybe green and gold."

I nodded. "Sweet. What flavours does Mummy like?"

There was a pause.

Then: "Ehm…she likes…cake?"

The next morning, Kunle sent a text:

Slight problem. Mummy is asking too many questions. She suspects something.

I replied, 'Is she asking about the cake? '

No. But she just told my sister, 'My spirit is telling me something is happening this Sunday.'

I sighed. Then texted back: *Kunle, does she like surprises?*

He went quiet.

Then: *She doesn't hate them.*

I put my head on the table.

Kunle sent another text on Friday evening.

Mummy just called me. She said, 'Kunle, what are you hiding?'

I rubbed my temples.

Kunle, if she finds out before Sunday, I am charging you stress allowance.

Finally, Sunday afternoon came. We arrived early at a luxurious hall in Ikeja, where the event was scheduled to take place.

The cake was flawless. Three tiers of vanilla and coconut sponge, hand-painted floral details, green with gold-trimmed edges. We were almost done setting up the cake table in front of the hall. The guests had begun to arrive. Everything was perfect.

Until…

"MUMMY IS HERE EARLY!"

The hall erupted into panic.

The DJ cut the music. People dived behind tables. One uncle tripped and nearly fell as he ran into the bathroom.

I grabbed Cynthia. "Where's the celebrant supposed to enter from?"

"The back."

I turned.

Mummy was already in the front.

Kunle's sister ran toward her. "Mummy! What are you doing here?"

Mummy, unbothered, walked up to the cake. "Am I not the owner of the birthday?" she asked.

She scanned the room, taking in the entire setup. Decorations. Caterers setting up a buffet. Cake. Guests holding balloons mid-air.

She exhaled.

"I knew it."

Everyone started laughing.

Ten minutes later, after hugs, dancing, and amusement that nobody could surprise her, Mummy took the microphone.

"My children tried," she said, shaking her head. "But you cannot hide this kind of thing from a mother."

There was laughter and applause.

Then she turned to me and beamed. "The cake is very nice."

Kunle exhaled like a man who had just escaped police trouble.

"Dayo," he whispered, "bill me extra."

I smiled. "I already did."

Next time?

I'd just tell Mummy the truth. It's easier.

13. The Expensive Cake

Sometimes, expensive does not mean better. Sometimes, expensive just means premium heartbreak. And that's exactly what happened when Madam Evelyn walked into my shop.

Evelyn was the type of woman who didn't need to say she was rich.

You could tell from her designer bag, her diamond-studded nails, and the way she said, "I don't do regular cakes."

She flipped open her iPad.

"I'm having a party for top socialites in Lagos. I want a cake covered in edible gold. Real gold. Not that 'Lagos gold dust' nonsense."

I nodded slowly. "Okay...gold accents?"

She sighed. "No. The whole cake must shine like money."

Ah.

"Ma, real edible gold is very delicate. And expensive."

She waved her hand. "Money is not my problem."

I smiled.

After the consultation, I emailed her the price. A ridiculous amount.

She replied immediately: *Expensive. But fine. I'll pay.*

I was stunned.

No negotiation. No "reduce it for me".

We sourced imported edible gold sheets.

The supplier laughed. "Hope your client won't cry when this thing melts?"

Cynthia muttered, "She won't cry. But Dayo will."

The day before the party, I got to work and made the cake as if my entire reputation depended on it.

When it was done, we all stepped back and admired it. The cake was stunning. Three tiers of vanilla-almond sponge, covered in pure gold leaf, smooth as luxury.

"This cake looks richer than my bank account," Morayo whispered.

Cynthia nodded. "This is not cake. This is generational wealth."

I took pictures. It was perfection on all sides. Nothing could go wrong, or so I thought.

On Friday afternoon, delivery was set. We loaded the cake into the van gently. We begged Mohammed to go slowly and carefully. Then Lagos betrayed us.

The sun was unhinged, the heat aggressive. The air conditioner in the van was not working effectively.

At Oworo, just before we hit the Third Mainland Bridge, Cynthia gasped.

"Dayo..."

I turned.

And saw it.

The gold leaf had begun to melt.

I called out to Mohammed.

"STOP. PULL OVER AND FIND SHADE."

We pulled into a nearby supermarket and begged for fridge space.

The staff stared.

"Madam, na pure gold dey fall from this cake?"

"Yes. And it's not mine," I cried.

After about an hour, the cake had cooled sufficiently, and the traffic had improved, so we decided to resume our delivery. We arrived in Ikoyi just in time.

Madam Evelyn walked in excited. She gasped when she saw the cake.

"Oh my God! It's beautiful!"

I exhaled. Crisis averted.

Then she squinted.

"Wait...why is the bottom part looking patchy?"

Silence.

The gold hadn't melted completely, but some parts were dull.

I forced a smile. "Ma, Lagos weather isn't friendly to gold."

She frowned.

"Can't you just...spray paint it back?"

Cynthia coughed loudly.

"Spray paint?" I repeated.

She nodded, serious.

"Ma, you cannot spray paint edible gold."

She sucked her teeth.

"Well, next time, let's try it."

Next time? I smiled.

Despite the melting mishap, the guests loved it.

Everyone took photos of the cake all evening, and the pictures flew everywhere.

Madam Evelyn was happy. After the event, she sent me a text.

Cake was amazing! But next time, let's add more shine.

I smiled and closed my phone.

And ate a regular, non-gold, stress-free slice of cake.

Because sometimes, simple is better.

14. The Cake Hustlers

Every baker has a favourite kind of client. Mine are the decisive ones. The bride who walks in with her Pinterest board, groom in tow, smiling, ready to pick a flavour and transfer a deposit within 30 minutes.

But unfortunately, Lagos isn't full of decisive people.

Some come in, sample everything, and disappear. Others ghost after requesting quotes. And then...there are the ones like *them*.

It started innocently. One Friday afternoon, a cheerful couple strolled into the shop. He wore round glasses and a polo shirt. Her braided hair was worn in a bun. They wore matching sneakers.

"Hi!" she chirped. "We're getting married, and we saw your cakes on Instagram!"

Lovely.

"Congratulations," I said, motioning them to the tasting table. "Would you like to try some samples?"

"Oh yes, please! Vanilla, chocolate, and red velvet, if you have."

Standard. I gave Morayo a look. She brought the tray.

They ate like people who hadn't seen cake in months.

Mouths full, nodding enthusiastically.

"This red velvet!" the man exclaimed, eyes closed as he sampled the dessert. "It's giving destiny."

The woman smiled, licking frosting off her finger. "It's so soft and moist."

After finishing, they thanked me profusely.

"We'll go and talk to our parents and come back next week to finalise."

No problem. This is Lagos. You learn not to expect too much.

Except...

They came back the very next week.

"Hi again!" she said, all smiles. "We just wanted to try the lemon and coconut flavours this time."

Still polite, I brought out the samples.

They devoured them.

Again. And said again, "We'll be back soon to finalise."

By the third visit, I knew something was off.

"We're not sure if we want buttercream or fondant," the woman said, chewing thoughtfully. "Can we try the caramel filling too?"

Cynthia leaned in as I plated the samples.

"Are they serious customers?" she whispered.

I frowned. "They've never picked a design. Never asked about price."

Morayo added, "They always leave with the extra slices of samples packed away."

Suspicious.

So, I made a plan.

On their fourth visit, I smiled sweetly.

"Welcome back! We have new flavours to try today…just a small charge for the premium tasting tray. Only three thousand naira."

The man's face changed. The woman's smile froze.

"Sorry…you said…charge?"

I nodded. "Yes. After three complimentary tastings, we offer curated sessions for serious couples."

Silence.

Then awkward laughter.

"Ah! We didn't realise. We're, um… still finalising some things."

They backed away, hands in pockets.

"Thanks so much, though!" she said, already halfway to the door. "Your cakes are amazing!"

Cynthia waved. "Bye-bye, o. Enjoy the rest of your date."

They never came back.

Later that week, Morayo sent me a screenshot of a tweet. It read:

"Pro tip: if you and bae are broke, go wedding cake tasting. Free cake, AC, and love vibes. Works every time."

The poster was the "bride" that had been in our shop. Same braids. Same sneakers.

I sighed.

Cynthia muttered, "We should start selling popcorn in this shop. The drama is endless."

15. The Other Cake

Some weddings are marked by last-minute madness and drama. Sometimes, it's the weather. Or traffic. Or missing rings.

But nothing prepared me for the day my cake went into battle against another cake.

It was Seun and Doyin's wedding, the sweet couple who knew what they wanted, had tried the samples, and paid early. The bride requested a five-tier white fondant cake with lace piping and edible orchids. Elegant and classy.

The morning of the wedding, I delivered the cake to the reception hall in Ikeja.

Everything was running smoothly. Until I saw her.

Middle-aged Aunty. Loud lipstick. Traditional iro and buba wrapped with purpose. And standing next to her was another cake.

Three tiers. Pink buttercream. Slightly leaning to the left. Covered in plastic wrap and pride.

"Hello," I said politely. "Can I help you?"

She turned, sniffed.

"I brought my nephew's wedding cake from our family baker. We don't trust all these fancy Lagos vendors."

I blinked. "I'm the official baker."

She blinked back. "So am I."

Cue confusion.

Bisi, the event planner, came over.

"What's going on?"

I pointed. "This woman brought a second cake."

Aunty Bunmi patted her gele.

"Abi I cannot bake cake again in my own family?"

Then Seun, the groom, arrived.

"Ah, Aunty, thank you, but we already..."

She waved. "Ehn ehn. I know. But this one is from our side of the family. At least let it show small on the main stage."

Doyin walked in and saw the pink cake. She turned to her husband.

"Seun."

Seun swallowed.

"Please talk to your aunty."

What followed was a 15-minute family meeting at the corner of the reception hall.

I watched from behind my cake stand, arms folded.

Finally, the planner came over.

"We'll put your cake on the stage," she whispered, "and Aunty's own on the buffet table."

I exhaled. Problem solved, or so we thought.

As guests entered, Aunty redirected people.

"Ah ah, no o! Don't take picture there! Come to this side!"

She posed next to her pink cake, dragging the bride's cousins for photos.

Even the MC got confused.

"Let's cut the – wait - which one is the real cake?"

The bride snapped.

"If he calls the pink one again, I'll cut HIM."

Eventually, Bisi turned off the stage lights on Aunty's side.

Her cake sat quietly in the shadows, like a forgotten cast member.

My cake got the spotlight and the photos.

As it should be.

Later, the bride whispered to me:

"Thank you for handling that well."

I smiled.

Back at the shop, Morayo asked how it went.

"It was cake politics. One Aunty came with a family cake"

Cynthia shook her head. "Aunties with cake agenda."

16. Delivery Driver Woes

The worst part of running a bakery? *Not the all-nighters. Not the fondant frights. Not even the bridezillas.*

It's the cake delivery. Because once a cake leaves my shop, my blood pressure leaves with it. And no matter how carefully I prepare, there's almost always drama.

Especially when the driver is Sammy.

We met Sammy through Cynthia's cousin's friend's barber's brother, so that's already a red flag. However, our usual driver, Mohammed, had gone to Kano to visit his family, and he said he would be away for months, so we had little choice. Lagos delivery drivers are scarce, and he came highly recommended.

Morayo asked, "Can he handle delicate cakes?"

Cynthia shrugged. "He used to work in logistics."

I nodded. "Good enough."

It was not.

We had an order for a three-tier vanilla and coconut wedding cake. The destination: a reception hall in Victoria Island. Time: 2.00 pm sharp.

We packed it carefully, placed it in the van, and gave Sammy clear instructions.

Drive carefully. Avoid potholes. No loud music, vibrations can ruin the fondant.

He nodded seriously.

"I dey hear, madam. No shaking."

There was shaking.

I was checking the time. By 12.45 pm, the venue should have called to confirm the cake had arrived.

They hadn't.

I dialled Sammy.

No answer.

I dialled again.

Voicemail.

Cynthia muttered, "Hope he didn't enter Third Mainland Bridge traffic."

Morayo crossed her arms. "Or enter another venue by mistake."

I was sweating. Then my phone rang.

Sammy.

"Madam..."

Something was wrong.

"Sammy, where are you?"

He cleared his throat.

"Ehm…madam…I get small issue."

My heart stopped.

"What issue?"

"…I dey fix my tire."

Cynthia gasped.

"The cake! WHERE IS THE CAKE?"

Silence.

Then: "It fell."

I collapsed into a chair.

Apparently, Sammy had been speeding. He ran into a pothole and his tire burst.

The van jerked. The cake tumbled.

MY CAKE WAS ON THE FLOOR OF HIS VAN.

I clutched my chest. "Sammy…how bad is it?"

Pause.

"…Ehm…some small dent."

Cynthia snatched the phone. "SEND PICTURE. NOW."

A photo came in.

The two top tiers were leaning precariously. The fondant was torn. The bottom tier was crushed on one side.

Cynthia held her head. "Jesus."

Morayo covered her eyes.

Me?

I saw my life flash before me. We had less than an hour.

No time to rebake. No time to cry.

"Grab the fondant," I snapped. "We're doing emergency cake surgery."

Cynthia packed all the necessary equipment.

Morayo grabbed extra frosting.

I took deep breaths and said a short prayer.

Then we drove. FAST.

We met Sammy by the roadside, where he stood looking guilty, hands in pockets, beside his van.

We grabbed our tools like trauma doctors.

Morayo fixed the fondant tears, while Cynthia reinforced the structure with extra supports.

I prayed the wedding coordinator wouldn't notice.

By 1.45 pm, it was standing again. It was not perfect, but presentable.

I wiped my hands.

"Let's go."

We arrived at the venue just in time. Nobody knew the cake had fought for its life.

I sighed in relief. Then side-eyed Sammy.

"This can't happen again."

He nodded quickly.

"Yes, madam. No shaking."

Lies.

The following Monday, Sammy sent a text.

Good morning, madam. Do you still need me for more deliveries?

I stared, then replied:

Sammy, God bless you. But no.

Then blocked his number.

17. The Bakery Proposal

Running a bakery means that I get to witness all kinds of love stories unfold in real time. Some are sweet. Some are stressful. And some? Some happen right in the middle of my shop.

Like what happened last Thursday.

It was rush hour. The shop was bustling, and the aroma of fresh pastries was in the air.

Morayo was boxing cupcakes. Cynthia was managing a fussy customer ("Madam, I can't make the icing less sweet..."). I was in the kitchen, finishing a wedding cake order.

Then the door chimed. A nervous-looking man walked in.

Cynthia greeted him. "Good evening, sir. What can we get you?"

He cleared his throat. "Uh...I need a small cake."

Cynthia smiled. "Great! Birthday? Anniversary?"

He hesitated.

Then said, "Proposal."

Cynthia's eyes widened.

She turned to me slowly.

I stepped out. "Sir, you want to propose?"

He nodded. "Right here."

I blinked. "In the shop?"

"Yes."

I looked around.

"Are you sure?"

He nodded again.

"She loves this place. She comes here all the time."

Cynthia gasped. "Aww, a bakery romance!"

"Which of our regular customers? Can you show us her photo?"

He brought out this phone and showed me a photo of his girlfriend. I recognised her.

Nancy who liked our muffins.

But I was still processing. "Sir, does she know?"

"No," he said. "It's a surprise."

Red flag.

We had one hour. We quickly organised a small red velvet cake, and piped "Will You Marry Me?" on it. Cynthia found some extra roses, and Morayo put on a subtle romantic playlist for background music.

Everything was ready.

Now we just needed the bride-to-be.

Nancy walked in, clueless, wearing jeans and a big smile.

"Ah! My favourite bakery!" she said.

Then she saw the flowers, the cake, and her boyfriend kneeling, holding a ring.

She froze.

Then said, "What is this?"

The entire shop held its breath.

The man smiled nervously. "Babe…will you marry me?"

Her face changed.

I knew it.

This wasn't a happy surprise.

This was an *I-will-kill-you* surprise.

She folded her arms. "Did I ask you to propose?"

SILENCE.

The man laughed awkwardly. "I thought you'd love this."

Her eyes narrowed. She turned to me.

"Dayo, did you know about this?"

ME?!

I stammered. "Uh…he just ordered a cake…"

She turned back to him.

"Chuka, you don't listen! I said we should talk first!"

The man stood up quickly. "But babe, I love you!"

She grabbed her bag.

"And I love sense."

She turned and left the shop.

The man stood there, stunned.

Cynthia whispered, "Jesus wept."

The man left quietly.

I whispered, "What do we do with this cake?"

A customer muttered, "This is why I don't trust love."

Cynthia sliced into the untouched cake. "No point wasting it."

I took a bite. "At least the cake was good."

Morayo nodded. "Better than his planning skills."

Because even if love fails, cake never does.

18. The Bride Who Pretended to Be Broke

Every bride has a budget. Some are realistic. Some aren't. And others? There are brides who pretend they don't have money at all. Until the wedding day. This is the story of one such bride.

She walked into my shop wearing plain Ankara, no makeup, and the humble aura of someone about to play hardball with my prices.

"Good afternoon," she said sweetly.

"Good afternoon," I replied.

She sat down. Smiled shyly.

"I'm getting married next month," she said, "and I really love your cakes."

I beamed. "That's great! What design are you thinking of?"

She sighed dramatically.

"Ah…something simple o. Just small cake."

I pulled out my iPad.

"Do you have a theme in mind?"

She hesitated.

"Maybe…four tiers?"

I nodded. "Nice. Do you like fondant or buttercream?"

She winced.

"Ah, fondant is fine, but please, no gold accents o! It's too expensive."

"Okay," I said, typing. "What flavour?"

She looked around nervously.

"Simple vanilla. No red velvet! My budget won't reach that one."

Then came the real problem.

"How much?" she asked, batting her eyelashes.

I gave her the price.

She gasped.

"Ah! Dayo, please na! I'm just a simple bride! We're managing things!"

Managing things indeed.

I sighed.

"Okay," I said. "I can do a small discount."

She clapped happily.

"God bless you, my sister!"

I smiled.

But something felt off.

Cynthia and I arrived at the venue in Lekki, carrying the cake.

We stepped inside. And I froze.

This was not a "small wedding." It was a lavish *owambe*.

I'm talking massive floral installations hanging from the ceiling. Live band with backup dancers. Ice sculptures. Waiters serving champagne in crystal flutes.

Cynthia whispered, "Dayo, are we in the right place?"

I clenched my teeth.

"Oh, we are."

Because right in the middle of the luxury madness was my "humble" bride glittering in what looked suspiciously like pure Swarovski stones.

She saw me and smiled innocently.

"Dayo! My cake is here!"

I placed the box down firmly.

"Wow! The decoration is beautiful," I said sweetly. "How much was it?"

She laughed nervously.

"Ahn ahn, my sister, it's just small touches."

Cynthia scoffed. "Small ke?"

I crossed my arms.

"So…ice sculptures are affordable, but cake is expensive?"

Her smile faltered. Then, she tried it.

"Ah! Don't be angry! It's not like that! Cake is not priority na."

I stared at her.

Cynthia whispered, "Dayo, I know that face. Don't fight here."

I inhaled and smiled.

Then said, loudly, "Well, since cake is not a priority, I guess you won't mind if we take this back."

Her eyes widened.

The wedding planner turned. "What's happening?"

I smiled sweetly.

"This bride said she didn't have money for my cake. But she has money for live band, imported decor, and ice sculptures."

Guests started watching.

The bride grabbed my arm.

"Wait, wait, wait!" she whispered. "Let's not do this here!"

I raised a brow. "Oh, now you care about the cake?"

She gulped.

The MC walked over. "Sister, what's wrong?"

The bride panicked.

Then her mother appeared.

She eyed her daughter. Then me.

She sighed.

"Dayo, how much did my daughter pay you?"

I folded my arms. "Half price."

Her mother exhaled.

Then turned to her daughter.

"Funke, why are you embarrassing the family?"

The bride froze.

"Ah! Mummy, it's not like…"

Her mother raised a hand. "I don't want to hear it."

Then she pulled out her wallet and counted the cash.

Pressed it into my hand.

"Take this, my dear. Full price."

I smiled. "God bless you, ma."

I placed the cake on the table, standing proud and paid in full.

The bride? She couldn't even look at me.

Cynthia grinned. "Dayo, you just won."

I smirked. "Oh, I always do."

19. The Ghanaian Instagram Order

Social media is both a blessing and a curse. Some days, it brings you real customers. Other days, it brings you confusion.

Like the woman who tried to order a cake from Ghana.

I was sipping coffee when Cynthia gasped.

"Dayo, see this message."

She turned on her phone.

A DM from a lady named Akua.

OMG! I love your cakes! I've been following you for months! Your work is beautiful!

Cynthia smiled. "Aww. Sweet."

Then she scrolled down.

Can you deliver to Accra?

I blinked. "Accra as in Ghana?"

Cynthia nodded.

I replied, *Hello, Akua! Thank you! But we are based in Lagos, Nigeria. We don't currently deliver to Ghana.*

She replied immediately.

Can't you just send it by flight?

I blinked.

Cynthia snorted. "Does she think we can check cake in as hand luggage?"

I typed carefully.

Cakes are delicate. They won't survive a flight.

Her next message?

Can't you wrap it in bubble wrap?

She was determined.

I don't mind paying for priority shipping. I will even book an extra seat for the cake.

I choked on my coffee.

Cynthia laughed. "She wants the cake to have a boarding pass."

I sighed and sent my reply.

Thank you, Akua, I love your enthusiasm. But cake cannot do international travel. Maybe find a Ghanaian baker?

She went silent.

I added another message: *I can guide a Ghanaian baker to replicate it. I'll even send a recipe!*

Silence.

Then: *Hmm. I don't know… your cakes just hit different.*

I sent her a list of top-rated bakers in Accra.

Finally, she replied, "*Okay, I'll check them out. But if you ever open a branch here, I'll be your first customer!*"

I smiled.

We ended the chat peacefully.

Days later, Akua posted a picture of a beautiful cake on Instagram.

Tagging me. "Inspired by @SweetCravingsLagos! My mum loved it. Maybe one day, I'll get the real thing."

Cynthia smiled. "Aww, so she found a Ghanaian baker?"

I smiled back.

"Well, at least we expanded our brand without even leaving Lagos."

But she did give me an idea. Maybe one day, Sweet Cravings Accra won't be a joke.

20. The Precious Birthday Cake

Children's cakes are fun to make. Bright colours and cute designs. But the thing about five-year-olds? They can be very attached to their cakes.

And last Saturday, I met the most attached child in Lagos.

The mother, Mrs. Bassey, had walked into the shop looking excited.

"My daughter, Jasmine, is turning five! She wants a princess cake."

I smiled. "That's lovely. What's her favourite princess?"

"Not just one," she said. "She wants all of them."

Pause.

"All of them?"

She pulled out a printed photo from Pinterest.

A four-tier cake.

Each tier dedicated to a Disney princess.

Cynthia peered at the picture. "So...Cinderella, Ariel, Belle, and Elsa?"

Mrs. Bassey nodded proudly.

"She loves them equally."

I sighed. "Okay. What flavour?"

She smiled. "Chocolate, vanilla, strawberry, and red velvet. One per tier."

I laughed. "Let's make magic."

We wrapped up everything a day before the party. The resulting cake was stunning.

Blue Cinderella base, with a tiny glass slipper.

Purple Ariel tier, with fondant seashells.

Gold Belle tier, with a little enchanted rose.

And a final Elsa layer with snowflakes and edible glitter.

Cynthia stepped back.

"This is not a cake. This is a masterpiece."

I nodded.

We took so many pictures. What could go wrong?

The cake arrived at its destination – a mansion in Lekki.

The garden was set up for a princess-themed party. There were massive balloons, a bouncy castle, face painting, the works. And in the middle of it all was Jasmine in a lovely pink dress and tiara.

The moment she saw the cake, she let out a scream.

"MY PRINCESS CAKE!!!"

Then she did something unusual.

She ran to the cake table.

And hugged the cake.

Gently. Carefully. Like it was her best friend.

All the adults *awwwed*.

It was cute.

The party went smoothly, with dancing, games and happy children.

Then cake time.

The MC grabbed the mic.

"Everyone, it's time to cut the cake!"

The kids cheered, and the parents clapped. Everyone gathered around for photos. There were big smiles, cameras and phones flashed.

Afterwards, Mrs Bassey brought a tray to cut and serve the cake.

Jasmine suddenly grabbed the cake stand.

And shouted: "NOOOOOO!"

Mrs. Bassey laughed nervously. "Jasmine, it's okay! We're just cutting the cake."

Jasmine hugged the table tighter.

"DON'T TOUCH IT!"

Cynthia whispered, "Dayo, I think we have a situation."

I pinched the bridge of my nose.

The MC tried again.

"Jasmine, sweetheart, let's cut it so everyone can eat."

Jasmine collapsed onto the table, wailing.

"NOOOOOO! MY PRINCESSES! DON'T HURT THEM!!!"

The other kids looked confused. One little boy whispered, "Why is she crying?"

Mrs. Bassey tried everything. Bribes. Promises. Sweet words.

But Jasmine was unshaken. The cake was her friend.

I sighed. "Let me try."

I knelt beside Jasmine.

"Sweetheart," I said gently, "your princesses want to go to the castle in your tummy."

She sniffled.

"Huh?"

I nodded. "Yes! They want to live inside you, so you can be a real princess too."

Her tears slowed.

"You mean...Elsa wants to be in my tummy?"

I smiled. "Yes."

She thought about it.

199

Then whispered, "Even Cinderella?"

I nodded firmly.

"Cinderella most of all."

She wiped her face.

"Okay. But only a small piece."

We cut exactly one piece.

Jasmine watched closely.

She took one bite.

Then nodded. "Okay. Other people can have *small-small* pieces."

The party cheered.

Mrs. Bassey hugged me.

"Dayo, you saved us."

I laughed. "Next time, maybe just one princess."

She sighed. "Never again."

21. The Baby Shower Gender-Reveal Cake

Some cake orders are straightforward, while others are stressful. Sometimes, the work involves baking a cake inside another cake. Sounds tough, right?

I was just finishing a batch of banana muffins when my phone rang.

"Hello, Sweet Cravings Bakery."

A bright, excited voice filled my ear.

"Hi! My name is Titi, and I need a cake for my sister's baby shower-slash-gender-reveal this weekend."

I smiled. "Congratulations! What design do you have in mind?"

She giggled.

"That's the fun part! I want a cake that's a surprise inside a surprise."

I frowned. "Meaning?"

She giggled again.

"My sister and her husband don't know the baby's gender yet. I'm the only one who knows, because I got the ultrasound photo. So, I want a cake that's plain on the outside but reveals the colour inside when we cut it."

I blinked.

"So... you want me to bake a gender-reveal cake... inside another cake?"

She clapped. "Exactly!"

Cynthia, who was eavesdropping, snorted.

I sighed.

"Hmmm, this is complicated."

She giggled louder.

"I know. That's why I picked you. I heard you love a challenge."

I closed my eyes.

"I'll send an envelope," she said, whispering like we were in a spy movie. "Inside, you'll find a note: 'Pink' for girl, 'Blue' for boy."

I sighed. "Okay."

She paused.

"Oh, and make sure it tastes amazing. My sister loves lemon."

"Lemon sponge, got it."

Then she added, "But she also hates food colouring. So the pink or blue must be natural."

I rubbed my temples. "You mean...I have to bake a naturally pink or blue cake?"

"Yes! See you Saturday!"

She hung up.

Cynthia wheezed. "Dayo, did she just say 'natural blue'?"

I stared at the ceiling. I needed a miracle.

I spent hours researching.

Beets make cake pink. Butterfly pea flower makes cake blue.

Problem solved. Or so I thought.

Because when I baked a test batch...

The pink looked fine. But the blue? Turned out more like green.

Morayo stared at it.

"So...you're saying if the baby is a boy, we'll cut the cake and see Shrek colour?"

Cynthia cackled.

I sighed deeply.

Back to square one.

After several stressful hours, I found the answer.

Pink? Beetroot puree.

Blue? Blue spirulina powder.

Natural. Safe. No green surprises.

Titi eventually sent the note, and we baked the gender-reveal cake. Then, I baked it inside a larger vanilla cake.

Everything was set. Now, we just had to deliver it. And pray.

We arrived at the baby shower, a pastel dreamland in Lekki. Everywhere, there were pink and blue balloons. Guests dressed in "Team Boy" and "Team Girl" shirts.

Lola, the glowing mum-to-be, screamed when she saw the cake.

"OH MY GOD! IT'S PERFECT!"

I smiled. "I just hope the inside is perfect too."

Because at this point? I was praying the cake colours inside had stayed intact.

When it was time for the Big Reveal, everyone gathered around.

Lola grabbed the knife, shaking with excitement.

Her husband held her waist, grinning.

"3…2…1…CUT!" the guests chanted.

She sliced through.

The knife slid in smoothly.

A piece lifted. First it was cream…then a layer of brown…

And then finally…

PINK!

Everyone cheered. Titi popped a giant balloon, and pink glitter went everywhere.

I exhaled. The surprise had worked.

After the reveal, Cythia and I left.

The next day, Lola sent a text.

"Dayo, thank you. The cake was amazing. Baby is a girl, and I can't wait!"

I laughed and showed the message to Cynthia. "If only she knew how I was praying..."

Cynthia smiled. "At least, thank God it wasn't green."

22. The Bank Order

Corporate cake orders are usually dull. Logos. Generic messages. Nothing exciting.

So one day, when a woman named Ngozi called from Prestige Capital Bank to place a large order for cakes and meat pies, I wasn't expecting anything different. I was wrong.

"Good morning. We'd like to place an order for our bank's customer appreciation day."

I pulled up my notes. "What kind of order?"

She listed it out:

Three large cakes (vanilla, red velvet, and chocolate).

200 meat pies.

50 assorted cupcakes.

I nodded. Straightforward.

Then she added, "Oh, and our executive director loves lemon cake. Can you add a special one for him?"

I smiled. "Of course."

Cynthia and I arrived at Prestige Capital Bank HQ in VI, carrying carefully packed boxes of cake and meat pies. Security let us in.

A receptionist directed us to a conference hall where a few employees were setting up.

One of them, a tall, ridiculously handsome man in a navy-blue suit, turned as we entered.

He smiled and walked over.

"Good morning," he said. Deep voice. Clean shave. Smelled like money and good decisions.

I blinked.

"Uh…hi."

The man gestured to the boxes. "This must be the cake and snacks we ordered."

I nodded, still trying to find words.

"Yes. Cakes. Pies. Sugar. You know, bakery things."

Cynthia choked on air.

The man chuckled. "I'm Tade, by the way."

I shook his hand. Firm grip.

"Dayo."

His smile widened. "Nice to meet you, Dayo."

Lord. Was I blushing?

As we arranged the cakes and pies, Ngozi walked in, checking her clipboard.

"Everything looks perfect! Except…"

She frowned.

"Where's the executive director's lemon cake?"

Cynthia gasped. "Wait. It's not here?"

I checked the box list.

One cake missing. The special lemon cake.

For the most important man in the bank. Oh no!

Cynthia whispered, "Dayo, we forgot the ED's cake. We're finished."

Tade noticed our panic.

"What's wrong?"

I sighed. "One of the cakes is missing."

But then Tade smiled.

"Don't worry. I'm the ED."

I blinked and stared at him.

"You're the executive director?"

He grinned. "Yes."

Ngozi was still panicking. "Sir, we can reorder…"

But Tade raised a hand.

"No need. I'll accept an apology in the form of coffee and a fresh slice of lemon cake…made just for me."

I stared. Was this man…flirting?

I swallowed.

"Deal."

Back at the shop, I baked another special lemon cake.

Small. Elegant. Perfectly glazed.

Then, at 6:00 p.m., I walked into Prestige Capital Bank's headquarters again.

Tade was waiting in the lobby.

He smiled.

"I was starting to think you wouldn't show up."

I handed him the cake box. "I keep my promises."

He smirked.

"Good. So do I."

Then he handed me a small white envelope.

"What's this?"

He winked. "My number."

Back at the bakery, Cynthia screamed.

"Dayo, did a man just give you his number... in an envelope?"

Morayo clutched her chest. "That's Executive Director romance!"

I smiled. Well, well.

Maybe cake wasn't the only thing getting delivered.

MEMOIRS OF A LAGOS TAXI DRIVER

A Collection of Flash Fiction Stories

MEET LADI

My name is Oladipupo, but everyone calls me Ladi. I'm 29 and a graduate of Ogun State University, and once upon a time, I was a banker. I wore suits, processed transactions, and acted like I had my life together until the bank merged and I became redundant.

To be honest; it messed me up. One day, I had a steady salary. The next, I was unemployed, watching my savings disappear like Lagos power supply.

I needed a plan. Fast.

So, I did what Lagos people do, I hustled.

I took what was left of my savings, borrowed money from my friend's dad, and bought a Toyota Corolla. Registered for one of those ride-hailing apps. And just like that, I became a Lagos taxi driver.

Some people say driving in Lagos is hell. They're not wrong. Between fuel shortages and queues, LASTMA, police checkpoints, danfo drivers, okadas, keke napep and passengers who think your car is their personal therapist's office, this work is not for the weak. But somehow, I survive.

I live in Ajah, sharing a three-bedroom house with my ex-work colleague and two university friends. Every other

Sunday, I visit my parents in Ogba, where my mother never fails to remind me that I should have married by now.

Speaking of women, there was Tolani.

The one that got away. Or the one who left me when life got rough. Lagos relationships are like danfo buses. If you miss your stop, another one will come, but the ride may not be smooth.

Now, I spend my days picking up strangers. And in Lagos, strangers come with stories.

Lagos is a city where anything can happen. One day, you're driving a CEO who won't stop ranting about his workers. The next day, you're helping a pregnant woman whose water just broke in your back seat. Some days, you're a getaway driver for a celebrity dodging paparazzi.

This is my life. These are my memoirs.

1. The Morning Commute from Hell

It was 7.00 am on a Tuesday, and Ajah traffic was already making me question my life decisions. I had just dropped off my first passenger, a quiet guy who smelled like too much aftershave, when a new request came in. The pickup location was at a residential estate nearby.

I pulled up in front of a gate and honked twice. A woman in a power suit emerged, dragging a suitcase behind her. She looked like she could run a multinational company with one hand while texting with the other.

"Morning," I said as she slid into the back seat.

"Morning," she replied without looking up from her phone. "Victoria Island, please. I have a meeting in an hour."

I mentally calculated the trip. If we were lucky, we'd make it on time. If not, well...this was Lagos.

We hit the Lekki-Epe Expressway, and for the first few minutes, everything was fine. The morning sun was rising, the radio was playing Burna Boy's *Last Last*, and my passenger was busy typing furiously on her phone. But Lagos traffic had other plans.

Just as we approached the Lekki Toll Gate, everything came to a screeching halt. Cars weren't moving. People were

213

honking as if the sheer force of their horns could clear the road.

"Traffic," I said, glancing at her through the rearview mirror.

She sighed, still typing. "I noticed."

Five minutes passed. Then ten. The cars ahead moved just enough to give us false hope before stopping again. My passenger finally looked up from her phone. "What's the hold-up?"

I shrugged. "Could be anything. Construction, accident, or maybe someone decided to turn the expressway into a market."

She wasn't amused. "I have a presentation at 9.00 am."

I checked Google Maps. The app wasn't helping, it just showed a sea of red lines mocking me. I was about to suggest a detour when a man knocked on the passenger-side window.

I rolled it down slightly. "Yes?"

"Boss, do you need fuel?" the man asked, holding a jerrycan and pointing at a makeshift fuel station set up on the side of the road.

I shook my head. "We're fine."

My passenger burst out laughing as I rolled up the window. "Did that guy really just try to sell you fuel in traffic?"

"Anything and everything happens in Lagos," I said, chuckling.

We sat in silence for a moment before she spoke again. "Is this what you do every day?"

"Pretty much," I said. "Lagos traffic is a full-time job on its own."

She sighed. "I used to work in New York. I thought I had seen the worst traffic in the world, but this is next level."

"New York doesn't have *danfos*," I said. "Or *okadas* that can appear out of nowhere."

We finally inched forward, only to stop again when a man pushing a wheelbarrow full of yams tried to cross the road. My passenger shook her head. "This is insane."

"Lagos isn't for the weak," I replied with a grin.

Eventually, we made it to Victoria Island, pulling up in front of a sleek glass building just five minutes before her meeting. She exhaled and smiled for the first time since the ride began. "You did it, Ladi."

I laughed. "It wasn't easy, but we survived."

As she stepped out, she handed me a tip. "Thanks for the adventure. Next time, I'll give myself an extra hour."

"Good plan," I said, watching her disappear into the building.

As I pulled back onto the road, another request came in, this time from a guy in Lekki Phase 1. I sighed, cranked up the radio, and prepared for the next adventure.

Just another day in Lagos.

2. The Mysterious Suitcase

It was 10.00 pm and I was ready to end my shift. My flatmates were already texting about *suya* and football matches, and I was eager to join them. But when a new request came in from a bar in Lekki Phase 1, I sighed and accepted it. One last trip, I told myself.

When I finally pulled up outside the bar, the street was alive with activity. The bass from the club vibrated throughout my car as people spilt onto the sidewalk, laughing and shouting over the music. A few minutes after I arrived, my passenger stumbled out of the bar, clutching a large suitcase that looked like it had been dragged through a battlefield.

"Mainland," he slurred, tossing the suitcase into the trunk before collapsing into the back seat.

"Mainland where, Sir?" I asked, trying to ignore the heavy scent of whiskey that lingered on his breath.

"Anywhere," he mumbled, leaning against the window.

I sighed. *Anywhere* wasn't exactly a location, but I figured we'd sort that out once we were on the road. I started driving toward the Third Mainland Bridge, hoping he'd sober up enough to give me a specific destination.

The suitcase in the trunk kept nagging at me. It was too large for a casual night out, and the way he guarded it earlier made me suspicious. My imagination ran wild. Was it full of stolen money? Contraband? Something worse? Lagos has a way of making you think the worst, and I wasn't in the mood to end my night with a police investigation.

I cleared my throat. "What's in the suitcase, sir?"

He chuckled, the sound bitter and hollow. "It's my wedding suit. And gifts for my fiancée."

"Ah, wedding preparations?" I asked, trying to sound casual.

"There's no wedding," he said, his voice breaking. "She called it off this morning."

I winced. "I'm sorry to hear that."

"Don't be," he muttered. "She did me a favour."

We drove in silence for a few minutes, the city lights casting shadows across his face as we passed street vendors and *okada* riders weaving through traffic. His phone buzzed on his lap, but he ignored it. I figured it was probably friends or family trying to check on him, or maybe even the ex-fiancée. Either way, it wasn't my business to ask.

As we neared the bridge, he sighed deeply. "You ever loved someone who didn't love you back?"

I chuckled softly. "Hmmm. Lagos has a way of teaching you those lessons. But I'm surviving."

He laughed; a genuine one this time. "You're lucky. Maybe I will survive this."

We sat in companionable silence as the car cruised over the bridge, the cool night breeze drifting through the open windows. I glanced at him through the rearview mirror. "What are you going to do now?"

He shrugged. "I don't know. Maybe go to my friend's place on the mainland, maybe get a hotel. Start over, I guess."

"You'll be fine," I said, surprising even myself. "Heartbreak sucks, but it doesn't last forever."

He leaned back, closing his eyes for a moment. "Thanks, Ladi. You're a good listener."

When we arrived at his destination, a modest apartment complex in Yaba, he fished through his pockets and handed me a generous tip.

"Not just for the ride," he said. "For the therapy."

I laughed. "I'll add 'unlicensed therapist' to my resume."

I watched him walk toward the building after he stepped out of my cab and retrieved his suitcase, his silhouette disappearing into the shadows. For a moment, I felt a pang of empathy. Lagos is a tough city, but heartbreak is tougher.

I drove off, turning up the radio as Davido's *Unavailable* started playing on Cool FM. By the time I got home, my flatmates had already devoured the *suya* and were arguing over football highlights. I collapsed onto the couch, replaying the events of the night in my head.

3. The In-Law Showdown

I had carried many passengers, but none like Madam Blessing.

She entered my car carrying a shopping bag, a basket of fruit, and the confidence of a woman on a mission.

"Driver, how much if I book you for the whole day?"

I blinked. "Uh, where are we going Madam?"

"Ogun State," she said. "I'm going to fight my in-laws."

I adjusted my seatbelt. Ah.

"They have been stressing my sister," she continued, munching chin-chin. "They don't want to refund her bride price after she left their useless son."

"So, we're going to collect money?"

She grinned. "Something like that."

We agreed on a price and hit the express, and she sang along to all the songs on my playlist, offering me lots of snacks from her bag. She had plantain chips, biscuits and roasted peanuts. She was also very chatty, and she told me a lot of stories about her family, her sister and the husband her sister had fled from.

When we arrived, she stepped out of my cab like a Nollywood queen ready for battle.

Two women rushed out of the old house we had just parked in front of. One looked like she had been waiting for this fight since January.

"Blessing, you came here to make trouble?"

Madam Blessing didn't flinch. "Where is my sister's money?"

The second woman, a younger sister, folded her arms. "She left our brother; she should forget the money!"

Madam Blessing removed her earrings.

"Eh? Say it again."

I swallowed. "Madam, should I be worried?"

She patted my shoulder. "Relax, my brother. I came prepared."

I stepped back. This was above my taxi driver salary.

The three women faced each other, voices raised, insults flying. Neighbours rushed to the compound when they heard the commotion.

Thirty minutes later, after a lot of noise, accusations, denials, a few slaps, and the intervention of three village elders, the in-laws reluctantly handed over a wad of cash.

Madam Blessing smiled victoriously. "Driver, let's go."

As I turned to leave, one of the women hissed.

"Useless woman! You think you've won?"

Madam Blessing smirked. "I always win."

We got into the car and drove back to Lagos. She laughed all the way, excited by her victory. We made a stop at a supermarket in Gbagada, where she went in to buy some groceries, and she even bought me a large loaf of fresh bread.

Then she tossed me ₦10,000 extra when I dropped her off at her house.

"I like you, driver," she said, leaning against the passenger side window. "If you ever need someone to help you fight, call me."

I nodded. Because who knows, one day I might really need a woman like her to fight for me.

4. The Preacher

It was almost 8 o'clock on a Sunday, and there was no food in the house. I could've gone back to sleep, but my growling stomach and dwindling account balance told me otherwise. So, I grabbed my car keys and convinced myself that a few trips before church wouldn't hurt. I could make enough for a nice breakfast and still catch the 10.30 am service.

The first ride request came in just as I got to the main road. The pickup location was in Ajah, not far from my flat. When I pulled up, my passenger was standing by the gate of a modest-looking bungalow with a large Bible tucked under his arm. He was wearing a crisp blue buba and sokoto that looked freshly ironed, complete with a matching cap that sat perfectly on his head. I already knew what kind of ride this was going to be.

"Good morning, sir," I said, greeting him as he slid into the back seat.

"Blessings to you, my brother!" he said, his voice booming like the preacher on one of those early-morning gospel programs my mum used to watch.

I smiled and nodded, hoping this wouldn't be the kind of ride where I'd have to explain my entire life story.

We were barely five minutes into the journey when he leaned forward, rested one hand on the back of the passenger seat and said, "Young man, do you know that your soul is precious to the Lord?"

Here we go.

"Yes, sir."

"Have you accepted Jesus as your personal saviour?"

"Yes, sir," I said again, keeping my eyes on the road. Maybe if I agreed with him enough, he'd run out of things to say.

He chuckled and shook his head. "You answered too quickly. When were you saved, and by whom?"

I blinked. "By...Jesus, sir."

He laughed again, but this time it was more of a "you can't fool me" kind of laugh. "When last did you read your Bible?"

"Last week," I said, hoping that would satisfy him.

He didn't look convinced. "Do you know the story of the prodigal son?"

"Yes, sir."

"Recite it."

"Excuse me?" I asked, glancing at him through the rearview mirror.

"Recite it," he repeated like he was a teacher giving a pop quiz.

I sighed internally. This man was determined to test me. "There was a man who had two sons," I began hesitantly. "One of them asked for his share of the inheritance, left home, and wasted everything on..."

"Wasted everything on *what*, my brother?" he interrupted, raising an eyebrow.

"On... riotous living," I said, proud of myself for remembering that detail.

"Ah, you know it! Praise God!" He clapped his hands, making me jump. "But do you know what that story is really about?"

I was about to answer when a *danfo* cut me off, nearly scraping the side of my car. I slammed on the brakes and honked, muttering under my breath.

"Patience, my brother," the preacher said calmly. "Even when the enemy tests you, you must remain steadfast."

I bit my tongue and kept driving.

By the time we got to Lekki, he had moved on to quoting scriptures at lightning speed. "Romans 10:9 says, 'If you declare with your mouth, "Jesus is Lord," and believe in your heart that God raised him from the dead, you will be saved.'"

"Yes, sir," I said again, my voice now robotic.

We were getting closer to his destination when he suddenly said, "Young man, pull over."

I frowned. "Here?"

"Yes, right here," he insisted.

I parked by the side of the road, confused. Was he about to buy something? Maybe some snacks or a newspaper?

He leaned forward and placed his hand on my shoulder. "Let me pray for you."

I stiffened. "Sir, I appreciate it, but..."

"Don't worry, it won't take long."

Before I could protest, he launched into a prayer loud enough to make passersby turn their heads. "Father Lord, we thank you for this young man. Bless him and guide him. May he leave behind any sinful behaviour and find favour in your eyes."

I sat there awkwardly, nodding along as he prayed for my soul, my future wife, my unborn children, and even my car. When he finally said, "Amen," I breathed a sigh of relief.

"Amen," I echoed.

He smiled, satisfied. "I feel the Spirit moving in you already."

I didn't have the heart to tell him that what I was feeling was hunger. I started the car and drove the final stretch to his church, where he handed me a pamphlet titled *10 Steps to Eternal Salvation* before stepping out.

"Thank you, my brother," he said, beaming. "I'll see you in church one day."

"Maybe," I said with a weak smile.

As I drove off, I tossed the pamphlet into the glove compartment. Lagos never disappoints.

When I got home, my flatmates, Seyi and Kunle, were already eating *akara*.

"Did you get bread?" Kunle asked.

"No," I replied, collapsing onto the couch. "But I did get a sermon."

5. Impromptu Photoshoot

It was a Friday afternoon, and I had just taken a short break to eat *gala* and drink cold *La Casera* at a roadside stand. The traffic wasn't too bad for a Lagos Friday, and I figured a few more trips before rush hour would earn me enough for a decent weekend. As I leaned back in my Toyota Corolla, enjoying the breeze, my phone pinged. A new ride request from Ikoyi.

I wiped my hands on a napkin, accepted the ride, and drove to the pickup location. It was a luxury apartment complex with security guards who didn't even flinch when I pulled up. They waved me in like they had seen too many ride-hailing drivers to care.

I parked outside the lobby, and a woman wearing designer sunglasses and a glittery dress strutted toward the car, phone in hand. Her heels clicked against the pavement like she was on a runway. She didn't even glance at me before sliding into the back seat.

"Good afternoon," I said, starting the trip.

She waved dismissively. "Just a moment." She was live-streaming. "Hey guys! I'm heading to the most exclusive event in Lagos today. It's going to be fabulous, and of

228

course, I'll give you all the behind-the-scenes content." She winked at her phone, blowing a kiss to her followers.

I chuckled under my breath. *Another influencer.*

As I pulled onto the main road, she kept the live stream going, switching between showing her makeup and giving updates about her outfit. "This dress is from Luxe Boutique," she said, pouting at the camera. "You guys can get a discount if you use my code."

I tried to focus on the road, but her constant narration made it difficult. "Ladi, slow down!" she suddenly exclaimed.

I nearly hit the brakes. "What's wrong?"

"The lighting is bad. I need better light for this shot."

I sighed but eased off the accelerator. Lagos traffic wasn't forgiving, and the last thing I needed was someone honking behind me because we were moving too slowly.

She angled her phone, tilted her head, and finally seemed satisfied. "Perfect," she muttered, then continued her live broadcast. "We're heading to the event now. I can't wait to meet all the celebs!"

I wasn't sure who she was but judging by the way she was promoting herself; she was either famous or desperately trying to be.

We hit a small traffic jam near the Lekki Toll Gate. "How long will this take?" she asked, frowning.

"It's Lagos," I replied. "Could be five minutes or thirty."

"Ugh, I can't be late," she said, typing furiously on her phone. "This is a VIP-only event, and if I miss the red carpet, my followers will be disappointed."

I didn't know how to respond to that, so I kept quiet.

After about fifteen minutes, the traffic eased, and I managed to get her to the event venue in Lekki just in time. I parked outside, expecting her to hop out and disappear into the glamorous world of influencers. But instead, she tapped my shoulder.

"Can you park somewhere for a minute? I need good lighting for my arrival pictures."

I raised an eyebrow. "You want me to wait?"

"Yes, please. I'll give you a good rating," she added, flashing a smile that probably worked wonders on her Instagram followers.

I sighed and found a spot under a streetlight where the lighting was decent. She stepped out and inspected the car like it was part of her outfit. "Okay, we'll use this angle."

I watched as she posed dramatically, flipping her hair and adjusting her sunglasses. After a few selfies, she approached my window again. "Can you take a few pictures of me?"

I hesitated. "Me?"

"Yes! Just hold the phone and make sure you get the car in the background. I'll pose."

I took the phone and snapped a few photos as she leaned against the car, blew kisses, and pouted at the camera. "Make sure you get the heels," she said, lifting one leg slightly.

I took a deep breath and adjusted the frame. After about five minutes, I handed the phone back. "That should do it."

She scrolled through the pictures, nodding approvingly. "These are great! Thanks, Ladi."

"No problem."

As she finally prepared to leave, she added, "What's your Instagram handle? I'll tag you."

I chuckled. "I don't have one."

Her jaw dropped. "No Instagram? What kind of driver are you?"

"The kind who just drives," I replied with a grin.

She laughed, waved goodbye, and strutted toward the entrance of the event. As I drove off, I shook my head. Lagos never fails to deliver entertainment, even when I'm not looking for it.

Later that night, my flatmates asked about my day. "I met an influencer," I said.

"Did she give you a shout-out?" Wale asked.

"Nope."

"User," Kunle said, laughing.

"Na she sabi," I replied and laughed. Just another day's work in Lagos.

6. The Juggling Passenger

It was a quiet Thursday evening, and the traffic gods had finally shown mercy. The roads weren't as congested, and I had just dropped off a passenger in Victoria Island when a new request came in. The pickup location was a fancy hotel that screamed *big man energy*, the kind of place where the cost of their cheapest room could fund my entire month's rent.

I pulled up to the entrance and waited for a few minutes. My passenger emerged wearing a perfectly tailored suit, carrying a sleek briefcase, and glanced around like someone expecting to see a familiar face. His cologne wafted into the car as he slid into the back seat.

"Evening, sir," I greeted.

"Evening," he said, already on his phone.

We pulled onto the main road, and for the first few minutes, the only sound in the car was the low hum of the engine and the occasional notification pings coming from his passenger's phone. Then, the calls started.

The first one came in just as we passed the Lekki Toll Gate. He answered it with a smooth, charming tone. "Darling, I'm on my way home."

I tried to focus on the road, but it was hard not to eavesdrop.

"Yes, yes. I'll be there soon. I just had a business meeting that ran late." He chuckled softly, the way people do when they're trying to sound romantic.

Maybe he's just a busy man with a loving wife, I thought. *No big deal.*

Then, not even two minutes after ending that call, his phone rang again.

"Hello, baby," he said, switching to a slightly different tone, this one softer, more affectionate. "How's your day going?"

I frowned, glancing at him through the rearview mirror. *Didn't he just call someone 'darling'?*

"Yes, I'm still in traffic. You know how Lagos can be," he continued, laughing. "I can't wait to see you this weekend."

He hung up, and I shook my head slightly. *This guy is living dangerously.* But before I could dwell on it, his phone rang a third time.

"Sweetheart!" he exclaimed, this time sounding breathless like he was starring in a Nollywood romance.

I almost hit a man on an okada. I couldn't believe this guy. Three different women in less than ten minutes? He was juggling them like a circus performer. I adjusted the rearview mirror to get a better look at him. He was completely calm as if this was just another day at the office.

"Yes, yes, I miss you too," he said, lowering his voice. "I'll see you tomorrow night."

He ended the call and finally looked up from his phone, meeting my gaze in the mirror. He must have noticed the slight smirk on my face because he raised an eyebrow. "What's funny, driver?"

I hesitated, but curiosity got the better of me. "Sir, no offence, but you're a very busy man."

He laughed, a deep, hearty laugh that filled the car. "You don't know the half of it."

I chuckled. "Three calls, three different women. You're living life on the edge."

He shrugged, leaning back in his seat. "Lagos is small, my brother. Discretion is key."

"Small world, indeed," I replied. "Aren't you afraid they'll find out?"

He smirked. "I'm careful. I never mix them up."

I shook my head, amazed at his confidence. "I hope you're not heading to meet any of them now."

He laughed again. "No, I'm going to see a friend. One of the few people who knows my secrets and won't judge me."

As we approached his destination, a high-end restaurant in Lekki, I couldn't resist giving him one last piece of advice.

"Sir, with all due respect, you might want to slow down."

He smiled and handed me cash for the ride, along with a generous tip.

"I appreciate the advice, Ladi. But trust me, I know how to handle surprises."

Then I watched as he strolled into the restaurant, briefcase in hand, exuding the kind of confidence that only someone living on borrowed time could have. I shook my head and drove off, chuckling to myself.

7. Sleeping Beauty

It was 1.00 am, and I was ready to call it a night. My eyes were heavy, my back ached from hours of driving, and my stomach grumbled because I had skipped dinner. But Lagos has a way of testing your limits, so just as I was about to log off the ride-hailing app, a new request came in.

The pickup location was a nightclub in Lekki. I debated ignoring it. Nightclub pickups were unpredictable, sometimes fun, often chaotic. But the thought of a little extra cash for the weekend convinced me to hit 'accept'.

I pulled up outside the club. The music was so loud, I could hear it from almost 50 metres away. People loitered on the sidewalk, some shouting into their phones, others staggering toward waiting cars. It was the usual Friday night scene in Lagos. My passenger was supposed to be a woman named Eniola. None of the people loitering outside looked like they were waiting for a ride, so I waited a few minutes.

Then I saw her.

A woman in a glittery dress and sky-high heels stumbled out of the club, her makeup slightly smudged, but still looking like she'd just stepped off a fashion runway. She wobbled toward my car, waving her phone lazily. "You're my taxi driver, right?"

"Yes, ma'am," I said, jumping out to help her with the door.

She collapsed into the back seat, laughing to herself. "Take me to Ikoyi...by Banana Island," she mumbled, slurring her words.

I nodded and started the trip. For the first few minutes, she hummed along to the soft afrobeats playing on the radio. Then, just as we got to the Lekki Toll Gate, she went quiet. I glanced in the rearview mirror and saw her head leaning against the window, eyes closed.

She's asleep. I sighed. It wasn't the first time a drunk passenger had fallen asleep in my car, but it was always awkward trying to wake them up when we arrived. I turned down the radio and focused on the road, hoping she wouldn't be difficult.

Lagos at night was both peaceful and eerie. The usual chaos of the day was gone, replaced by the occasional sound of a distant car horn or an okada zipping past. As I drove through the dimly lit streets, I thought about my plans for the weekend, catching up on sleep, visiting my parents in Ogba, and maybe finally working on my tech certification.

Twenty minutes later, we arrived in Ikoyi, and I parked outside the gated estate she had mentioned.

"Madam," I called, gently tapping the headrest, "We're here."

Nothing.

I turned around and called again, a little louder this time. "Madam, wake up. We've arrived."

Still nothing. She was out cold, her head resting against the window, one shoe dangling off her foot. I sighed and rubbed my temples. This wasn't in the job description.

I considered my options. I couldn't leave her in the car, and I definitely couldn't carry her to her doorstep. Imagine the rumours that would spread if someone saw that. My best bet was to call someone she knew.

Her phone was on her lap, the screen lighting up occasionally with notifications from WhatsApp and Instagram. I hesitated, knowing I was about to cross a boundary, but desperate times called for desperate measures. I unlocked the phone using her fingerprint and scrolled through her recent calls.

The contact labelled "Bestie 🖤" seemed like a safe bet.

I hit dial, and after two rings, a groggy voice answered. "Eniola, what's going on?"

"Good evening, ma'am," I said quickly. "I'm her taxi driver. She's asleep, and we're outside her estate."

There was a pause. "She's asleep? Drunk again?"

"Uh…yes."

"Okay, give me five minutes. I'm coming."

True to her word, a woman in pyjamas and slippers appeared at the gate, five minutes later. She opened the back door and gently shook Eniola awake. "Babe, get up. You're home."

Eniola groaned but didn't resist as her friend helped her out of the car.

"Ladi, right?" the friend said, glancing at me.

"Yes."

"You're a lifesaver. If she'd passed out in the club, it would've been a whole different kind of drama. Thank you for bringing her home."

"No problem," I said, watching as she guided Eniola toward the gate.

As they disappeared inside, I leaned back in my seat, exhaling.

It was definitely time to call it a night.

8. The Forgotten Laptop

The Monday morning traffic on the Lekki-Epe Expressway was crawling at a snail's pace. The air was heavy with humidity, and the occasional honk from impatient drivers only added to the stress. My first few rides had been uneventful, just people staring at their phones, barely acknowledging my greetings.

Then I got a new ride request: pickup from a hotel in Victoria Island. Destination, Ikeja. Long trip, a decent fare. I accepted it immediately.

When I pulled up to the hotel, a sharply dressed man in a navy blue suit stepped out, carrying a briefcase. His shoes were polished to perfection, and his tie looked like it had been tied by a professional. This man exuded the kind of confidence that could only come from knowing you had an important meeting to dominate.

"Morning, sir," I said as he slid into the back seat.

"Good morning," he replied, already opening his phone to check emails. "Ikeja, please. I have a meeting at 10."

I nodded and pulled into traffic. For the first fifteen minutes, we drove in silence with the passenger typing furiously on his phone while I focused on navigating the chaotic roads.

Everything was going smoothly until we hit a small traffic jam just before the Third Mainland Bridge.

That's when the passenger sighed loudly and muttered, "Lagos traffic."

"Always reliable," I said with a chuckle, trying to lighten the mood.

Then, just as we were inching forward, he sat up straight, eyes wide. "Wait. Where's my laptop?"

I glanced at him through the rearview mirror. "Sir?"

"My laptop!" he repeated, frantically checking the back seat and his briefcase. "It's not here. Oh God, I left it in the hotel room."

My stomach sank. This wasn't just a minor inconvenience, this man looked like his entire career was riding on that laptop. I knew what he was going to say before he said it.

"Ladi, we have to go back," he pleaded. "Please."

I checked the time. It was already 8:45. Going back to Victoria Island would take at least 40 minutes, plus another hour to get back to Ikeja if traffic was merciful, which it rarely was. "Sir, if we go back now, you might miss your meeting."

"I know," he groaned, running a hand through his hair. "But I can't show up without that laptop. My entire presentation is on it."

There was no point arguing. I made a U-turn at the next junction, breaking several traffic laws and earning a few angry honks from other drivers.

"We'll get it," I said, stepping on the accelerator. "Just hold on."

The return trip was a blur of lane changes, near-misses, and muttered prayers. I weaved through traffic like I was competing in a Fast & Furious movie. The businessman sat in the back, tapping his phone and muttering under his breath. I caught snippets of his frantic calls to colleagues: "Tell them I'm on my way... No, I didn't forget on purpose... Yes, I'll be there."

We arrived at the hotel at 9.15 am. He jumped out before the car had even come to a full stop, sprinting toward the entrance like an Olympic athlete. I waited, drumming my fingers on the steering wheel and hoping this detour wouldn't cost me the rest of my day.

Five minutes later, he returned, clutching the laptop like it was a newborn baby. He slid back into the car, slightly out of breath but relieved. "Got it."

"Good," I said, pulling out of the hotel driveway and heading back toward Ikeja.

The ride back was quieter. He spent most of it reviewing his presentation, occasionally muttering key points under his breath. I focused on navigating the traffic, which had gotten worse since we left. The sun was now fully out, and the heat combined with the stop-and-go movement was testing my patience.

By some miracle, we made it to his office building at exactly 10.02 am. I pulled up to the entrance, and he jumped out, briefcase in one hand, laptop in the other.

"Thank you," he said, handing me cash for the ride and a tip that was almost as generous as the fare. "You saved me today."

I laughed. "Don't forget your laptop next time, sir. Lagos traffic won't always be this forgiving."

He chuckled. "Lesson learned."

9. The Rude Flirt

Lagos passengers come in all sorts. There are the silent ones, the chatty ones, the prayer warriors, and then the rude and entitled ones. These are the ones who think taxi drivers are their personal slaves.

It was a Monday morning, and my phone buzzed with a ride request from Ikoyi to Victoria Island. I was just about to complete a trip nearby when the messages started flooding in.

Customer: "Driver, where are you?"

Customer: "Are you blind? I've been waiting!"

Customer: "You want me to cancel, abi?"

I sighed. Here we go again.

I pulled up in front of the pickup point to see a woman in a fitted corporate dress standing there and tapping her foot aggressively. Her wig was laid to perfection, but her face was set in a scowl that I could see even with her huge sunglasses.

"You took too long," she snapped at me as she got in.

"Good morning Madam," I muttered, pulling into traffic.

She ignored me and kept typing furiously on her phone, probably composing an angry email to ruin someone's day.

After the first ten minutes, she sighed dramatically, shifted in her seat, and muttered, "Useless drivers," under her breath.

I focused on the road. Not today, Satan.

Then, just as we crossed Falomo Bridge, she exhaled deeply and put her phone down.

"So, do you drive full-time?" she asked.

I raised an eyebrow. "Yes."

She nodded. "That's impressive. I like hardworking men."

I nearly swerved into a danfo.

Wait, what?

Was this not the same woman who just called me useless five minutes ago?

She crossed her legs and leaned forward. "You look familiar. Have we met before?"

"No ma. I don't think so."

"Well," she said, flipping her hair. "You have a nice smile, you know. If you play your cards right, you could be working for me."

Before I could respond, she added, "Or maybe I can introduce you to something that pays more than driving."

I forced a smile. "No, ma."

She took off her sunglasses as if she was studying me closely.

"You have nice skin. Do you use special products?"

My grip on the steering wheel tightened.

"Just soap and water, ma."

Her lips curved into a smirk.

"You don't have to keep calling me 'ma.' My name is Tara."

I nodded but kept my eyes on the road. Focus, Ladi.

She leaned forward again.

"So, do you have a girlfriend?"

Ah. It has finished.

I almost burst out laughing. "Madam, you started this ride by insulting me."

She giggled.

"You didn't answer my question."

I cleared my throat. "I'm just focused on work right now."

"Maybe we should talk after your shift," she purred. "I do business. Maybe you can make extra money."

I exhaled. "Madam, eh sorry, Tara, we've reached your destination."

She grinned. "I like men who can handle me."

I shook my head and repeated: "Madam, we have arrived."

She pouted. "No number?"

I smiled broadly and pointed at the app. "Five-star rating, please."

She pouted but handed me a ₦5,000 tip.

"Text me. You never know where opportunities come from."

I laughed all the way home. Lagos women. Fear them.

10. Passenger Playing Smart

I f there's one thing that I hate more than Lagos traffic, it's passengers who think taxis should be a free service.

It was a regular Wednesday night, and I was about to call it quits when I got one last ride request. The pickup location was a lounge in Lekki, and the destination was somewhere in Surulere. I figured it was a good way to end the night.

I pulled up outside the lounge, where a young guy in ripped jeans and designer sneakers sauntered toward the car. He was holding a bottle of Hennessy, half-empty, which already told me everything I needed to know about how this ride was going to go.

"Ladi, my guy!" he greeted, sliding into the back seat like we were old friends.

I sighed internally. I didn't know him, but Lagos guys have a way of acting like they've known you since primary school.

"Good evening, sir," I said. "We're heading to Surulere, right?"

"Yeah, yeah, straight to the place," he mumbled, taking a sip from the bottle.

I shook my head and started driving. The trip was mostly quiet, apart from him humming along to the Wizkid song playing on the radio. Everything was fine until we got to Surulere, and I pulled up to his destination, a dimly lit street where a group of guys stood around chatting.

"Alright, sir. That'll be ₦7,500," I said, showing him the fare on the app.

He patted his pockets, suddenly looking confused. "Ah, guy, I forgot my wallet inside the club."

I blinked. "Excuse me?"

"No wahala, I'll just sort you later," he said casually, reaching for the door handle.

I immediately locked the doors. "Oga, no 'later'. Where's my money?"

He laughed like I had just cracked a joke. "Baba, no vex. I didn't plan for this, but I fit do you transfer tomorrow."

I sighed, gripping the steering wheel. "If you didn't plan for this, why did you request a ride?"

He shrugged. "I thought my guy would be home to settle me, but he's not around."

By now, his friends had noticed something was off. One of them walked up to the car. "Wetin dey happen?"

"Your guy doesn't want to pay me," I explained.

The friend turned to him. "Ah ah, Mide, no disgrace us na."

Mide sighed dramatically and fished through his pockets. He pulled out his phone and started typing. "Oya, I'll transfer."

I watched carefully as he tapped his screen, but the moment I heard the classic Lagos scam line, I knew what was coming next.

"Ah, network wahala! The transfer isn't going through."

I sighed. "Sir, you're not leaving this car until I get my money."

His friends, now amused, shook their heads. "Mide, just pay abeg."

After another minute of grumbling, he finally sent the transfer. I waited for the alert before unlocking the door.

He stepped out, taking another sip of his drink. "Ladi, no vex. You be my guy."

I didn't even reply. I just drove off.

Lagos will test your patience every day, but this city will never see me work for free.

11. The Woman and the Spirits

When I accepted the ride, I thought it was just another regular trip. The pickup was in Yaba, and the destination was Ikeja. Simple.

I pulled up outside the address, and a woman in traditional attire got into the back seat. She was elderly, maybe in her late sixties, and she carried the strong scent of sandalwood and something herbal.

"Good evening, ma," I greeted.

She nodded but didn't reply.

I started driving, keeping an eye on the road while listening to the quiet hum of her breathing. Everything was normal until she started whispering.

At first, I thought she was speaking to me. "Sorry, ma, did you say something?"

She didn't respond.

Then I glanced in the rearview mirror and realized she wasn't talking to me. She was talking to someone…or something… that wasn't there.

"Hmm… Yes… I see," she murmured, nodding. "They will not stop me. My enemies will not succeed."

I gripped the steering wheel tighter.

"Ma…are you okay?"

She kept whispering. "Hmm…Ejo wa ni orun…Omo aye o mo nkan kan…" (The spirits are speaking…The people of the earth know nothing.)

At that moment, I contemplated parking and running for my life. But Lagos was too expensive for me to abandon my car, so I kept driving.

She reached into her handbag, pulled out a small calabash, and started shaking it.

That was it.

"Ma, we're here!" I announced, even though we weren't.

She looked up as if she had just remembered where she was. "Oh, thank you, my son. The spirits say you are a good man."

I forced a smile. "That's great, ma."

She handed me cash and stepped out, still whispering as she walked away.

I took the money and sped off but spent the rest of the night wondering if I had just been blessed or cursed.

Lagos will show you things.

12. Runaway Man

Some people request long-distance trips in advance. Others make spontaneous, life-changing decisions in the back seat of a taxi. This was one of those days.

I picked up a man from a restaurant in Victoria Island. He was dressed in a kaftan, looking rich and respectable, but his body language told a different story. He kept glancing over his shoulder like he was expecting someone to appear out of nowhere.

As soon as he got in, he spoke in a hushed tone. "Oga, can you take me to Ibadan?"

I frowned. "Ibadan? As in Oyo State?"

"Yes."

I checked the app. "Sir, I don't see a trip request for Ibadan."

"I know, I know," he said quickly. "Just drive. I will pay you in cash."

Now, see, I'm not a curious person, but this felt off. Who just wakes up and decides to flee to another state in the middle of the day?

"Sir, I need to know why you're going," I said, watching him through the mirror.

He hesitated, then sighed. "It's woman trouble."

I raised an eyebrow. "What kind of woman trouble?"

He shook his head. "Oga, just drive before my wife finds me."

I let out a long breath. "Sir, I don't think I want to be involved in this."

He sighed. "I'll add an extra ₦60k."

I started the engine.

Lagos is expensive. Principles don't pay rent.

13. The Ghost Rider

It was almost midnight when I got the request. It was a pickup in Yaba with a drop-off in Ikoyi. Odd time for a ride, but occasionally, late-night trips meant surge pricing, so I accepted it.

When I arrived, the street was eerily quiet. The passenger stood near a lamppost, dressed in a black hoodie and jeans, hands in his pockets.

"Good evening," I said.

He nodded silently and got in.

I checked the app. "Going to Ikoyi, right?"

A pause.

Then, in a low voice, he said, "Yes."

Something about his tone gave me chills, but I told myself to relax. People take late-night rides all the time.

I started driving.

A few minutes in, I tried small talk. "Busy night for you, sir?"

No response.

I glanced in the mirror. He was staring straight ahead, expressionless.

I swallowed. Okay. No problem. Maybe he's just tired.

We got to Third Mainland Bridge. The water below looked darker than usual.

Then, suddenly...

"Driver, stop the car."

My heart nearly stopped. "Here? On the bridge?"

He nodded.

I hesitated. "Sir, this place is not safe."

He turned to me, eyes cold. "Just stop."

I obeyed, gripping the wheel tightly.

For a moment, he just sat there, breathing heavily.

Then he opened the door.

I panicked. Was he about to jump?

"Sir! Are you okay?"

He turned back and smiled. A slow, eerie smile.

Then he stepped out.

And vanished.

I swear. He disappeared into thin air.

I blinked. My heart slammed against my chest. This is a dream. It has to be.

I looked around. No sign of him. No footsteps. Nothing.

I looked at my phone. The ride had been cancelled.

I checked the seat. No imprint. No trace.

For a full minute, I just sat there, shaking.

Then I did the only thing that made sense. I floored the accelerator and sped off like my life depended on it.

I didn't stop until I got home.

I burst into the house, breathless, my heart still racing. My housemates, Wale, Seyi, and Kunle were gathered in the living room, watching football highlights.

Kunle looked up. "Omo, Ladi, why you dey sweat like this? You run from LASTMA?"

I dropped my car keys on the table and collapsed onto the couch. "Guys…I think I just carried a ghost."

Seyi scoffed. "Which kind ghost? Abeg, no start."

I shook my head. "I swear! The guy disappeared. Poof! Just like that. One second, he was there, next second, nothing!"

Wale sat up. "Wait. Where did this happen?"

"Third Mainland Bridge."

Kunle's eyes widened. "Ha! Omo, you don go jam spirit."

Seyi laughed. "Abeg, abeg. You sure say the guy no just do 'now you see me, now you don't'?"

I shot him a glare. "Do I look like I'm joking?"

Wale rubbed his chin. "You know say e get one story wey I hear. Some people say they don pick ghost for that bridge before."

I sat up. "Wait, what?"

Kunle nodded. "Yes, nau! Dem say one man wey suppose marry woman for 1985, but he die before the wedding. Since then, people don claim say dem see am for that bridge, dey stop taxi. Some say if you drop am for Ikoyi, by the time you reach, he no go dey again."

I stared at them. "So, I just carried a ghost that's been hitchhiking since 1985?"

Seyi burst out laughing. "Omo, if na true, that ghost don get Taxi Plus subscription."

I glared at him. "Seyi, I dey serious."

Kunle shrugged. "Did you check your back seat?"

A chill ran down my spine. "Why?"

He smirked. "Because sometimes, dem no dey go alone."

I jumped off the couch. "Kunle, you wan kill me?!"

The guys burst into laughter.

I shook my head and grabbed my phone. "Omo, I dey sleep with light on tonight."

Seyi chuckled. "Pray make your ghost rider no order another ride."

I threw a pillow at him.

That night, I locked my door, put my Bible under my pillow, and slept with one eye open.

Lagos will stress you, but Lagos ghosts will introduce you to a whole new level of fear.

14. The Airport Hustle

I had just dropped off my first passenger of the day when a ride request popped up with pickup at Murtala Muhammed Airport. I groaned. Airport trips could be a blessing or a curse, depending on the passenger.

I accepted the request and maneuvered my way through the ever-chaotic Lagos roads, dodging *danfos* and *okadas*. I finally got to the International Arrivals terminal where my passenger, a middle-aged woman in a flowing Ankara gown, stood waving frantically like I was a long-lost son.

"Driver! You're here! Thank God!" She dragged two massive Ghana-Must-Go bags toward my car.

"Good morning, ma," I greeted her and stepped out to help.

"My son, help me put these in the boot," she said, barely pausing to acknowledge me before shouting at a young man who had been following her with a trolley.

"Ehn ehn! You! Move away from my bag! God will judge all you airport thieves!"

I lifted one of the bags and nearly threw out my back. What on earth was inside?

"Ma, these bags are heavy o."

"Ah! I bought small provisions from America," she said nonchalantly, squeezing into the back seat. "Take me to Lekki Phase 1."

I winced. Traffic to Lekki at this time? Lord have mercy.

As I eased the car onto the expressway, she began a detailed commentary on Nigerian customs officers and their love for bribes.

"You won't believe it, my son. After all the stress of travelling, these people stopped me at customs and asked for 'something for the boys.' Ha! Do I look like Santa Claus? I told them, 'Madam no dey drop shishi!'"

She clapped her hands dramatically.

I chuckled. "So, they let you go just like that?"

"Ah, my dear, I had to beg small o. I told them I was a widow, and they should have pity on me."

I glanced at her in the rearview mirror. She looked far too energetic to be pitied.

As we approached Third Mainland Bridge, she suddenly leaned forward. "Driver, do you have a Bible in this car?"

"Uh, no ma."

"Ehn? How can you be driving in Lagos without a Bible? Don't you know the enemy is always at work?"

I opened my mouth to respond when, as if on cue, a LASTMA officer stepped into the road, flagging me down.

"Ah! See what I'm saying! Devil at work!" she hissed. "Don't stop o! Press the accelerator and go!"

"Ma, I can't..."

"Go, jare! They just want money! If you stop, you're finished!"

But before I could decide, the officer smacked his palm on my bonnet. "Oga, park well."

I sighed and pulled over, rolling down my window.

"Good morning, officer," I said, feigning politeness.

"Morning," he replied, peering into the car. "Your papers dey?"

"Yes," I said, handing him my documents. I kept my face neutral, knowing any sign of impatience could turn a five-minute stop into a twenty-minute extortion exercise.

The officer studied the papers, tapping them against his palm. "Oga, you dey drive one-way just now."

"One-way? Officer, I no drive one-way o. This road na normal route."

"Na you go tell me? You wan argue?"

I groaned internally. Here we go.

Before I could respond, my passenger leaned across the seat and poked her head out of the window. "Officer, you this man! How much do you want? Stop wasting our time!"

I froze. Ah. O ti tan. It has finished.

The officer's eyes lit up. "Madam, you dey insult me?"

She folded her arms. "See, my flight was delayed, I've been standing in customs for two hours, and now you're here wasting my time. Will ₦1,000 make you happy so we can go?"

I nearly choked. Who sent her?

The officer straightened. "Madam, you just admitted to trying to bribe a government officer."

I buried my face in my hands.

Five minutes, three arguments, and one reluctant handshake later, I handed over ₦2,000 and drove off before the officer could change his mind.

As soon as we hit the road again, my passenger sat back and sighed dramatically. "You see why I said you need a Bible?"

I shook my head, already exhausted. It wasn't even noon.

This city will humble you.

15. The Job Offer

Some rides change your life. Others almost do.

It was a humid afternoon in June when I picked up a well-dressed man from a high-rise in Marina. He looked like a big *oga*, the type who had people running when he entered an office building.

"Good afternoon, sir," I said, greeting him.

"Ah, young man," he said as he settled in the back of the taxi. "How is work?"

"It's fine, sir," I replied.

We drove in silence for a while until he suddenly said, "You're well-spoken."

I glanced in the mirror. "Thank you, sir," I replied.

"You don't sound like a regular taxi driver," he said, returning my gaze in the rear-view mirror.

I sighed. "I used to work in a bank before I lost my job."

He nodded, interested. "Which bank?"

I told him.

His eyes lit up. "Really? Which school did you finish from?"

"Lagos State University."

He smiled. "Good. I'm a director at one of the new-generation banks. We need smart young men like you."

I almost slammed the brakes. Did I just enter a divine connection?

"Sir, I would love to work in banking again."

He nodded. "Give me your number. Come to my office on Friday for an interview. I'll see what I can do."

I could have done backflips.

I arrived home that night like a man who had just discovered oil in his backyard. My housemates hyped me up.

"Ladi, if you enter that bank, we must celebrate!"

I ironed my best shirt, polished my shoes, and set ten alarms.

Then on Friday morning, I woke up with a fever.

My body felt like someone had put it inside a washing machine and pressed 'spin'. My temperature was through the roof, and my head pounded like an overzealous talking drum.

I took medicine, drank garri, and told myself it was just nerves, then I got dressed for the interview.

By the time I reached the bank, I was sweating like a goat in a pepper soup pot.

The receptionist looked at me like I was a health hazard.

"Who are you here to see?"

I managed to whisper the director's name.

She frowned. "Oh, sir. He travelled last night."

I nearly collapsed.

"Did he leave any message?" I croaked.

She shook her head. "No, sir."

I went home in silence. That evening, I texted him.

No response.

I called.

"This number is switched off."

By evening, the fever broke, and I rushed back to the office on Monday morning. I was told he was still not back from his trip to Abuja.

Just like that, my big break vanished.

Lagos giveth, Lagos also taketh away.

16. The Holy Ghost Slap

It was a bright Wednesday afternoon when the ride request came in, pickup at Lekki Phase 1, drop-off in Ikeja. The long-distance meant good money, so I accepted it immediately.

I arrived at the pickup location and saw my passenger standing by the roadside, talking on the phone. He was tall, light-skinned, and heavily bearded, dressed in designer from head to toe, Gucci slides, a Fendi shirt, and sunglasses that probably cost more than my car battery. He had one Air Pod in his ear and a suspiciously large bundle of cash in his hand.

As soon as I parked, he slid into the front seat. Red flag. Lagos passengers hardly sit in front unless they're planning to talk your ear off or run from the police.

"Baba, how far?" he said casually.

"I dey," I responded, pulling into the road.

He continued his phone conversation, speaking in hushed but urgent tones.

"Guy, no fall my hand o! Just tell the client say the wire don go. No long talk. Omo, na 5K dollars be this one, no go dull."

I bit my tongue and focused on driving. Lagos traffic had taught me one thing, **mind your business.** But it was hard to ignore when my passenger was clearly negotiating fraud inside my car.

He ended the call and sighed. "Omo, this work no easy o."

I glanced at him. "Which work?"

He grinned. "You go know."

I chuckled nervously and turned up the volume on my radio. No be me go hear FBI case today.

We were just approaching Ikoyi Bridge when he suddenly turned to me. "Baba, make I run you small package?"

I frowned. "Which package?"

He lowered his voice. "Na one small hustle. No shaking. I just need make I use your account collect one small wire, I go give you 20 percent."

Blood of Jesus.

I gripped the steering wheel. "Oga, I no dey do that kind thing."

"Ah-ah! Why you dey dull yourself?" He laughed. "See, I fit send you $3,000 now. You go just use your account receive am, withdraw small, then give me the rest. Easy money."

I inhaled deeply. "Oga, abeg, I be taxi driver. I no want wahala."

He scoffed and waved his hand. "No worry. If you change your mind, just let me…"

Before he could finish, his phone rang. He glanced at the screen and his expression changed.

"Omo, wahala don dey."

"What happened?" I asked before remembering I didn't want to know.

"It's my guy. He say EFCC dey sweep Lekki."

I nearly slammed the brakes. "Eh?"

He started shifting in his seat. "Omo, driver, I go drop here."

"You never reach Ikeja."

"No worry, I go find another way."

I pulled over reluctantly. He reached for the door handle, then hesitated. "Baba, just reason my matter. The package legit."

I shook my head. "Oga, abeg, comot from my motor."

He sighed dramatically. "You too dey fear." Then he stepped out, slammed the door, and blended into the crowd like a ghost.

I exhaled, relieved. That was close.

I adjusted my mirror, ready to drive off when I heard another voice from the backseat. "Driver, follow that man!"

I almost jumped out of my skin.

I turned around and saw a short, elderly woman sitting in the backseat, wearing a large gele and clutching a leather handbag. Where did she come from?!

"Madam, how did you..."

"No time for story! Follow him! The Holy Spirit says I must deliver a message!"

I stared in shock. "Ah?"

She leaned forward, eyes blazing. "Driver! I say follow him!"

I had two choices, argue with a determined Nigerian woman, or obey. I sighed and put the car in motion, trailing after my former passenger.

We followed him down a side street. He walked briskly, looking around nervously, probably checking if he was being watched.

Then, just as we pulled up beside him, the woman threw open the door and stepped out. "Young man!" she barked.

He froze. "Ah, Mama, wetin happen?"

She pointed a stern finger at him. "The Lord sent me to you!"

He laughed nervously. "Mama, abeg, I no get change."

She ignored him and continued, voice loud enough for the heavens to hear. "Repent, my son! The Holy Spirit says your hands are unclean!"

I nearly choked. Is this a Nollywood movie?

The guy's eyes darted around, clearly embarrassed. "Mama, abeg, no dey disgrace me."

But the woman was just getting started. "Disgrace? Do you know disgrace? When EFCC catches you, that is disgrace! When your mother sees your face on TV paraded as a criminal, that is disgrace!"

A small crowd started gathering. Lagos people and their love for drama.

"Madam, please, I dey go..." he started.

Then it happened.

She slapped him.

A thunderous, Holy Ghost-filled slap that sent his sunglasses flying off his face.

The crowd gasped. I gasped.

"Jesus!" he yelped, holding his cheek.

"Let that slap deliver you from yahoo yahoo!" she declared.

People started clapping. One man shouted, "Preach, Mama!"

The guy looked genuinely shaken. "Mama, you no need to slap me nau."

"My son, I slap you because I love you," she said, adjusting her gele.

At that moment, a police siren blared down the road. The guy didn't wait. He picked up his Gucci slides and ran.

The woman dusted her hands. "The devil will not have his soul."

She turned to me. "Driver, take me home."

I nodded quickly, not wanting to be the next recipient of her Holy Ghost slap.

As I drove off, she sighed. "This is why you need to be prayerful, my son. Be careful of the company you keep."

I shook my head, exhausted. "Yes, ma."

I comported myself well throughout the drive to her house.

17. The University Students

One Saturday afternoon, I got a request from Ojota Motor Park.

Two guys and two girls, all dressed like they had just stepped out of a TikTok dance video, piled into my car.

"Driver, how far now?" one of them asked, sliding into the car.

"I dey," I responded.

"Ah! AC, AC! Omo, Lagos taxis sweet o!" one of them shouted.

I adjusted my mirror. "Good afternoon. Where are we going?"

"Ilashe Beach!"

I hesitated. Ilashe was far. And from the way they looked, I had a feeling their bank accounts weren't as strong as their energy.

"You know how much that will cost?" I asked.

One of them, a slim girl with dyed red hair, grinned. "We go settle you."

I sighed and started the car.

As we drove, they switched from gossiping about their classmates to analysing their course lectures to ranking Lagos beaches. I expected noise, but these students were smart. They spoke in crisp English, switching seamlessly between Yoruba and Pidgin, and debating the economy with more intelligence than some politicians I'd carried.

"Driver, are you married?" one of them suddenly asked.

I chuckled. "No."

"Ah!" Another one said with a clap. "See fine boy! Lagos girls no sabi choose good men."

"Driver, you don go university before?"

"Yes," I said. "I went to LASU."

She gasped dramatically. "Ha! Omo, see alumni!"

The whole car burst into laughter.

Then the guy in the front seat, a quiet one with glasses, said, "I heard LASU's computer science department is good."

I nodded. "Yes. You dey study comp science?"

He smiled. "Something like that."

The ride continued, full of loud music, jokes, and energy. Then, as we neared Lekki, they started discussing their courses.

One of the guys bragged, "Me, I don tire for Engineering. Too many formulas."

Another laughed. "Guy, na you gree do am. I dey manage Mass Comm jejely."

When we finally arrived at the boat terminal where they would take a ferry to Ilashe Beach, they paid me my fare without stressing me.

"Take this," one of them said, handing me a ₦2,000 tip. "For your troubles."

I nodded. "Enjoy the beach."

As they walked away, one of them turned back to me and said, "Driver, if Lagos stress too much for you, come to Ibadan! We sabi enjoy too."

I laughed as they disappeared into the crowd.

Ibadan people were different.

18. Fellowship at Hotel

It was a quiet Sunday evening when a request came in for a pick-up at a high-end restaurant in Ikeja. The drop-off was a hotel.

I arrived a short time later to see a man standing near the entrance of the restaurant. He was middle-aged with a potbelly and was dressed like a 1980s music producer.

As soon as he entered the car, he adjusted his wristwatch and leaned back. "Young man, let's go." He smelled of expensive perfume and bad decisions.

I nodded. "Where to, sir?"

"Rockview Hotel."

I started driving.

Then his phone rang.

"Hello, baby! I'm on my way," he cooed. "You're at Rockview, right?"

I didn't mean to eavesdrop, but the car wasn't soundproof.

"Ehn?! Which Rockview?" His voice rose. "Ikeja? Not Victoria Island?!"

I gripped the wheel tighter.

"My dear, you said Rockview! How am I supposed to know which one?!"

I kept my face straight. Lagos had two Rockview Hotels. He had picked the wrong one.

"Baby, don't be angry," he continued, his tone softer. "I will come now."

He ended the call and sighed deeply. "Driver, we need to turn back."

I nodded, already turning the car around.

Then his phone rang again. A different number.

"Hello?" His voice dropped an octave.

A pause.

"Ah, my wife! I was just about to call you."

I nearly crashed into a *keke*.

He cleared his throat. "No, no, I'm still at the men's fellowship…Yes, we just finished prayers."

I bit my lip to keep from laughing.

"Alright, my dear. I'll be home soon. God bless you too."

He ended the call and exhaled. "Driver, drive fast."

I stepped on the gas, but in my head, I was laughing and thinking about how I would gist my flatmates about the "Men's Fellowship at Rockview Hotel."

19. The Mainland Madam and Sunday Visit

Sundays were for church and my biweekly visit to my parents in Ogba. It was a tradition I upheld, mostly because my mother called me at 7.00 am sharp to remind me as if she thought I'd forget where I came from.

That morning, I went to church in Ajah where I endured a sermon on the dangers of laziness (ironic, considering I had worked till 2.00 am the night before), and then started to drive towards Ogba.

I got a ride request from a certain "Madam Folabi" for drop-off in Surulere. The name alone sounded like trouble, but I thought it would be worth it since I was going to Mainland anyway.

I arrived at the location and saw my passenger, a Mainland Madam in her mid-40s, wearing a lace blouse, gold earrings that could be traded for land in Epe, and a face set in permanent disapproval.

"Driver, this your car is too small. Don't you have a Prado?"

I forced a smile. "No ma, but this Corolla is very comfortable."

She rolled her eyes and got in. "Anyway, just drive carefully. I don't like rough drivers."

I nodded and pulled into traffic. Barely five minutes in, she pulled out her phone and started talking loudly.

"I am telling you, Funke, these Lekki men are all mad! Imagine, I took one young boy to dinner, and he ordered only rice! No meat! No drink! Just rice! What kind of poverty mindset is that?"

I swallowed a laugh.

"Can you imagine? I even told him, 'Order whatever you like, my dear.' He said, 'Aunty, rice is okay.' Ha! If I wanted a hungry person, I would have adopted a child from the village!"

I focused on driving, but Madam wasn't done.

"And guess what, Funke? After the meal, this idiot had the audacity to say, 'So how do we split the bill?' Split which bill?! Was I not the one who called him out?!"

I bit my lip to keep from laughing.

She exhaled dramatically. "Anyway, I just blocked his number. Nonsense."

We got to Surulere, and she gave me a ₦2000 tip. "Young man, take. Use it to buy meat with your rice."

I chuckled. Madam was wicked, but at least she was generous.

I continued my journey to Ogba, but Lagos traffic was doing its best to delay me. By the time I parked outside my parents' compound, my mother was already waiting at the door.

"Oladipupo, you're late!" she called out, hands on her hips.

"Good afternoon, Mummy," I said as I stretched and yawned.

She shook her head. "Look at you. Always tired. What kind of work are you even doing sef? Are you still carrying passengers up and down?"

Before I could answer, our neighbour, Mummy Chinyere, a woman who had an advanced degree in amebo, peeked from her balcony.

"Ah, Ladi! My son! You don come visit?" she beamed.

"Yes, ma."

She leaned on the railing. "So, when are we coming to eat rice? Your mother says you don't have a wife yet."

I sighed. Here we go.

My mother jumped in. "You see? Even the neighbours are concerned! You're almost 30! You should at least be engaged by now."

I groaned. "Mummy, let me eat first."

But she was just warming up. "Look at Kunle, our neighbour's son. Married with a child. Look at Bode, he's even in Canada with his wife! You, what are you doing?"

"Driving passengers up and down," Mummy Chinyere supplied helpfully.

I exhaled and marched inside.

Inside, my father was already seated with his tablet. "Your mother has started again, abi?"

I nodded.

He chuckled. "Eat first. Then you can run before she starts the second round."

I took his advice. Lagos passengers and traffic were stressful, but dodging marriage talks with my mom on Sunday? Even worse.

20. NON-ENGAGEMENT RING

One slow Monday evening, I got a request from Ikoyi to Ikeja. When I arrived in Ikoyi, my passenger, a sharply dressed man in a navy blue suit holding a small velvet box, was waiting.

"Good evening, sir," I greeted him.

He nodded, but his expression was tense. "Ikeja, please. I need to do something important tonight."

We hit the road.

After a few minutes of silence, he sighed. "I'm proposing tonight."

I smiled. "Ah, congratulations in advance, sir."

He nodded absentmindedly. "I just hope she says yes."

I smiled again.

Halfway through the journey, my passenger started checking his phone. I watched him in the rear-view mirror and saw his face twist.

"What the hell?" he muttered.

I glanced at him. "Everything okay, sir?"

He didn't answer. Instead, he frantically scrolled through his phone, his face getting darker by the second.

Then, without warning, he demanded, "Driver, stop the car!"

I pulled over, confused. My passenger sat frozen, staring at his phone.

Then he laughed. It was not a happy laugh. It was a painful, wounded laugh.

"Sir?" I asked cautiously.

He shook his head. "She's at a hotel. With another man."

I blinked. Omo.

He exhaled deeply. "Can you take me there?"

I hesitated. "Sir, are you sure?"

"Yes."

I sighed and drove toward the hotel.

When we arrived, he sat still for a while, gripping the engagement ring like it was a weapon. Then, slowly, he stepped out.

I debated whether to leave, but curiosity got the best of me, so I stayed.

A few minutes later, the hotel doors swung open, and a woman ran out, half-dressed and panicking.

Right behind her was my passenger. He was holding a shoe.

"Driver, let's go."

I didn't ask any questions.

We sped off in silence. Then finally, he spoke. "She said she wasn't ready for marriage."

I glanced in the rearview mirror. "I'm sorry to hear that."

He exhaled. "I dodged a bullet."

I nodded.

Lagos, another day, another drama.

21. Baby That Wasn't Mine

I got a request from Yaba to Ajah on a quiet Thursday afternoon. When I arrived at the pickup location, I found a young woman standing by the roadside with a baby in her arms.

She climbed in and smiled. "Good afternoon."

"Good afternoon, ma. Off to Ajah, right?"

"Yes."

I pulled into the road. Her destination was close to my street, so I knew the area well.

As we drove, she sighed dramatically. "Men are scum."

I glanced at her. "Ah. Sorry, ma."

She shook her head. "You men will deny pregnancy, deny responsibility, and still sleep peacefully at night."

I swallowed. "Eh...okay."

She eyed me. "You don't even remember me, do you?"

I almost crashed into a keke. "What?"

She scoffed. "Typical."

"Madam, I don't know you o."

She sighed. "Sure. Just like you didn't know me nine months ago when you left me with this baby?"

I gripped the steering wheel. Ah?

"Madam, I swear, I don't know you."

She shook her head. "Don't pretend, Ladi."

My soul left my body. She knew my name.

My mind raced. What was going on?

Then she burst out laughing.

"Relax, driver. I'm joking!"

I exhaled so hard that I nearly passed out. "Jesus!"

She laughed harder. "See your face! You looked ready to jump out of the car."

I shook my head. "Madam, Lagos no fit give me this kind stress."

She smiled. "Don't worry. The real father is hiding in Lekki. I'm just going to my sister's house. She's your neighbour."

I chuckled weakly.

Lagos women. For a second there, I was about to have a heart attack.

22. The Chatty Bird

The ride request came from Surulere. I pulled up, expecting a regular passenger. Instead, I got a man holding a bright green parrot in a cage.

I blinked. "Sir, did you order a ride?"

"Yes," he said. "Is there a problem?"

I hesitated. "Uh, no. But…the bird?"

He smiled. "Oh, this is Caeser. He's harmless."

Before I could respond, the parrot squawked, "HELLO! HOW MUCH IS FUEL?"

I opened my mouth in shock. "He talks?"

The man chuckled. "He picks up random things."

I laughed and started driving.

For the first few minutes, it was peaceful. Then Caeser started again.

"WATCH OUT FOR LASTMA!"

I choked on air. "Sir, where did he learn that?"

The man shrugged. "I take taxis a lot. And we watch TV together, so he hears a lot of repetitive words."

The parrot continued. "NO LIGHT!"

I covered my mouth, laughing. This bird had seen Lagos.

Halfway through the ride, we stopped at a pet shop.

"I need to get food for Caeser," the man explained. "And some of my other pets."

As he went inside, Caeser turned to me: "THIS MAN IS BROKE."

I continued laughing and turned to the bird. "What else can you say?"

"GIVE ME MY CHANGE!" the bird squawked.

The man returned, carrying a bag of bird food and some other items. "I see you two are bonding."

I pointed at the parrot. "He said you're broke."

The man chuckled. "Ignore him. He's dramatic."

I shook my head, laughing.

By the time we reached his house, I had enjoyed chatting with the bird and the random things it was saying.

As he got out, Caeser looked at me and squawked, "FIVE-STAR RATING, OGA!"

I gave them a five-star rating. For comedy.

23. The Lagos Avoidant

One cool Sunday evening, I got a ride request from Banana Island. I pulled up in front of a luxury apartment where a young guy with a fresh haircut, wearing an expensive watch and a designer outfit swaggered out, carrying a duffle bag.

"Driver, na Lekki we dey go," he said.

"Yes, sir."

As I pulled into the road, he made a call.

"Babe, I'm on my way."

I tuned him out and focused on the road.

A few minutes into his call, I heard him say, "I don't know what you're talking about. What do you mean you're pregnant?"

Ah.

I immediately knew where this was going.

The conversation escalated quickly.

"You sef, why didn't you use protection?" he snapped.

I nearly slammed the brakes. Oga, is it not both of you?

"I'm not ready for this," he continued. "You should just take care of it."

My ears perked up.

Silence on the other end.

Then the woman's voice, cold, sharp through the loud volume of the phone said, "I'm keeping the baby. And guess what? I'm outside your house."

My passenger froze. "Wait, what?"

"I'm waiting for you."

I saw him check his phone.

He looked at me. "Driver, change the route. We're going to VI."

I shook my head and sighed. Lagos men.

24. The Forgotten Past

It was on one of those rare quiet mornings in Lagos that I got a ping requesting a ride from Surulere to Ikorodu. The name on the app was simply "Baba O."

When I arrived, there was an elderly man, probably in his 70s, waiting. He wore a faded Agbada and carried a small leather bag.

"Good morning, sir," I greeted him and stepped out to help him in.

"Ah, my son. Thank you," he said, smiling warmly.

As we hit the road, he looked out the window, sighing deeply.

"Ah, Lagos," he murmured. "It used to be different."

I smiled. "Sir, you've lived here long?"

He chuckled. "I was born here. Before these new express roads. Before danfos took over. Before…"

He paused, his smile fading.

"What happened, sir?"

He exhaled. "I left Lagos 40 years ago. Today, I am returning to see…if she still remembers me."

I frowned. "Who, sir?"

He hesitated, then pulled out an old, folded photograph.

A young woman, beautiful, smiling, stood in front of a small shop.

"Her name was Folake," he whispered. "I was supposed to marry her."

I felt my chest tighten.

"What happened?" I asked.

He looked out the window. "I left for London. Promised to return. Sent letters. But by the time I came back years later… she was gone. No trace."

I swallowed.

"She used to sell fabric in Ikorodu," he continued. "That's where we're going. Maybe… maybe someone remembers her."

We drove in silence.

When we arrived, I helped him get out. He stood looking around like a man searching for ghosts.

"Sir, do you need help?"

He shook his head. "No, my son. Some things, you must do alone."

I watched him slowly walk away.

And for the first time in a long while, I realized some journeys are not just about distance. They are about time.

25. The Billionaire's Daughter

Lagos is unpredictable, but that Thursday morning, I wasn't ready for what was about to happen.

I had just accepted a ride request from Banana Island to Eko Atlantic. The name on the app? "Princess B." Ah, Lagosians and their names.

I arrived at a massive mansion, the kind that looked like it belonged to an oil tycoon. The gate slid open, and my passenger stepped out, a young woman dressed in designer from head to toe. Gucci sunglasses, a Prada handbag, and the kind of confidence only old money could buy.

"Good morning, ma," I greeted her.

She barely looked at me as she got in. "Let's go."

We hit the road. She was scrolling through her phone, barely paying attention, which was fine by me. Then, halfway to Eko Atlantic, she suddenly sighed dramatically.

"Ugh. Lagos men are so broke."

I nearly hit the brakes.

"Sorry, ma?"

She exhaled. "Imagine! This guy had the audacity to ask me out, and when I checked his Instagram, he still lives with his parents in Surulere."

I swallowed a laugh.

"You know," she continued, "if you don't have at least two properties and a yacht, why are you even talking to me?"

I nodded slowly. People dey try for this Lagos sha.

We approached a junction where traffic had built up when out of nowhere, three guys jumped in front of the car.

Before I could react, one of them yanked open the passenger door.

"Madam, no shout. Give us everything."

Jesus.

The girl gasped. "Oh my God!"

The second guy leaned in through my window. "Oga, just cooperate. Bring your wallet."

I exhaled and quickly handed over my wallet. Lagos Wisdom 101 - your life is more important than your wallet. Thankfully, my ID was in my other pocket.

But my passenger? She made a mistake.

She laughed.

"You think you can rob me?" she sneered. "Do you know who my father is?"

The guys exchanged looks.

"Ah. We don hear that one before," one of them said.

She folded her arms. "Fine. I won't give you anything."

The leader nodded. "Okay. Oya, bring her down."

My blood ran cold.

"Madam, give them something!" I hissed.

But she scoffed. "They can't do anything to me."

One of them grabbed her arm.

"Wait!" I yelled. "Take my money. Just let her go."

They hesitated.

The girl huffed. "Driver, shut up."

The leader eyed her. "You dey craze?"

Then, as if sensing an opportunity, he yanked off her designer wig and ran.

The other two burst out laughing and sprinted after him.

The girl sat frozen for a moment.

Then "MY WIG! DO YOU KNOW HOW MUCH THAT COST?!"

I sat there speechless as she jumped out of the car and started screaming at random passersby.

"Chase them! My wig!"

Passersby and even people in other cars were amused by the whole drama.

I sighed and looked up at the sky. She looked funny, and even though it was a tense situation, I was glad we were unharmed.

I tried to calm her down and suggested that we return to her house so she could get another wig. She agreed.

The things my eyes see on these Lagos roads.

26. Chance Encounter with Tolani

It had been months since I last saw Tolani. My ex. The one who left me when things got tough. The one I wasn't supposed to still be thinking about.

But Lagos had other plans.

It was a Saturday night, and I had just dropped off a passenger at a popular lounge in Lekki when another request popped up from the spot just two minutes away.

I accepted.

When I pulled up to the location, three ladies were standing outside, laughing. They were all dressed in their Saturday night finest.

And smack in the middle of them?

Tolani.

My heart did a small backflip.

She turned, locked eyes with me, and froze.

I cleared my throat. "Uh, ride for... Tola?"

One of her friends, tall, loud, with the confidence of a Lagos aunty at a wedding grinned. "Yes, that's her!"

Tolani looked like she wanted to disappear.

"Hey, Ladi," she said, her voice cautious.

I nodded. "Long time."

Her friend raised an eyebrow. "Wait, you two know each other?"

Tolani shot her a warning look. "Let's just go."

They piled in. The friend, still curious, kept pressing. "So, how do you know our dear Tola?"

I smirked. "We used to date."

Tolani groaned. "Can we not do this?"

The car fell silent.

Then her friend burst into laughter. "Oh! So, you are the Ladi!"

I glanced at Tolani. "You've been talking about me?"

She sighed. "Can we just get to Ikoyi?"

The friend wasn't done. "You broke his heart, Tola. And now, fate has brought him back to drive you."

Tolani shot me an apologetic glance. I just smiled.

"Life is funny like that."

The rest of the ride was quiet.

When we got to their stop, Tolani's friends got out while Tolani lingered.

"Ladi... I..."

I held up a hand. "It's fine. Really."

She hesitated. "Take care, okay?"

I nodded. She left.

As I drove off, I let out a breath I didn't realize I was holding in.

27. The Paparazzi Escape

On a slow Tuesday night, my app pinged with a ride request for a pickup from Eko Hotel. The drop-off was at a "Private Residence." No specific address, just "Private Residence."

I raised an eyebrow. That was already suspicious.

I arrived at the hotel's back entrance, where a tall figure in a hoodie and face mask slipped into the backseat.

"Good evening, sir," I greeted.

"Drive. Fast."

I blinked. Okay, this was either a robbery or a Nollywood movie scene.

I pulled out smoothly, trying to figure out who my passenger was. His voice sounded familiar. I stole a glance in the mirror and then it clicked, I was carrying Blaze Benny, the Afrobeats superstar.

Omo!

I swallowed my excitement. Stay professional, Ladi. Don't mess this up.

We hit the road, but barely five minutes later, he cursed under his breath.

"Damn it. They're following."

I checked my mirrors. Two cars, one black, and one silver, were tailing us.

Paparazzi.

"Sir, should I…"

"Lose them."

Ah. F1 mode activated.

I took a sharp right, then another left, dodging through smaller roads in VI. The paparazzi weren't joking, they followed us at full speed.

"Lagos drivers," Blaze muttered. "These people drive like they have nine lives."

I smirked. "Me too."

I swerved into a narrow street, then suddenly cut through a filling station and emerged on another road. The cars behind me got stuck in traffic.

Silence.

Then Blaze let out a low whistle. "Damn, bro. You've done this before."

I grinned. "Lagos will teach you."

We finally arrived at his hidden location, and before stepping out, he reached into his pocket and handed me an extra ₦20,000 tip.

"Good work, my guy. Keep this."

I tried to stay cool. "Thank you, sir."

As he slipped into the house, I sighed, thankful for the money.

Lagos. One night you're dodging traffic, the next you're a getaway driver for a superstar.

28. The IJGB Reality Check

Sunday afternoon. Traffic-free roads. Just vibes.

I got a request from the airport, for a passenger heading to Lekki. The name? "Tunde Japa."

Japa? I already knew what was coming.

I arrived and saw a guy in designer sweats, wheeling two large suitcases, smiling like someone who had just escaped from prison.

He got in, inhaling like he was absorbing fresh air.

"Ah, Lagos! My city!"

I smiled. "Welcome back, sir."

He nodded. "You won't understand. I've been in Canada for six years. No jollof rice, no proper suya. Just snow and stress."

I chuckled. "So, you missed Lagos?"

"Of course! Lagos is home! Everything works here!"

I almost hit a pothole from laughing.

"I can't wait to visit cool new places! Eat some real food!"

We drove into Lekki, and as if Lagos heard him, wahala started.

First, a danfo driver cut me off aggressively.

Tunde gasped. "Wait, this is still happening?"

I nodded. "E never change."

Then, at a traffic light, an area boy knocked on his window.

"Bros, welcome back! Anything for the boys?"

Tunde turned to me. "Omo, I forgot about these guys."

I smirked. "Dem miss you."

We got to his street, only to find that the street was flooded.

He blinked. "Wait, it didn't even rain today."

I shrugged. "Lagos has its own water system."

As I parked, he exhaled deeply. "Maybe I should've stayed in Canada."

I patted the dashboard. "Welcome home, bros."

Lagos doesn't change. It just waits for you.

MEMOIRS OF A LAGOS JUNIOR BANKER

A Collection of Flash Fiction Stories

Tolulope Popoola

MEET ONOME

If anyone had told me that working in a Lagos bank would be like signing up for a reality TV show packed with stress, drama, and questionable life choices, I would have laughed and asked them to stop exaggerating.

But after a few weeks on the job, I realised the truth. Banking in Lagos is not for the weak. It is a daily grind.

I, Onome Eferogho, a fresh graduate from Babcock University, never imagined that my first job would be this chaotic.

I thought I would be wearing nice suits, working in a beautiful office, and handling important financial deals. Instead, I found myself hiding to avoid my creepy manager, dealing with all sorts of crazy customers, dodging office politics, and watching my dreams of early retirement fade away with every stressful day.

But in the middle of the madness, I have learned a few things, and I have written them down in my memoirs. So, this is my life in the trenches of Lagos banking.

Brace yourself. It's going to be a wild ride.

1. First Day Fiasco

I adjusted my blazer for the fifth time, staring at my reflection. My first official day as a full-time employee at Prestige Capital Bank, and I *had* to make a good impression. I had spent the last ten months as a youth corper in the Opebi branch, and I was now due to resume at the head office in Victoria Island. Recalling how hard I worked to be retained, I knew that transitioning to employee meant I had to keep proving myself. Only two of us, I and another corper named Samuel, had been offered full-time employment with the VI office.

"Onome! Your friend is here!" My mother's voice echoed up the stairs.

I grabbed my handbag and folder and rushed out to meet Oyinkan, my work bestie, waiting impatiently in her cherry-red Toyota.

Oyinkan and I met during my NYSC, when she was at the Opebi branch and had been assigned to me as a buddy, as she had joined the bank fourteen months before I did. She moved to the VI branch six months ago, and I was excited to be working with her again.

"Onome, if you make us late on your first day, I will personally assign you to the help desk for eternity," she warned.

"Sorry...sorry", I said as I slid into the car.

It was almost 6.15 am, and the morning drive to Victoria Island was the usual battle for survival. There were hawkers weaving through traffic, okadas breaking every law, and Oyinkan expertly dodging danfo buses.

"Ready to experience head office banking in all its soul-crushing glory?" she asked.

"You've only been here a year longer than me, don't act like a veteran," I laughed.

"In Nigerian banking, one year equals ten anywhere else."

She wasn't wrong.

The moment we arrived, trouble started. The security guard waved Oyinkan through but stopped me.

"ID card, madam?"

"I'm new," I said, forcing a smile. "First day."

"No ID, no entry."

"But I'm here to get the ID *nau*."

"Management directive."

After fifteen minutes of calls to my team lead and the Head of Security, and mentally drafting my resignation letter, I was finally allowed inside.

"First lesson of banking," Oyinkan muttered, as we arrived at our desks. "Always make friends with security personnel."

Before I could breathe, a voice loomed over me.

"Onome Eferogho? Orientation started five minutes ago in the conference room."

I turned to see Mrs Asiogu, the Operations Manager.

I grabbed my notebook and ran.

Conference Room 3 was dark and locked.

A cleaner passing by snorted. "New staff? That one na for Conference Room 7, fifth floor."

I arrived panting, sweaty, and late.

"Ah, Ms. Eferogho finally joins us," the HR Manager quipped. Eight faces turned to stare.

I wanted to disappear.

The orientation session was a blur of compliance rules, dress codes, and warnings about lateness, which felt personal. I took some notes, but I was mostly bored and counting down to lunchtime.

When I was finally able to escape the conference room, I met up with Oyinkan at the staff canteen. Then I realised I'd left my wallet on my desk.

I whispered in panic. "Oyinkan, I forgot my money."

She rolled her eyes and pushed her tray toward me. "Share mine. But you owe me lunch for a week."

As I chewed my meat pie and fried chicken, a tall, well-dressed man approached.

"That's Femi Adekoya," Oyinkan whispered. "Head of Corporate Banking. Workaholic. Gorgeous. Rich. Husband material."

I choked.

"Ladies, enjoying lunch?" he asked smoothly.

"Yes, sir," we chorused.

He turned to me. "You must be one of our new recruits."

"Yes, sir. Onome Eferogho, Retail Banking."

"Retail," he said, smiling slightly. "The frontlines. If you ever consider Corporate, let me know. We're always looking for fresh talent."

As he walked away, Oyinkan gripped my arm.

"Did you see that? He was totally checking you out!"

"He was being professional!" I protested but couldn't stop myself from smiling.

After lunch, I was heading back to my desk when I turned a corner too fast and collided with someone holding a steaming cup of coffee.

Splash.

I gasped. "Oh my God, I'm so sorry!"

Then I looked up. Straight into the furious eyes of Mr Ogundare, the Branch Manager.

Coffee dripped from his pristine white shirt and mine.

Silence.

"Ms. Eferogho, isn't it?" he said coldly.

"Yes, sir. I'm so, so sorry, sir. I'll pay for dry cleaning..."

He held up a hand. "First day?"

I nodded, terrified.

"Then I suggest you find a change of clothes. Prestige Capital expects excellence. Including how we present ourselves."

I wanted to cry.

Back at my desk, I texted Oyinkan in full panic mode.

Emergency. Need spare blouse now!

She appeared minutes later, holding a blouse from her gym bag.

"What happened?"

I changed quickly, muttering, "I spilled coffee on the Branch Manager."

She howled with laughter. "On your first day?! That's impressive!"

"He's going to hate me forever."

"Probably," she chirped. "But hey, at least you made an impression."

The rest of the day crawled by with more trainings, form signings, and meeting too many people to remember.

By 6.00 pm, my feet were aching, and my head was spinning.

As we drove home, I stared out the window, questioning all my life choices.

"So, first-day reflections?" Oyinkan asked.

"It was a disaster."

"It's banking, babe. It gets worse."

"Hei God."

"Don't worry, you'll survive. See you at 6.00 am sharp!"

At home, my family gathered for my first-day report.

"So? How was your first day as a proper banker?" my father asked eagerly.

My mother beamed. "Our daughter, the banker!"

Ovie, my brother, barely looked up from his phone. "Did they give you vault access yet? I have some business ideas."

Ufuoma rolled her eyes. "Did you meet any cute guys?"

I collapsed into a chair, exhausted.

"Let's just say, banking is going to be an adventure."

2. The Teller Trials

"Next customer, please!"

I fixed my best customer service smile as a woman in a bold ankara outfit strutted up to my teller window. It was week three into my job at Prestige Capital, and I was now confident and capable of handling customers on my own.

"Good morning, ma. How may I help you?"

The customer dropped a heavy handbag on the counter. "I want to withdraw one million naira."

I nodded. "Do you have your withdrawal slip and ID, ma?"

She waved a dismissive hand. "I don't need all that. I've been banking here for twenty years. Just give me my money."

"Ma, we require proper documentation for large withdrawals."

Her voice rose instantly. "Do you know who I am? Call your manager!"

As if summoned by drama, Mr Ogundare, my coffee-stained nemesis, appeared.

"Is there a problem here?"

"This small girl is asking me for ID! *Me!* Chief Mrs. Adebisi!"

Ogundare turned to me with a raised eyebrow.

"She wants to withdraw one million naira without documentation, sir," I said, keeping my voice calm.

To my shock, he nodded. "Ms. Eferogho is absolutely correct. Even our most valued customers must now follow Central Bank regulations."

Chief Mrs. Adebisi huffed but reluctantly presented her ID.

As Ogundare walked away, he gave me a slight approving nod. Maybe he didn't hate me after all.

The rest of my morning was a parade of all sorts.

A man swearing his account had been credited (it hadn't).

A student locking his ATM card after six wrong PIN attempts.

An elderly man who narrated his entire financial history before withdrawing ₦5,000.

By lunch, my cheeks hurt from forced smiling.

"How's the front line treating you?" Oyinkan asked, biting into her sausage roll.

"It's wild," I muttered. "One woman brought in loose cash in a rice sack and got angry when I said I had to count it."

"Welcome to retail banking," she laughed. "Where the customer is always right, especially when they're completely wrong."

As I chewed my jollof rice, a tall, well-dressed man laughed at a nearby table with Ogundare.

"Who's that?" I asked.

"Deji Adewale," Oyinkan whispered. "Assistant Branch Manager. Transferred from Enugu last week. Single, ambitious, and rumour has it, looking for a banker wife."

"Not interested," I said immediately.

"You haven't even met him!"

"I'm saving for my Masters. No distractions."

After lunch, I was assigned to the Foreign Exchange desk.

Within minutes, a man approached the desk with a briefcase.

"I need to send $5,000 to my son's school in America!" He opened the briefcase to show me the cash.

"Certainly, sir. I just need some ID and proof of school admission."

His face fell. "Proof? I never needed that before!"

"New CBN regulations, sir..."

"This is nonsense!"

As I tried to pacify him, I noticed Deji watching from nearby.

Great. An audience for my suffering. To my surprise, he walked over, smiling.

"Sir, these are actually new directives from the Central Bank," he explained smoothly. "But I can help you with the process."

The customer calmed down instantly. He agreed to return with proper documents.

"Well handled," Deji said, turning to me. "Forex customers can be tricky."

"Thank you, sir."

"Please, call me Deji. 'Sir' makes me feel ancient." He smiled. "You're Onome, right? I've heard you're doing excellent work."

"You have?"

He laughed. "Don't sound so surprised. Talent gets noticed."

Then he lingered. "Listen, some of us are having drinks on Friday night. Team bonding. You should come."

I hesitated. "I usually catch a ride home with Oyinkan..."

"Bring her too. 7.00 pm at Crossroads."

And with that, he walked away.

I cornered Oyinkan in the break room.

"Did you know about drinks on Friday?"

"Of course. Most of us are going. Why?"

"Deji just invited me."

Her eyes widened. "I told you! Banker wife material!"

"Stop it! He was just being nice."

"Nice, specifically to the pretty new girl."

"I'm not dating a manager."

"We'll see," she sang, returning to her desk.

At closing time, I was balancing my cash drawer when I noticed I was exactly five naira short. It was an infuriating discrepancy that took thirty minutes to track.

I was near tears when Mr Ogundare appeared.

"Still here, Ms. Eferogho?"

"Cash balancing issue, sir. But I found it."

He nodded. "Customer-facing roles are the foundation of banking. Not everyone has the temperament for it."

I braced for criticism.

Instead, he said, "You handled Chief Mrs. Adebisi well today. Others in your place would have buckled."

I blinked. Was that a compliment?

"Thank you, sir," I said, stunned.

He nodded. "Banking is about relationships as much as rules. Remember that."

Then, as he walked away, he added:

"And try not to spill coffee on any more managers."

Did Ogundare just make a joke?

On the drive home, Oyinkan was already planning my outfit.

"What are you wearing on Friday? You need something professional but cute. Banking cute, not club cute."

317

"I haven't decided if I'm going yet," I muttered.

"Of course you're going! Networking is everything in this industry."

"Oh."

"Besides, Deji invited you personally."

"As a colleague," I said.

"Just saying," Oyinkan teased. "A banker husband is the best investment."

I rolled my eyes. No distractions, remember? I was here to work, save, and leave.

At home, my mother beamed proudly.

"Onome the banker! How was your day today?"

I hesitated.

"Well... today was busy. And there's a team gathering on Friday night..."

My mother perked up. "Should I iron your blue dress?"

"Mum, it's just drinks with colleagues. Not a matchmaking event."

Still, I couldn't ignore the tiny flutter in my stomach.

By Friday, I was exhausted, but Oyinkan had threatened to drag me to drinks by force, so I had no choice. She came to my desk as I was logging out of my computer.

"Change into this," she said, handing me a sleek black top.

I thought you said "banking cute," not "club cute?" I teased.

"Yes, but also - look at Deji."

I glanced across the office. He looked effortlessly sharp in a dark blue blazer, speaking with Mrs. Asiogu.

I swallowed. It's just networking. Nothing more.

By 7.15 pm, we walked into Crossroads Bar. Half the office was already there, nursing cocktails and talking about nothing work-related.

Deji spotted me immediately.

"Glad you made it, Onome," he said, flashing that easy smile.

"Thanks for the invite, sir."

"No 'sir.' It's just Deji."

I nodded, unsure why my pulse had picked up.

He signalled to the waiter. "A mojito for her. Light ice."

I raised an eyebrow. "How do you know what I drink?"

"Educated guess. Refreshing but not too sweet. Like you."

I blinked. Was this flirting? Or just workplace charm?

Either way, Oyinkan was watching everything like a Nollywood detective.

As the night went on, I relaxed.

We laughed about customer dramas, shared horror stories about system failures, and listened to the juicy office gossip.

I was still giggling when I felt Deji lean closer.

"How are you finding banking so far?"

I sighed. "Honestly? It's exhausting. But I like the challenge."

He nodded. "That's how I felt when I started. If you ever need guidance, let me know."

I met his gaze. Warm and genuine.

"I appreciate that, Deji."

3. Training Day Troubles

"**S**ix Banking Principles for Customer Excellence," the presenter droned, clicking to the next PowerPoint slide.

"Promptness!"

"Promptness," we all muttered, sounding half-dead.

"Accuracy!"

"Accuracy," came an even weaker response.

I stifled a yawn. Three hours into another training day, and we'd barely scratched the surface of compliance updates and customer service protocols. Still ahead? Anti-money laundering, cybersecurity, and digital banking.

"Someone kill me now," I whispered to Oyinkan, who was discreetly online shopping under the table.

"Just pretend to take notes," she whispered back. "Ogundare keeps looking this way."

Sure enough, Mr Ogundare sat near the front, surveying the room, probably taking note of those looking disengaged.

My phone vibrated. A message from Deji.

Thrilling stuff, isn't it? Dinner later to recover from this torture?

Since the Friday drinks three weeks ago, Deji had been friendly and charming, and was now texting me during training.

I sighed and typed back: *Sorry, family dinner tonight.*

"Communication!" the trainer bellowed.

I repeated it weakly, praying that lunch break could come soon. It was taking so long.

"For our next session, we'll be doing group activities!"

A collective groan rippled through the room.

We counted off into groups, and by some twist of fate, I ended up with Deji, Blessing (a friendly but overwhelmed cashier), Mr. Ekwueme, head of Treasury (older than CBN itself), and worst of all, Lola from Credit.

"Great," Oyinkan whispered, heading to her group. "Watch your back. Lola is a snake."

My group's task was to create a skit demonstrating excellent customer service.

"I'll be group leader," Lola declared immediately, flipping her expensive weave. "I have experience in drama."

Deji smirked but said nothing.

"What scenario should we act out?" I asked.

"A fraud attempt." Blessing suggested.

"Perfect," Lola said. "Deji, you'll be the branch manager. I'll be the heroic officer who catches the fraud. Mr. Ekwueme, you're the security guard. Blessing, the teller."

I waited.

Lola turned to me.

"You'll be the fraudster."

I blinked. "Why am I the criminal?"

Lola smirked. "You have the right…energy for it."

Before I could respond, Deji intervened.

"Actually, I think Onome would make a better account officer. She has great attention to detail."

Lola's smile tightened. "Fine. Then I'll be the branch manager."

By the time we got to the final script, it had devolved into pure madness, involving international wire fraud, fake passports, and a highlight moment where Lola single-handedly stopped a criminal by tackling them to the ground.

"This is ridiculous," I whispered to Deji as I watched the display. "No banker physically stops a fraudster."

"Just go with it," he whispered back. "It's only a skit."

When our turn came, Lola delivered an Oscar-worthy performance, dramatically "catching" Blessing (playing the fraudster) and throwing her to the floor.

The entire room gasped.

Mr. Ekwueme forgot his lines entirely, and Deji nearly lost it.

It was a disaster, but at least the other groups were worse.

Group 1's skit about a power outage ended in awkward singing, while Group 4's robbery scenario somehow turned into a dance off.

"That was... creative," the trainer said, looking physically pained. "Let's break for lunch."

I had just joined the line for lunch when Lola cornered me.

"Your performance lacked commitment," she sniffed. "If you want to succeed in banking, you need to be more assertive."

"Like physically assaulting customers?" I replied sweetly.

She narrowed her eyes. "I've noticed Deji paying special attention to you. Just remember, office romances rarely end well."

I frowned. "There's nothing between us."

"Good," she said smoothly. "Because there are already enough rumours about how some people advance their careers."

Before I could respond, she sauntered off.

"What was that about?" Oyinkan appeared, holding a plate of jollof rice.

I sighed. "Lola being Lola. Apparently, people are talking about Deji and me."

"Well, he does hover around your desk."

"Because I handled a VIP client issue. That's it."

"Mmhmm," Oyinkan said sceptically. "And your face card has nothing to do with it?"

"Can we change the subject?" I groaned.

"Fine. Let's talk about how I'm surviving the next four hours without sleeping."

After lunch, we had a cybersecurity session led by an IT specialist who spoke in robotic monotone.

I zoned out.

Then...

"Ms. Eferogho, can you name three warning signs of a phishing email?"

My heart stopped.

The entire room turned to me.

I racked my brain. "Um... Suspicious sender address. Urgent language. And...grammatical errors?"

"Correct," the IT guy nodded, looking slightly disappointed that I didn't embarrass myself.

I let out a slow breath, catching Deji's approving smile from across the room.

Even Ogundare gave a slight nod.

At 5.30 pm, just when we thought we were free, Mr Ogundare ruined everything.

"There will be a test on today's material next week. This counts toward your quarterly performance review."

Outside, I was waiting to be joined by Oyinkan when Deji appeared beside me.

"Survived another training day," he grinned. "Sure I can't convince you to grab dinner? There's a great seafood place nearby."

"Thank you, but family obligations," I said politely.

"Rain check, then."

He handed me a business card.

"By the way, I have a friend who might be interested in custom jewellery. She's looking for something exclusive for her daughter's wedding. I thought of you."

I froze. I hadn't told him about my side business.

"I remember you mentioning it at drinks," he added. "And I figured it might help your savings goal."

Before I could respond, Oyinkan pulled up.

"Think about it," Deji said. "And about dinner. Some other time?"

As soon as we were in the car, Oyinkan demanded details.

"What did Manager Charming want?"

"Nothing," I said, tucking the card into my bag.

"He just handed you a rich client for fun?"

"Maybe he's just being nice!"

"Nice specifically to you?"

"Can we not talk about this? My brain is fried from training."

"Fine. But I will get the truth out of you."

She pulled into an ice cream shop.

"After a day of corporate torture, we deserve this."

I agreed.

4. Staff Bus Chronicles and More Training

It was a Monday morning, and this week, I was taking the staff bus because Oyinkan's car was at the mechanics. I was running late. The staff bus was supposed to leave at 6.00 am sharp, and I was still in my room, trying to find a matching pair of earrings.

My mum yelled from the kitchen, "Onome, if you miss that bus, you're on your own o!"

I finally found the earrings, grabbed my bag, and sprinted out the door. The bus was already pulling away when I got to the bus stop, but I waved frantically, and the driver mercifully stopped. I climbed on, panting, and found a seat next to Oyinkan.

"Cutting it close, huh?" she said, smirking.

"Don't start," I muttered, adjusting my skirt.

The staff bus was a unique experience. It was a mix of sleepy colleagues, whispered gossip, and the occasional argument over the air conditioning.

As the bus crawled through Lagos traffic, I noticed a guy sitting across from me. He was tall, with a sharp jawline and a confident air that made him stand out. I nudged Oyinkan.

"Who's that?" I whispered.

"That's Tunde. He works in Treasury. Cute, right?"

I nodded, trying not to stare. Tunde caught my eye and smiled, and I quickly looked away, pretending to be very interested in the traffic outside.

The bus ride was uneventful until we got to the Third Mainland Bridge. That's when the drama started.

A woman at the back of the bus suddenly started yelling at the driver. "Why are you driving so fast? Do you want to kill us?"

The driver, a no-nonsense man in his 50s, shot back, "Madam, if you don't like my driving, you can walk!"

Different people started arguing. Some people sided with the woman, others with the driver, and a few just yelled at everyone to shut up and stop disturbing their sleep. Oyinkan and I exchanged looks, trying not to laugh.

"Welcome to the staff bus," she said.

By the time we arrived at the office, I was already mentally exhausted. But the day was just beginning. I had a training session at 9.00 am, and I was determined not to be late. I arrived at the conference room at 8.45 am., hoping to snag a seat at the back where I could discreetly check my phone or even take a nap.

But Mrs Chukwuma, the no-nonsense woman who looked like she hadn't smiled since 1997, had other plans.

"Onome, sit at the front. You need to pay attention," she said, pointing to a chair directly in front of the projector screen.

I groaned internally but obeyed, plastering a fake smile on my face.

She introduced herself as a "customer relationship expert" with over twenty years of experience. I glanced at the PowerPoint slide, which had a stock photo of a handshake and the words *"Building Trust and Loyalty"* in Comic Sans. This was going to be a long morning.

Mrs Chukwuma started her presentation with a story about how she once calmed an angry customer by offering them a cup of tea.

"It's all about empathy," she said, pacing the room like a motivational speaker who'd lost her mojo. I tried to focus, but her monotone voice was like a lullaby. My eyelids grew heavy, and I started to drift off.

That's when Samuel, my other fresh hire counterpart, slid into the seat next to me. He had a mischievous grin on his face and a notebook filled with doodles instead of notes.

"Onome, if I die of boredom, tell my family I loved them," he whispered.

I stifled a laugh and tried to focus, but Samuel wasn't done. He spent the next hour passing me notes with increasingly ridiculous jokes.

"Why did the banker break up with her boyfriend? He couldn't handle her interest rates!"

I snorted, drawing a glance from Mrs Chukwuma. Samuel was incorrigible, but at least he made the session bearable.

By the time Mrs Chukwuma got to the part about "emotional intelligence," I was ready to scream. She asked us to pair up and role-play a scenario where we had to handle an irate customer. Samuel volunteered to be the customer, and within seconds, he was yelling at me like I'd personally stolen his life savings.

"Where is my money?!" he shouted, slamming his hand on the table.

I panicked and blurted out, "Sir, please calm down. Would you like a cup of tea?"

The entire room burst into laughter, and even Mrs Chukwuma cracked a smile.

The session finally ended at 2.00 pm, and I practically ran out of the room. Mrs Chukwuma stopped me on my way out.

"Onome, you need to take these trainings seriously. They're important for your growth."

I nodded, but all I could think about was lunch.

As I sat in the staff canteen with Oyinkan, I couldn't help but laugh about the morning's events.

"At least you got a certificate," she said, trying to cheer me up.

I rolled my eyes. "A certificate for surviving boredom," I replied.

But deep down, I knew Mrs Chukwuma was right. These trainings were part of the job, and if I wanted to succeed, I had to take them seriously.

Still, I made a mental note to bring extra coffee to the next training session, and maybe earplugs.

5. The Side Hustle Shuffle

"That'll be thirty-five thousand naira, ma," I said, carefully placing the handcrafted necklace into a small gift box. "I can accept transfer or cash."

Mrs Coker, an elegant woman in her fifties, nodded approvingly. "It's beautiful work. My daughter will love it for her engagement party. I'll transfer now."

We were seated in the corner of an upscale café in Victoria Island, far enough from Prestige Capital to avoid any accidental run-ins with colleagues. I had timed the meeting perfectly for my lunch break, with just enough time to close the sale and return before anyone noticed I was gone.

After much debating, I had decided to pursue this opportunity. Deji's high-net-worth referral was precisely the kind of exposure my jewellery business needed. Lagos' elite social circles? That's where the money was.

As Mrs Coker completed the transfer, I felt a mix of pride and anxiety. This was my biggest sale yet.

"Deji mentioned you're quite new at the bank," she said casually.

"Yes, ma. Just a few months now."

"But clearly ambitious." She gestured to the jewellery. "Banking and a business on the side. My late husband always said the best bankers understand entrepreneurship from experience."

I smiled. "I'm saving for my Masters. Hopefully, in Canada, I want to do Finance or Business Administration."

"Admirable. Though with talent like yours, I wonder if you'd be better off focusing on your craft."

Before I could respond, my phone buzzed. A message from Oyinkan:

WHERE ARE YOU?! Ogundare is looking for everyone. Emergency meeting!

I checked the time. Lunch hour had ended five minutes ago.

I shot up from my seat. "I'm so sorry, ma, but I need to get back. Duty calls."

Mrs Coker chuckled. "Of course, dear. But do send me photos when you have new pieces. I have friends who would love your work."

I thanked her hurriedly before grabbing my bag and running back to the bank.

By the time I reached Prestige Capital, I was sweating and out of breath. I slipped into the conference room where the Retail team was gathered.

"Nice of you to join us, Ms. Eferogho," Ogundare said smoothly.

"Sorry, sir. I was..."

"Having lunch, I assume. Like most people do during their lunch hour."

I froze. The way he said it made it clear that no further explanation was needed.

I nodded silently and sank into a chair. Beside me, Oyinkan slipped me a note.

Where were you REALLY?!

I took a deep breath. This was not the time for confessions.

"As I was saying," Ogundare continued, "we have a situation. The Central Bank examiners will be conducting a surprise audit. Starting tomorrow."

A collective groan filled the room.

"This is not a drill. They'll be reviewing everything, including compliance, customer documentation, and transaction records. Everything must be perfect."

He scanned the room. "To that end, all leave is cancelled. Expect to work late this week."

I barely had time to process the news before I was assigned a stack of customer files to review for missing Know Your Customer (KYC) documentation.

I returned to my desk and buried myself in work.

Then my phone buzzed.

Deji: *How did it go with Mrs Coker?*

I typed back quickly: *Very well, thank you. She bought the necklace and wants to see more pieces.*

Deji: *Told you she'd love your work. Dinner to celebrate?*

I barely had time to formulate another polite rejection before a shadow fell across my desk.

Ogundare.

I snapped my head up, phone still in hand.

"Ms. Eferogho," he said, voice low but sharp. "I need those files reviewed by 6.30 pm. All of them."

I glanced at the substantial pile.

"Yes, sir. I'm on it."

"Good. And I'd appreciate fewer personal messages during this critical time."

I nearly died. Heat rushed to my face as I quickly shoved my phone into my drawer.

The rest of the afternoon was a blur of paperwork. By 6.30 pm, my eyes burned from staring at customer files. Each document needed ID verification, proof of address, and employment records. Anything missing could trigger audit findings, resulting in extra scrutiny and additional work.

When I finally finished, Oyinkan appeared at my desk looking equally exhausted.

"Ready for the progress meeting?"

"As ready as I'll ever be."

The evening meeting was grim. Operations identified missing signatures on loans, and Credit discovered inconsistencies in risk ratings.

Ogundare's verdict? "Fix everything tonight. I don't care how late you stay."

Another groan filled the room.

Someone muttered, "I had dinner plans."

Ogundare's sharp hearing picked it up.

"Cancel them. Banking requires sacrifice. If you can't handle it, find another profession."

His gaze lingered on me. Was that my guilty conscience, or did he suspect something?

By 10.00 pm, I was finally leaving the office, starving and exhausted.

The staff bus had stopped running by 9.00 pm, and Oyinkan had somehow managed to slip away earlier, so I had to split a rideshare with three other colleagues.

"Welcome to audit season," said Philip, a veteran teller. "My first year, I slept at the bank for three nights straight."

"Please tell me you're joking," I muttered.

"I wish. Brought a toothbrush and everything."

When I finally got home, my father was still awake, reading in the living room.

"Banking hours are getting longer," he observed.

"Audit preparation," I sighed. "We'll be working late all week."

"Your mother saved dinner. It's in the microwave."

As I reheated my food, my phone buzzed again.

Mrs Coker: *My friends loved your necklace! Three of them want custom pieces. When are you available?*

Excitement flashed through me. But then, reality hit.

The audit. The long hours. There was no way I could meet customers this week.

I quickly typed back: *Thank you so much! Unfortunately, we have a bank audit this week with extended hours. Would next week work?*

She responded immediately. *I understand. Next Tuesday evening, my house? I'll host a small jewellery showcase for my friends.*

I nearly dropped my phone. A showcase? That meant preparing at least a dozen pieces.

How was I going to find time for that? But the opportunity was too good to pass up.

I typed back: *That sounds perfect. Thank you, Ma.*

Despite my exhaustion, I was smiling as I ate my late dinner.

This business was gaining momentum. The sacrifice would be worth it.

6. The Audit Storm

The next morning, by 6.45 am, I was already at my desk, wearing my most professional outfit. It was a navy-blue suit that cost a month's salary but made me feel like I could handle anything. I was sipping coffee while Oyinkan had already started drinking her first diet soda. The bank was buzzing with nervous energy.

The examiners from CBN were arriving today, and if there was one universal truth in banking, it was this: *Auditors do not come to be impressed. They come to find mistakes.*

I was double-checking my assigned customer files when Deji appeared beside my desk, looking far too relaxed for the chaos ahead.

"Ready for battle?" he asked cheerfully.

"As ready as humanly possible," I muttered, flipping through the paperwork.

"I heard you did excellent work yesterday," he said, leaning in slightly. "Ogundare was impressed. Though he'd never admit it."

I blinked. Ogundare? Impressed?

"Really?"

"Really." Deji smiled. "Listen, when this audit madness is over, you should let me take you to dinner. To celebrate surviving."

Before I could formulate another polite rejection, a commotion near the entrance stole everyone's attention. A group of serious-looking men and women in formal attire had arrived.

"They're here," Deji whispered. "Show time."

The next three days were the most intense of my banking career. The auditors reviewed everything, from customer files and transaction records to operational procedures. They randomly selected accounts and grilled us on the Know Your Customer (KYC) documents.

By day two, my brain felt like mush. I was questioned twice, once about a customer's incomplete address verification, and once about a large cash deposit I'd processed.

Both times, I managed to answer correctly. Even Ogundare nodded approvingly.

By the time the final meeting with the auditors came around on Friday afternoon, the entire branch was exhausted but hopeful.

They found twelve exceptions," Deji whispered as we sat in the conference room. "That's actually not bad, considering."

"What happens now?"

"We have thirty days to fix the issues and submit documentation proving we've resolved them."

The lead examiner, a stern woman with silver-rimmed glasses, stood at the front of the room.

"Overall," she began, "Prestige Capital's Victoria Island branch shows adequate compliance with regulatory requirements, with some areas of concern..."

We all held our breath.

The findings were mostly minor. Documentation issues, procedural inconsistencies, training gaps. Nothing catastrophic.

For the first time all week, I saw Ogundare exhale.

"Well done, everyone," he said. "We'll address these findings immediately. In recognition of your hard work this week, you may all leave at normal closing time today."

It was the first time in history that Ogundare willingly let people leave early.

As we packed up, Oyinkan threw her arms around me.

"We survived! Let's go get drinks!"

"I can't," I sighed. "I have jewellery to make for Mrs Coker's showcase next week."

"Your side hustle waits for no one," she laughed. "Need help?"

"You'd help me make jewellery?"

"I mean...I can string some beads. How hard can it be?"

"Thank you! You're the best."

That night, my room turned into a full-fledged production studio.

Beads, wire, chains, and tools covered every surface. I showed Oyinkan what to do, and she enjoyed assembling them. Even Ufuoma got involved; it turns out my younger sister was surprisingly skilled at making earrings.

"You should be selling these in a proper shop," my mother said, holding up a pair of intricate earrings.

"I'm not selling from my desk, Mum. Mrs Coker is hosting a showcase."

"Still," she said, looking concerned. "Banking and jewellery-making? It's a lot, Onome."

"It's temporary," I assured her. "Until I save enough for my Master's."

7. IT System Battles

Thankfully, the weeks following the auditors brought a return to regular banking hours. I was assigned to the operations team. By now, I had accepted that banking was a different kind of suffering. I had survived impossible deposit targets, tight deadlines, and entitled customers. However, I was not prepared for my latest adversary, the bank's IT system.

It all started on Monday morning when I arrived early, determined to be productive. I logged into my computer and clicked on the banking application.

"SYSTEM ERROR. PLEASE TRY AGAIN."

I frowned. Maybe I had typed my password wrong. I tried again.

"SYSTEM ERROR. PLEASE CONTACT IT."

I groaned. I knew what this meant. A long, painful battle with the IT department.

"Oyinkan," I said. "The system has locked me out."

She sighed like someone who had heard this complaint many times before. "IT wahala. Just call them now before your whole day is wasted."

I dialled the internal IT line. It rang 12 times before someone picked up.

"IT help desk," a bored male voice answered.

"Good morning," I said, forcing politeness. "I can't log in to the system."

"Have you tried restarting your computer?" he asked.

I exhaled. "Yes."

"Have you tried clearing your cache?"

I blinked. "What cache? This is a banking app."

He sighed like I was the problem. "I'll log a complaint for you."

"How long will it take to fix?" I asked.

He chuckled. That was my first mistake.

"Ah, it depends," he said. "Maybe today. Maybe next week."

Next week?

"Oga, I have customers to call! I need my account access now."

"Okay," he said. "Just restart your computer again and pray."

He hung up.

I stared at the receiver in shock.

Oyinkan smirked. "Welcome to your first IT battle."

While I was struggling with my computer system issues, Samuel was somehow having the time of his life.

"Ah, Onome, why are you frowning?" he asked, sipping his coffee like he had no worries in life.

"My system is locked, and IT is useless," I muttered.

He laughed. "So is mine. But I'm chilling, not stressing about it."

"So, what should I be doing in the meantime?" I asked.

"Just look busy and concerned", Samuel laughed, as he went to chat with another colleague.

Just as I was contemplating resigning and going home to make more jewellery, Mrs Asiogu called me to her office.

"Onome," she said, "you're coming with me to see a VIP client this afternoon."

My stomach clenched. VIP clients were high-net-worth individuals who had no time for nonsense. I quickly grabbed my notebook and followed her to the bank's executive floor.

The meeting was at 2.00 pm. By 2.30 pm, the customer had still not arrived.

I shifted uncomfortably in my chair.

"Madam, should we call him?" I asked.

She gave me a steady look. "Never rush a VIP customer."

At 2.47 pm, the door finally opened, and in walked Chief Balogun, a sixty-something-year-old businessman wearing a well-starched agbada and holding two phones.

"Good afternoon, sir," we greeted.

He barely looked at us. "I only have five minutes," he said.

I sat up straight, ready to make a good impression.

Mrs Asiogu smiled. "Sir, we would like to discuss your account and explore ways to see how we can better serve you."

He waved a hand. "I don't have time for all that. Just make sure my money is safe."

"Yes, sir," she said. "Would you also be interested in some investment opportunities?"

He frowned. "Let me ask you something," he said, turning to me.

I straightened. "Yes, sir?"

"Have you ever lost ₦500 million before?"

I choked. "Sir?"

"Exactly," he said. "So don't talk to me about investments unless you've lost money before."

I blinked. What kind of logic was that?

Mrs Asiogu smiled and tried again. "Sir, we also offer premium banking services that…"

He raised a hand. "I don't need premium service. I just need no stress."

Before we could say anything else, his phone rang. He picked up immediately.

"Hello? Yes, bring my car to the entrance."

He stood up and nodded at us. "Alright. Good meeting."

Then he walked out.

Just like that.

I turned to Mrs Asiogu. "Ma...what just happened?"

She sighed. "That was actually a successful meeting."

I stared at her. "But we didn't say anything."

She shrugged. "Rich people just want to feel important. As long as he stays with our bank, we've done our job."

I rubbed my forehead and mentally took notes.

By Wednesday, my IT issues were still unresolved, and I was running out of ways to look busy. The only consolation was that the technical bug had now affected several other colleagues as well. One by one, everyone started grumbling as they got locked out.

Samuel, who had been chilling earlier in the week, was now almost in tears because he was assigned to the FX desk for the day.

"Onome, this is not fair," he complained.

"What happened to 'just chill'?" I teased.

"FX customers don't chill o! They want speed, they want urgency, they want dollars!" He wiped his forehead dramatically. "And my system is hanging every two minutes."

From the corner of my eye, I saw two of our relationship managers sharing a bottle of water. Their systems were also frozen, and they had given up pretending.

By 2.00 pm, we were all just moving around aimlessly, giving customers 'forms' to fill out and hoping IT would save us soon.

At 3.00 pm, a sheepish-looking Somto from IT finally walked into the banking hall.

"Sorry about this outage," he said, laughing nervously. "We are working on it. Hopefully by Monday, everything will be restored."

The way customers and staff alike stared at him, he knew he would soon be eaten alive, and he quickly disappeared up the stairs.

I turned to Samuel. "Maybe you're right. Maybe the best strategy is just to chill."

He nodded, defeated. "Exactly. Chill and pretend."

8. The Banking Hall Madness

The following week, I had barely settled at my desk when Mrs Asiogu called my name.

"Onome, you'll be working in the banking hall today."

I frowned. "Banking hall?"

"Yes," she said. "We're short-staffed."

I turned to Oyinkan. "What does that mean?"

She gave me a pitiful look. "It means you are going to suffer."

I didn't fully understand what she meant until five minutes later, when I stepped into the banking hall.

The first thing that hit me was noise. Customers were shouting. Someone was arguing with a security guard. An elderly man was banging the counter, demanding to see "the MD himself."

I barely had time to find my place behind the cashier's desk when the first customer attacked.

A woman in gele and dark sunglasses stormed up to me.

"You people are very wicked!" she shouted before I could even say "Good morning."

I blinked. "Sorry, ma. What happened?"

She threw a crumpled slip of paper at me. "I have been here since 7.00 am, and I am still in this queue!"

I checked the time. It was 8.45 am.

"Ma, please, let me check your number in the queue."

"I don't care about numbers! I need to withdraw my money NOW."

I forced a smile. "Ma, I understand your frustration, but the queue system…"

She clapped her hands. "Did I come here for frustration? Ehn? Is it your money?"

I sighed. This woman would slap me before 9.00 am.

Just as I was trying to calm her down, an old man cut the queue and appeared beside her.

"Small girl," he said to me, tapping the counter, "I need to collect my pension."

I tried to be polite. "Sir, please join the queue…"

He raised a finger. "I am a retired director of Nigerian Airways. I cannot queue with these small children."

But before I could argue, Gele Woman turned on him.

"Baba, who is a small child? I was here before you!"

"Madam, respect your elders," the man fired back.

"Which elder? You cannot fly a plane to the front of this queue!"

The two of them started shouting at each other, and I tried to calm them down so that we could actually solve their problems. Eventually, another cashier called the retired director to her desk, and I could deal with the woman in peace.

After dealing with angry customers for two hours, I was already exhausted. However, a new kind of stress soon entered the bank.

A man in an oversized suit walked up to me.

"I need to withdraw ₦500,000," he said.

"No problem, sir. Please insert your card and enter your PIN."

He did.

"Incorrect pin. Please try again."

He frowned. "Wait. Let me try again."

"Incorrect pin. Please try again."

I glanced at him. "Sir, are you sure it's the right PIN?"

"Ah, of course!" he said, pressing the buttons confidently.

"Incorrect pin. CARD BLOCKED."

He stared at the screen in shock.

"Sir, you've entered the wrong PIN too many times. The system has blocked your card."

He blinked. "Ehn? But I always use this PIN!"

I sighed. "Sir, do you have another card?"

"No, this is my only one."

I rubbed my forehead. "Sir, when was the last time you used this ATM card?"

He paused. "Maybe…two years ago?"

Oh dear.

I inhaled deeply. "Sir, you'll have to reset your PIN."

He clutched his chest. "But I don't remember the PIN at all!"

I sighed again. "Do you remember your security questions?"

His face went blank.

I handed him a form to fill out for a PIN reset. He looked at the paper, then looked at me.

"My wife filled this form when we opened the account," he confessed.

Just as I was recovering from the PIN man, another man in a designer suit and loud perfume strolled in like he owned the bank.

"Good morning," he said smoothly.

"Good morning, sir. How may I help you?"

"I need to withdraw ₦1 million."

I nodded. "Please provide your account number."

He handed me his ATM card. I typed in the details.

Account Balance: ₦1,754.20.

I blinked and checked again.

Still ₦1,754.20.

I looked up at him. "Sir, there are…insufficient funds in your account."

He frowned. "That's impossible! I have money there."

I turned my screen to show him. "Sir, this is your balance."

His eyes widened. "Are you saying I don't have ₦1 million?"

"Sir, you don't even have ₦2,000."

He suddenly laughed.

"Ah! My dear, I was just testing you. I wanted to see if you're sharp."

I just stared.

He took his card and casually walked out like nothing had happened.

I turned to Oyinkan, who had been watching the whole thing.

"Did that just happen?" I asked.

She nodded. "Big man with zero balance. Classic."

By the end of the day, my head was pounding.

As I packed up to leave, Mrs Asiogu walked up to me.

"Well done today, Onome," she said.

"Thank you, ma," I said weakly.

She smiled. "You'll be back in the banking hall again tomorrow."

I froze.

"Tomorrow?" I repeated.

"Yes," she said, walking away. "You handled today well."

I turned to Oyinkan in horror. "How do people do this every day?"

She patted my back. "Welcome to real Lagos banking, babe."

Hei God.

9. The Missing Office Laptop

Lunchtime at the bank was sacred. It was the only time of the day we had some freedom to breathe before the next wave of stress and customers flooded in. But today, just as I was about to enjoy my fried rice, my phone buzzed.

Incoming call: Mr Ogundare.

I sighed. *So much for peace.*

"Yes, sir?" I answered, already feeling the tension.

"Onome, where are you?"

"In the canteen, sir."

"Come to my office. Now."

I hung up, groaning. "Why is he calling me when I'm supposed to be eating?"

Oyinkan, munching on her meat-pie, didn't even look up. "Maybe it's your promotion."

I shot her a look. "After seven months? You think this is Google?"

Dragging myself to the Branch Manager's office, I knocked once and entered. Ogundare sat behind his large desk, looking unusually serious. Beside him stood James, my least favourite colleague, with his signature *I am innocent* face.

"Onome," Ogundare started, "do you know anything about the missing office laptop?"

I blinked. "Laptop? Which laptop, sir?"

"The one assigned to James."

I glanced at James, who immediately looked away.

"Sir, I don't know anything about it."

Ogundare exhaled loudly.

"James claims someone took the laptop from his desk on Friday after work. IT has checked, and it hasn't been logged into since."

I frowned. "But sir, why would I…"

James suddenly cleared his throat. "Sir, I'm not saying Onome took it, but…"

I turned to him sharply. "But *what*, James?"

He shifted. "I mean, she was one of the last people to leave on Friday. Maybe she saw something?"

I nearly lost it. "Wait, so because I stayed late to finish work that *you* left unfinished, you're now pointing fingers at me?"

James adjusted his tie. "I'm just saying…"

"Sir, if James had done his work during office hours instead of watching football highlights and gossiping with tellers, I wouldn't have had to stay late!"

Ogundare raised a hand. "Enough! We are reviewing the CCTV footage. If we don't find the laptop, the cost will be deducted from James's salary."

James let out a strangled sound. "Sir! That laptop is almost ₦500,000!"

"Then you'd better pray we find it."

At that moment, IT personnel knocked and entered. "Sir, we checked the camera. The laptop was last seen on James's desk, but at closing time, *he* walked out with it."

I turned slowly to face James, who was now sweating.

"James," I said sweetly, "do you have anything to say?"

He stammered. "I...I just remembered. I took it home!"

Ogundare folded his arms. "James, get out of my office. And don't let me hear that laptop is missing again."

James bolted. I turned to Ogundare. "Sir, can I go back to my lunch now?"

He chuckled. "You can go, Onome."

I marched straight back to the canteen, triumphant.

Oyinkan looked up from her phone. "So? What happened?"

I sat down and dug into my food. "James is a confirmed idiot. But we already knew that."

And just like that, another chaotic day continued.

10. The Office Party

By now, I had come to accept that Lagos banking was a combination of stress, unrealistic targets, and daily prayers for survival. But what I had not yet experienced was an office party, a gathering where banking professionals pretend to relax but somehow still manage to cause drama.

And so, when the bank announced a Friday evening "team bonding" event, I knew it would not end well.

"Are you coming to the party?" Oyinkan asked as we walked out for lunch.

I hesitated. "Is it compulsory?"

She laughed. "It's technically optional. But if you don't show up, managers will remember."

"Ah," I said, nodding in understanding. So it was "optional" in the same way that bringing in fifty million naira was "easy."

Samuel was excited. "Ah, Onome, you have to come o," he said, adjusting his tie. "These parties are where connections happen."

I raised an eyebrow. "Samuel, do you ever actually work?"

He grinned. "I work smart, not hard."

I sighed. There was no escaping this party.

The event took place in a luxurious rooftop lounge on Victoria Island. The bank had paid for finger foods, cocktails, and a DJ. I arrived with Oyinkan, mentally preparing for whatever nonsense awaited me.

As soon as we stepped in, I spotted Mr Adekunle near the drinks table. He looked like he was already on his third glass of wine. I quickly adjusted my dress and whispered to Oyinkan, "We need to avoid him."

She nodded. "Agreed. That man is looking for who to 'mentor' tonight."

We grabbed drinks and sat at a table, watching as Lagos bankers transformed into party animals.

Mrs Asiogu, who was usually strict, was suddenly dancing to Burna Boy. The HR Manager was drinking like she had no care in the world, and our salary budget to spend. And Samuel? Well... he was moving from table to table, networking like his rent depended on it.

Just as the party was getting into full swing, one senior manager decided to kill the vibe.

He grabbed the mic and started giving a speech.

"Good evening, everyone!" he slurred. "Tonight is not about work...but let's talk about work!"

A collective groan spread through the room.

"You all need to work harder," he continued. "Banking is about hustle, dedication, and bringing in deposits!"

Oyinkan muttered, "Even at a party, we cannot rest."

Samuel, who was now three cocktails deep, whispered, "This is why I don't stress. See how they are still preaching hustle at a party."

After five painful minutes, the manager finally ended his speech and raised his glass. "To banking!"

Nobody clapped.

The drinks were flowing, and people were getting loose. That's when the true confessions started.

One guy from IT was ranting loudly. "I don't even like this job! The system is outdated! Do you know we're still using software from 2010?"

Someone from HR whispered, "We don't have money to upgrade."

Then, one of the older bankers suddenly banged his table.

"I have been here for 15 years!" he declared. "They have not promoted me since 2012! But I'm still here! Loyalty!"

Mrs Asiogu cleared her throat and changed the subject. "DJ, play music!"

The DJ immediately blasted Asake's Lonely at the Top like he knew we were all suffering.

I had just started enjoying my drink when trouble arrived. Oyinkan had gone to get us small chops.

"Onome!" a voice called.

I looked up. It was Mr Adekunle.

I froze.

"Why are you sitting here alone?" he asked, smiling like a hunter who had spotted prey.

"I'm just…relaxing," I said, forcing a smile.

He sat beside me. Uninvited.

"You know," he said, leaning too close, "I have been observing you. You are very smart."

"Thank you, sir," I said, shifting my chair slightly.

"You should let me mentor you," he continued. "We can discuss over dinner. Or maybe a weekend trip?"

I nearly choked on my drink. A weekend trip? Ah, God, is this my life?

Just then, Oyinkan saved me.

"Sir!" she said, coming back with two plates. "Your car is blocking someone outside. The security guard is calling you."

He frowned. "My car?"

"Yes, sir! The security guard is very angry!"

He stood up, muttering, and walked toward the exit.

The moment he left, I turned to Oyinkan.

"I owe you my life."

She laughed. "Babe, we have to protect each other in this bank."

Meanwhile, Samuel was on another mission.

I saw him sitting with a rich-looking woman in a red dress.

"Oyinkan, who is that?" I asked.

She squinted. "Ah! That's Madam Bola! She's the owner of this lounge and two other clubs in Lekki."

Samuel was laughing and nodding like he was sealing a multimillion-dollar deal.

After a while, he returned to our table, grinning like a lottery winner.

"I have secured a client," he announced.

I frowned. "You? Samuel? A whole client?"

He smirked. "Madam Bola likes me. She said she will come and open an account with us, and I will be her Account Manager."

I gasped. "Samuel! Just like that?"

He nodded. "Soft work."

I shook my head. Samuel was an unserious human being, but somehow, he was winning.

Just when I thought the night was over, chaos struck.

The HR Manager who had been drinking heavily stood up to dance. As she twirled, her heel snapped. She fell backwards, straight into the drinks table.

Glass broke. Drinks spilled.

"Ah!" someone shouted. "HR Madam don fall!"

We all froze. Two ladies rushed to her aid. HR Madam slowly sat up and was helped back to her seat.

"Nobody should report this on Monday!" she warned.

We all knew better than to make the spectacle worse. Eventually, she recovered from the shock, and fortunately, she wasn't hurt. She took off her remaining shoe, grabbed another drink, and continued dancing barefoot.

At midnight, I was ready to leave.

"Let's go home," I told Oyinkan.

Samuel smirked. "Onome, you didn't dance."

"I danced with my problems," I muttered.

As we left, my phone buzzed.

"Hello, Onome. I saw you at the party, but I didn't get a chance to say hello. Hope you have a good weekend, and I'll see you on Monday. Deji."

I stopped in my tracks.

Oyinkan peeked at my phone. "Who is that?"

I showed her the text.

She gasped. "I told you he was checking you out!"

I shook my head. "He's just being friendly."

She laughed. "And you're in denial. I think you need deliverance."

As we got into her car, I sighed deeply. Another week in Lagos banking.

11. Fishy Phishing Email

There are three things I have learnt since working at Prestige Capital Bank: Never click on suspicious links, never believe emails from people claiming to be "The CEO." And never trust James with anything important.

It started around 9.45 am. I was in the middle of checking customer transactions when my email pinged.

SUBJECT: URGENT DIRECTIVE FROM MANAGEMENT

I frowned. Urgent directive? From who? I opened the email.

Dear Prestige Capital Bank Staff,

As part of an ongoing audit, all branches are required to immediately transfer reserve funds to a secured Treasury Holding Account.

Please ensure that ₦30,000,000 is transferred to the following account before noon today.

Account Name: Prestige Holdings Ltd

Bank: Global Trust Bank

Account Number: 39030753630

This transaction is highly confidential and must be completed immediately. Failure to comply may result in disciplinary action.

Signed,

Michael Okechukwu

Regional Director

I blinked. Something felt off.

Michael Okechukwu? The Regional Director's name was Michael O. Okechukwu.

This one was missing the middle initial. I quickly checked the sender's email.

m.okechukwu@prestigebank.ng.com

I frowned. "Ng.com? That wasn't our domain."

I hovered over the email and saw the real sender's address:

m.okechukwu@prestige-directives.com

Ah. Scam. 419. Fake Email Alert.

I sat up straight. Someone was trying to trick us.

I rushed to Treasury and saw James typing furiously. I saw his screen and almost fainted.

James was already processing the ₦30 million transfer.

I screamed.

"James, stop!"

He jumped. "Onome, why are you shouting?!"

I grabbed his mouse. "Who told you to process this transfer?!"

He blinked. "Erm...the email from management?"

I pointed at the screen. "James, this is a scam!"

He froze. "Wait...you mean this is not real?"

I covered my mouth in horror. "James, have you already submitted the transaction?"

He swallowed hard. "Erm...maybe?"

"Maybe?"

I ran straight to Ogundare's office.

"Sir, we have been scammed!"

He looked up. "What do you mean?"

"James wired ₦30 million to fraudsters!"

Ogundare jumped up. "Where is he?"

Before I could answer, James ran in, sweating.

"Sir, sir, sir! I just received a second email saying to transfer ₦50 million instead! But I already sent the first one..."

Ogundare's jaw dropped.

"You sent it?"

James panicked. "No, sir! I mean, yes...but I called IT, and they blocked it...I think?"

Ogundare grabbed his intercom.

"SUSPEND ALL TRANSACTIONS! NOW!"

Within five minutes, IT had confirmed that the transfer had been stopped.

James sat down, visibly shaking. "Jesus. I almost made us bankrupt."

I folded my arms. "Yes, James. You almost gave yahoo boys ₦30 million on a Thursday morning."

He held his head. "I will never open emails again."

Mrs Asiogu burst into the office. "I just heard that James tried to dash yahoo boys our entire salary fund! Is this true?"

Ogundare glared at James. "If Onome hadn't caught it, we would all be jobless."

James slowly turned to me. "Onome… you have saved my life."

I glared at him. "I want compensation. Buy me lunch for one month."

James nodded aggressively. "Done!"

Ogundare sighed. "James, get out of my office before I fire you."

James ran out of the office like LASTMA was chasing him.

The next day, IT sent a branch-wide memo:

SUBJECT: FRAUD ATTEMPT ALERT

Dear Team,

Yesterday, our branch narrowly avoided a fraudulent transaction due to a phishing email. Please be reminded to always verify sender addresses and confirm any financial directives with management before processing transactions.

Special thanks to Onome for detecting the fraud before any loss occurred.

Oyinkan read the email and nudged me. "Onome, you're now the official Anti-419 Queen."

David added. "If we ever get hacked again, you must collect salary increase."

I smirked. James owes me big time.

12. The Man Who Forgot He Had a Wife

There was one person in our office more dangerous than EFCC. More efficient than HR. More relentless than LASTMA officers. Her name was Aunty Agnes.

She was the unofficial Bank Gist Queen. If something happened at 9.00 am, the entire branch would be aware by 9.05 am.

So when she cornered me at the canteen, first thing in the morning, I knew I was in trouble.

"Onome!" she beamed, clutching her big cup of Lipton tea.

"Good morning, ma," I said cautiously.

She grinned. "So…when is the wedding?"

I frowned. "Whose wedding?"

She clicked her tongue. "Don't pretend! We all saw you laughing with Adekunle yesterday. Eh-hen! Is he the lucky man?"

I nearly choked. "Mr Adekunle?"

She nodded excitedly. "Yes, my dear! We saw him hovering around your desk like mosquito. That means love is in the air!"

I groaned internally. "Aunty Agnes, I was rejecting his dinner invitation."

She gasped. "Ehn? You rejected him? But why? He is a fine man, and he has a good salary!"

I sighed. "Because I don't like him."

She shook her head in disappointment. "Onome, you young girls of today don't know what you are doing. You will reject a potential husband and be looking for love up and down!"

I had to escape, or else she would start a full motivational speech.

I forced a smile. "Aunty Agnes, I have to attend to a customer."

She clutched my arm. "No wahala, but I will be monitoring you. If he proposes, let me be the first to know!"

I ran to the banking hall to face my customers. A well-dressed man in a fitted kaftan and expensive sunglasses strolled in and sat at my desk.

"Good morning, sir," I said.

He gave me a slow, lazy smile. "Good morning, beautiful."

I mentally rolled my eyes. *Here we go again.*

"I have an account here already, but I want to open a new one," he said.

"Alright, sir. Do you have your means of identification?"

He reached into his pocket and pulled out his driver's license. I took it and began entering his details into the system.

Then I saw it.

Marital status: Married.

I glanced up. He was still smiling at me.

"You know," he said, "I like the way you're handling my request. Very…efficient."

I hummed in response, typing faster.

"Are you single?"

I ignored him.

"Because," he continued, leaning in, "I can tell you are the kind of woman who deserves to be treated like a queen."

I slowly turned the screen toward him.

"Sir, is this you?"

He looked. "Yes."

I tapped the section labelled 'Marital Status: Married.'

"Sir, I don't think your wife will like this conversation."

He sat up straight. "Ah! Who put that there?!"

I stifled a laugh. "You put it there, sir. When you got married."

He suddenly became very interested in his wristwatch. "Ah…well…I mean, it's just small marriage."

I shook my head. "Sir, do you still want to open the account, or should I call Madam for you?"

He cleared his throat. "Ah! Just open it quickly."

From the corner of my eye, I saw Oyinkan typing furiously on her phone. I knew she was texting me.

Sure enough, my phone buzzed:

Oyinkan: "*Small marriage? Lagos men are MAD.*"

I couldn't stop laughing.

A few minutes later, I was reviewing a report when I heard someone clear his throat loudly at my desk.

I looked up to see a man in a faded polo shirt and jeans, holding a phone that appeared to have seen better days.

"Good morning, sir," I said.

He gave me a small, embarrassed smile. "Good morning, my sister. I need your help."

I sighed. "What's the issue, sir?"

He glanced around as if he was about to tell me a secret. Then he leaned forward, and, in a low voice, he said:

"Please, I need urgent 2K."

I blinked. "Sir?"

"Urgent 2K, please. Just small something to hold body."

I stared at him. "Sir, this is a bank. We don't dash money here."

He scratched his head. "Ah, but don't you people have customer appreciation?"

I stifled a laugh. "Sir, customer appreciation does not mean we give out free money."

He sucked his teeth. "Ahn ahn, even politicians dey do palliative. You mean Prestige Capital Bank cannot help me with small change?"

I took a deep breath. "Sir, we are not a charity. Do you want to apply for a loan?"

"Loan? Ah! So I should come and fill one hundred forms because of 2K?"

"Sir, that's how banks work..."

"God forbid! I will find another solution!"

And with that, he walked out, grumbling about how banks are wicked and don't help the common man.

Oyinkan, who had been listening the entire time, collapsed into laughter.

"Onome!" she gasped. "Urgent 2K?! From the bank?!"

I shook my head. "Wonders shall never end."

13. Friday and the Escape Plan

Fridays were supposed to be easy, a calm slide into the weekend. But in Nigerian banking, that was a foolish dream.

The chaos started just after 3.00 pm when an older woman, dressed in full lace iro and buba, with a gele that could knock down a toddler, stormed into the bank.

"Who is Onome?" she demanded.

I was mid-sip of my lukewarm tea when my name echoed across the banking hall.

I looked up cautiously. "Good afternoon, ma. How can I help you?"

She stomped to my desk and slammed her handbag on the counter. "You people have been stealing my money!"

My headache instantly doubled.

"Ma, please calm down. Let's check your account…"

"Calm down for what?! I came here last week, you said my money is intact, but I checked today, and it has reduced again!"

I pulled up her details and immediately saw the issue. She had a daily deduction for an investment package she signed up for three months ago.

"Madam, the deductions are for your Golden Savings Investment..."

"Which investment?!"

"The one you signed for, ma."

She blinked. "Me? Sign for deduction? God forbid!"

I turned the screen towards her, showing her the scanned copy of her signature.

She peered at it. Her lips tightened. Then she did what every guilty Nigerian does: she changed the argument.

"Even if I signed it, you people should have told me the money would be disappearing like this!"

"Ma, they explained it to you at registration..."

She cut me off with a loud clap of her hands. "It is a lie! You tricked me! This is fraud!"

The nearby customers turned to watch the free Nollywood performance. Even Musa, the security guard, adjusted his belt, preparing for intervention.

"Ma, please lower your voice..."

She smacked the counter. "I will not lower anything! You people will not turn me into a poor woman! If I don't get my money back, I will sleep in this bank!"

I closed my eyes for five seconds, took a deep breath, and forced a smile.

"Madam, let's go to the manager's office."

She folded her arms. "No need. Just reverse my money now."

"Ma, investment funds are non-refundable."

"Jesu! You see why I say you are a thief?!"

At this point, Oyinkan, who had been stifling laughter, coughed and sneezed loudly.

I covered my mouth to hide my laughter.

Mrs Asiogu came to see what was going on, and I explained. She managed to pacify the customer by offering to move her future deductions to a savings account instead.

She huffed, grabbed her bag, and stomped out, muttering, "May God judge you people."

As soon as she left, I slumped in my chair.

But before I could enjoy my temporary peace, I saw something worse than an angry customer – Mr Adekunle was approaching my desk.

"Onome!" he called out, grinning. "That woman was crazy, huh?"

I forced a smile. "Yes, sir."

"So... I was thinking. It's Friday night. Maybe you and I should go for dinner?"

I choked. "Eh?"

"Dinner. You know, just us two. Maybe a nice place on the Island."

Oh God.

I looked at Oyinkan, silently begging for help. She responded by sipping her coffee slowly, enjoying my suffering.

I needed an escape plan. Fast.

I widened my eyes like I just remembered something. "I have Bible study tonight!"

He raised an eyebrow. "Bible study?"

"Yes, yes. Very important one. In fact, I promised my pastor I would be there."

"You go to Bible study?"

I nodded aggressively. "Every first and third Friday of the month, sir."

He frowned. He wasn't buying it.

"Okay," he said. "Then let's do Saturday."

I gasped. "Saturday?"

"Yes."

I panicked. "Ah! No o. Saturday is my fasting and prayer day."

"Ah! Onome, which church do you go to?"

I faked a solemn expression. "A very deep one."

He stared at me for a long time, then sighed. "No wahala. Enjoy your Bible study."

As soon as he walked away, Oyinkan burst into laughter.

"Fasting and prayer?" she wheezed.

I rubbed my forehead. "I was under pressure!"

She wiped her eyes. "Just pray he doesn't see you eating amala at an *owambe* one Saturday."

I groaned. "God *abeg*."

Just another day in the life of a Lagos junior banker, dodging drama in and outside the office.

14. The Secret Office Romance

It was exactly 3.47 pm on a slow Tuesday afternoon when the internal memo dropped. Nobody was prepared for what we saw:

Dear Team,

We are pleased to announce the upcoming wedding of our dear colleagues, TUNDE and GRACE! Please join us in congratulating them as they prepare for this joyous occasion.

Signed,
Branch Management

I blinked. Tunde? Grace? How?

The entire office erupted into confusion.

"AHHHHH!" Somebody screamed.

Samuel nearly knocked over his laptop. "Wait, Tunde and WHO?"

Oyinkan grabbed my arm. "Grace! As in HR Grace?"

James, who was half-asleep, suddenly sat up straight. "What is happening? Why is everybody shouting?"

I turned to him. "Tunde and Grace are getting married!"

James frowned. "Which Tunde?"

I shook my head. "Tunde in Treasury!"

"Which Grace?"

"HR Grace!"

James screamed. "JESU!!!"

In less than five minutes, the bank turned into a fully operational gossip centre.

Some people ran to the breakroom. Others rushed to HR's office to confirm if it was "true love" or "sudden pregnancy." I grabbed my phone and opened WhatsApp.

Prestige Capital Bank VI Branch Group Chat:

David: "How did Tunde and Grace date for months and we didn't know?!"

Oyinkan: "Because they are FBI agents. Secret romance experts!"

Me: "How did they hide it from Aunty Agnes? She knows everything!"

At that moment, Aunty Agnes herself stood up from her desk and shouted, "I have been betrayed!"

The entire office erupted into laughter.

James wiped his eyes. "But how?! We work in the same building! How did they date under our noses?"

Samuel shook his head. "These people are smarter than EFCC."

Oyinkan gasped. "Wait. WAIT. Does this mean Tunde's girlfriend was inside this office all along?"

I laughed. "Ah! It was an under-g bank relationship!"

Samuel folded his arms. "And they want to invite us to the wedding after hiding the entire relationship?!"

James hissed. "We will attend...but we will not spray them money."

At 4.15 pm, we saw Tunde and Grace leave Ogundare's office.

They were smiling, but the moment they saw our judgmental faces, their smiles disappeared. The entire office turned to them at once.

"Explain yourselves!"

Tunde flinched. Grace grabbed his arm like he was about to be arrested.

David folded his arms. "Tunde, my guy, since when?"

Grace sighed. "Since last year..."

James shook his head. "Last year? Ha! You people have been dating for a year inside this bank!"

Grace nodded, looking guilty.

Samuel gasped dramatically. "Tunde, you used to tell us you were single!"

Tunde scratched his head. "Erm...I didn't lie. I just didn't... confirm anything."

I shook my head. "Grace, you used to advise us about men, and your own man was inside the bank?"

Grace covered her face. "I'm sorry, I'm sorry!"

Oyinkan was shaking her head. "This betrayal is deep."

Even Musa, our security guard, looked disappointed. "Oga Tunde, *na wa* for you."

Tunde laughed nervously. "Guys, please understand. We didn't want office drama."

James scoffed. "And now? Do you see what has happened?!"

David smirked. "Where was the first date? Near the ATM?"

Tunde sighed. "Mr. Biggs, Oniru."

We all burst into laughter.

"Awww! Old school romance!"

I shook my head. "HR Grace. Treasury Tunde. Who would have thought?"

James adjusted his tie. "Oya, tell us everything. Who made the first move?"

Grace smiled. "Tunde did."

David gasped. "How? He can barely talk to customers!"

Tunde laughed. "I sent her an email."

"An email?!"

I clutched my desk. "Tunde, you shot your shot by sending a mail?"

He shrugged. "It was professional."

"I need to see the subject line of that email!" David said.

Tunde shook his head. "No way!"

But at that moment, HR Grace betrayed him.

She grinned and said:

"Subject: Regarding your request."

"Ah! Corporate romance!"

David was howling. "Tunde, you proposed by sending 'REGARDING YOUR REQUEST???"

Oyinkan wiped her eyes. "This love story is sweet o."

A few moments later, the noise had died down. But then David clapped his hands.

"But wait o. Will one of you have to leave the bank after the wedding?"

"No, but Ogundare said one of us will have to transfer to a different branch," Grace replied.

"Ah, so who will go where?" I asked.

"I would likely move to the Oniru or Ajah branch," Tunde said.

"Awww," Oyinkan said. "But don't worry, we will look after Grace for you."

James said, "Okay, we have agreed, we will attend the wedding."

Tunde and Grace exhaled in relief. "Thanks, guys."

"But there are conditions."

They frowned. "Conditions?"

James stepped forward. "First of all, we need good souvenirs. No plastic buckets."

"Or keyholders!" I added.

Samuel nodded. "We need jollof rice and small chops served on time."

"And the puff-puff must be hot!" Oyinkan shouted.

Tunde and Grace laughed. "Fine, fine! Anything else?"

James grinned. "Yes. Give us VIP seating, since we suffered betrayal."

"Front-row chairs!"

Tunde rolled his eyes. "You guys are not the parents of the bride."

"No o, we are more important!"

Finally, they agreed to our "demands," and the conversation ended.

The next morning, the branch was still buzzing. People were already planning aso-ebi for staff. The Marketing department sent a "congratulations" cake. Aunty Agnes was still in emotional distress. And Grace spent the entire day blushing.

I nudged Oyinkan. "You know what this means, right?"

She smirked. "Tunde just made it harder for men in this bank."

Samuel sighed. "Ladies are about to start checking their inbox for 'Regarding your request.'"

And we all laughed.

15. The Persistent Toaster

Tunde and Grace's secret office romance had caused more problems for me. Ever since their "love story" went public, Mr Adekunle had doubled his efforts.

Before, he used to drop small comments like: *"Onome, let's have a mentoring session."*

"Onome, you're glowing today."

"Onome, let's discuss your future over dinner with me."

Now? This man was on a full-blown mission to get married. I couldn't breathe. I couldn't walk in peace. I couldn't *drink water drop cup* without him appearing beside me.

One Tuesday morning, I was at my desk, minding my business, when suddenly Mr Adekunle dropped a breakfast tray in front of me.

I frowned. "What's this, sir?"

He smiled, looking too pleased with himself. "Breakfast. For my future wife."

I blinked. "Future wife, sir?"

He leaned in and almost whispered. "Onome, Tunde and Grace have inspired me. Beautiful things can happen in this bank."

Oyinkan coughed loudly.

Mr Adekunle ignored her and continued. "I see so much potential in you. I could take you far. Hmmm?"

I didn't know what to say, so I just nodded.

"Good. I have a meeting now, but I will see you later."

Then he picked up his briefcase and walked upstairs.

Oyinkan, who had been stifling her laughter, looked up from her desk. "Onome, you're finished!"

Samuel, ever the instigator, rubbed his chin. "Onome, I think you and Adekunle would make a great couple."

I threw a pen at him. "All of you need prayers!"

James smirked. "Onome, stop resisting destiny."

I buried my face in my hands. "God, when will I resign?"

Oyinkan peeped at the breakfast tray. "Let's help you with this food, sef, let everything no waste."

For the next few days, I was dodging Mr Adekunle everywhere.

When I entered the breakroom?

"Onome, let me pour your tea. You need to be taken care of, my dear."

When I stepped outside for air?

"Ah, Onome, fresh breeze is good for our future children."

When I went to the canteen during lunchtime?

"Ah, Onome, can I buy you lunch?"

It was getting out of hand.

But the final straw came Friday morning.

Oyinkan and I walked into the office, and before I could sit, I saw there was a bouquet on my desk.

I froze.

Oyinkan clutched her chest. "Aww, isn't this so romantic!"

I gave her a look.

"Oya, sorry. But he is really serious o."

I picked up the flowers and dropped them on David's desk.

"David, please give these to your girlfriend."

"Eh, please o. I don't want Adekunle's wahala. He might think I am now his rival."

Samuel laughed, sitting on his desk. "Onome, you are on your own o."

I groaned. "God, why me?!"

I knew that if I didn't shut this down completely, Mr Adekunle would soon make it a bigger issue and get me in real trouble.

So on Friday afternoon, I pulled Oyinkan aside.

"I need your help."

She folded her arms. "Finally. What's the plan?"

I took a deep breath. "We need to make Mr Adekunle think I have a boyfriend."

She grinned. "Ooooh, we're about to play games! I love it!"

I whispered my plan into her ear.

She gasped. "Onome, you are wicked!"

I smirked. "Desperate times, my dear."

At 3.00 pm, when the banking hall was bustling, I went outside to get some fresh air, and I signalled Oyinkan. I knew Mr Adekunle would follow me. She was to call my phone.

I stood near the bank's entrance and answered my phone when it rang.

I spoke extra loudly, making sure Mr Adekunle could hear me.

"Yes, baby...I miss you too..."

He was smiling, then he froze.

I continued.

"Don't worry, love...I'll see you this evening...Maybe we can try that new restaurant?"

He frowned, and his mouth fell open.

"Okay, babe...Love you too..." I smiled sweetly, then hung up.

Mr Adekunle stepped forward slowly. "Onome... who was that?"

I flipped my hair. "My boyfriend."

His eyes widened. "Boyfriend?!"

I nodded. "Yes. The love of my life."

"But...but...since when?"

I smiled. "A year. Just like Tunde and Grace."

"I see. Eh, okay."

Oyinkan came outside.

Mr Adekunle eyed both of us and went into the building without another word.

That evening, Oyinkan and I walked out of the bank, victorious.

She nudged me. "So... are you going to actually get a boyfriend now?"

I laughed. "Nope. I just needed that man to leave me alone."

She shook her head, smiling. "You are a wicked girl."

I grinned. "Yes. But I am finally free."

16. The Office Witch is Transferred

There were two things everybody in Prestige Capital Bank office feared: losing network in the middle of a transaction and being transferred to the Idumota Branch.

Idumota was not for the faint-hearted. It was Lagos banking on steroids. A war zone where traders carrying bundles of cash shouted over each other, where area boys stood outside waiting for "commission" and where the smell of *akara* and puff-puff mixed with engine oil and body odour right inside the banking hall.

So, when we got the internal memo about staff transfers and saw Lola's name beside **"Transfer to Idumota Branch"**, we knew *wahala* was about to burst.

Now, let me explain something about Lola.

Lola was our resident Office Witch. Not the type that flew at night, but the type that carried gossip in her bag. She knew everything that was happening in the branch before even HR did. She was the one who reported staff to management for things like arriving five minutes late, laughing too loudly, or chewing gum while working.

Lola was the reason three people got warnings for "dress code violations". She was also the reason one of our colleagues, Kemi, had to delete her Twitter account because she tweeted that her bank job was draining her soul.

Lola had oppressed, frustrated, and terrorized all of us. But today? Today was judgment day.

At precisely 10.00 am, Lola saw the memo.

At 10.02 am, she let out the first wail.

"JESUUUUUUU!"

Everyone turned.

"NOOOOOO! This is a lie! It can't be me!"

She ran out of her office, memo clutched in her hands like an eviction notice.

"Who did I offend?" she screamed.

I exchanged a look with Oyinkan. "You have five seconds before she starts mentioning spiritual attack."

We were wrong. She lasted three seconds.

"This is village people! It's my enemies! They don't want me to prosper!"

The entire banking hall was watching. Customers stopped filling out forms. The tellers paused counting money.

Even Musa, the security guard, was biting his lips to stop himself from laughing.

Lola ran to Ogundare's office and barged in without knocking.

We all followed with our eyes, and some people stood near the glass walls, pretending to be busy while watching the live Nollywood movie.

"Sir!" she wailed. "What did I do to deserve this?"

Ogundare, who had zero patience for drama, barely looked up.

"Lola, kindly sit down…"

"Sir, I can't sit! My legs are shaking!"

"Then stand and shake quietly," he said.

She gasped. "Sir, please, you cannot send me to Idumota! Do you want me to die?"

Ogundare sighed. "Lola, staff transfers are normal."

"What about David? Why didn't he go?"

David, who had been minding his business, suddenly froze.

Ogundare rubbed his temples. "Lola, we transferred you because we believe your skills are needed there."

"It's a lie!" she screamed. "Sir, let me confess! I have enemies in this office!"

The entire office perked up. *Oh?*

"I know there are people praying for my downfall!" she continued. "I am a strong woman, but the forces against me are many!"

Someone coughed loudly to hide laughter.

Lola turned to us, eyes blazing. "It's you people!" she accused. "You all hate me!"

The office went silent. Nobody denied it.

She gasped. "Ah! So, you won't even pretend? JESU!"

Ogundare was losing patience. "Lola, you have two options. Accept the transfer or resign."

The silence that followed was louder than a NEPA transformer failure.

Lola's eyes widened like someone had poured hot pepper into them.

"Sir, resign? Me? No, sir, please, let's renegotiate!"

"There's nothing to renegotiate."

Lola collapsed into the chair dramatically. "Sir, just give me another branch. Any other place! Even Ikorodu!"

"Idumota," the Branch Manager repeated.

Lola started crying. Actual tears.

"Sir, I cannot work there! Do you know what happens in that branch?!"

Ogundare nodded. "Yes. That's why we're sending you there."

At that moment, every single person in the office knew the truth.

This was not a random transfer. This was punishment. And she deserved it.

Ogundare adjusted his glasses. "Lola, please return to your desk and prepare to resume at Idumota next Monday."

She sobbed loudly but stood up slowly.

As she walked out, her head bowed in defeat, the entire office pretended to go back to work.

But the moment she disappeared, everyone started texting.

Oyinkan: "Lola's village people have won!"

Me: "I think I just got saved from seven years of bad luck."

James: "Someone needs to film her first day at Idumota!"

The entire office secretly rejoiced.

By 3.00 pm, Lola sent an all-staff email.

"Dear Colleagues, I would like to formally express my disappointment and sadness at the recent turn of events regarding my transfer. I hope that one day, we will all understand the true meaning of fairness in the workplace. Thank you."

I turned to Oyinkan. "Should we reply with 'Safe journey'?"

She cackled. "No, let's wait until Monday and check if she comes back on crutches."

That night, I went home and slept peacefully. Lola's reign of terror was over.

17. School Fees Wahala

If there is one thing that exposes Nigerian parents, it is school fees. Every term, banking halls become war zones. People who were laughing last week suddenly remember they have three children in expensive schools that they can't afford.

But nothing prepared me for Madam Edith. This woman tried to scam her husband using our bank.

It was 10.30 am on Wednesday when a heavily perfumed woman in six-inch heels marched into the bank. She was dressed like a CEO and walked in like a landlady who was about to evict her tenants for owing rent.

She did not join the queue. She ignored the customer service desk. She stomped straight to my table and dropped a printed invoice in front of me.

"Young lady," she said. "Process this transfer immediately."

I glanced at the document.

It was an invoice for school fees from a high-class private school in Lekki.

I quickly did the math.

The total amount?

₦3.8 million.

"Ma, you are paying this now?"

She flipped her long wig. "Yes, my dear. My husband just sent the money, so let's do it fast."

I nodded and typed in her account number.

Then I froze.

Her balance was ₦2.3 million.

"Madam, you don't have enough money in this account."

She hissed. "I know."

I paused. "Okay... So, how do you want to complete the payment?"

She smiled sweetly. "Don't worry, darling. Just process ₦3.8 million. My husband will not check. He will just see 'School Fees' and assume it's correct."

"Excuse me, ma?"

She winked. "My husband is a busy man. He just asked me to sort out the children's school fees. He won't check the exact amount."

I stared at her. "Madam... You mean to tell me... that this school fee is less than ₦3.8 million?"

She waved her hand. "Ehn, the real amount is ₦2.5 million. But why should I suffer in this life? Let me add something small for myself."

"Madam, you are adding ₦1.3 million as... 'something small'???"

She rolled her eyes. "Young girl, one day you will marry. You will understand."

I cleared my throat. "Madam, I cannot process a transfer that exceeds your balance."

Her mood changed instantly.

"What are you saying? I told you my husband won't check! Just push it through and let it go into overdraft!"

I shook my head. "But you don't have an overdraft facility on this account, ma."

She placed her two hands on her head dramatically.

"God! What kind of useless bank is this?!"

People turned to look.

"Is it your money?!" she shouted. "Did I steal from the bank?! It is my husband's account!"

I exhaled deeply. "Madam, I still cannot process a transaction above the balance."

She leaned closer. "Okay, let's negotiate."

I frowned. "Negotiate what?"

She lowered her voice. "Let's remove ₦1 million. Just add only ₦300,000. You can even take small something for yourself."

Ha.

"Madam, are you trying to bribe me?"

Before she could respond, we heard a loud voice from the entrance.

"EDITH!!!"

The entire banking hall froze.

I looked up. A tall, serious-looking man in a crisp navy-blue suit had just walked in.

Her husband.

I knew instantly that we were about to witness a family meeting, live and direct.

The man stalked towards us, glaring at his wife.

"Edith, what are you doing here?" he demanded.

She froze. "Ah, darling! I was just handling the school fees…"

"I already paid it yesterday!"

Silence.

Even Musa, the security guard, stopped checking his phone.

Her husband turned to me. "Young lady, what was my wife trying to do?"

"Sir, your wife tried to add extra ₦1.3 million to the school fees."

He exhaled sharply. "Edith."

She clutched her chest like a widow in a Nollywood film. "Baby, it's not what you think!"

"So, what is it?!"

"I was going to use it to buy human hair!"

Her husband rubbed his forehead. "Edith...you wanted to use school fees to buy Brazilian hair?"

She sighed dramatically. "Darling, you know I like to look good! You work hard, and I need to represent you well!"

He just stared at her. "So your children's education is less important than your hairstyle?"

She pouted. "It's not like they won't go to school."

"Edith, go home! Just go home!"

She grabbed her purse and stormed out, muttering. "Bank people are too strict. In my mother's time, women could enjoy life!"

Her husband turned to me. "Thank you for not allowing this nonsense."

I nodded. "No problem, sir."

He sighed and left, still shaking his head.

The moment the door swung shut, the banking hall erupted in murmurs and laughter. Customers who had been paying attention to the drama started laughing.

David was laughing too. "Did you hear that woman?! She wanted to collect 'small something' for bone straight!"

Oyinkan clutched my arm. "Onome, you get the craziest customers."

I sighed and shook my head.

"This office is worse than a reality TV show."

18. The Return of Lola
the Office Witch

We all thought we were free. For an entire week, the office was peaceful. No unnecessary emails. No one getting reported for chewing gum. No evil eyes monitoring what time we arrived. We were happy.

Then, on Monday morning, at exactly 8.15 am, the office doors swung open.

And there she was. Lola.

Her wig was slightly askew. Her usually well-ironed blouse was wrinkled. Her eyes were red.

The entire office froze.

David whispered to me, "Did she escape from Idumota?"

Lola had returned from battle. And she was about to share the story.

She dumped her bag on her old desk that had been cleared out and assigned to a new colleague and sat down heavily.

Ogundare stepped out of his office, frowning. "Lola, what are you doing here? You were transferred."

She shot up like a wounded lioness.

"Sir! I cannot survive in that place!"

The entire first-floor office waited with silent excitement.

"Sir, do you know what I suffered last week?!"

Ogundare sighed and leaned against the door. "Lola, you were posted there for a reason. How bad could it have been?"

She let out a deep, traumatized sigh.

"Sir, on my first day, a trader walked in with a bag full of cash and poured it on my desk."

Ogundare didn't look impressed.

"₦3 million in dirty, smelly, crumpled notes!" she shouted. "It smelled like pepper soup and sweat!"

I had to bite my tongue to stop laughing.

Lola continued, pacing dramatically.

"Sir, do you know that in that branch, people don't queue? They just shout their transactions across the hall!"

James snickered.

"And the worst part?" Lola whispered, her voice breaking.

We all leaned in.

"They don't call me 'Ma' there."

I gasped. Oyinkan grabbed my arm. "They didn't call her ma?!"

Lola wiped a dramatic tear. "They called me Aunty! Or worse…Sister Lola!"

"Sister?" David choked.

"Sister Lola!" she screamed, flinging her hands into the air. "I lost all my respect in three days!"

I covered my mouth.

Ogundare rubbed his temples. "Lola, I warned you that branch is tough. But you needed the experience."

"Experience in suffering?! Sir, the Idumota branch is not banking. It is a local government office!"

She clutched her chest. "Do you know an agbero walked in and demanded a cash refund because 'POS swallowed his money'?"

I stifled a snort.

"And when I told him to wait, he brought out his cutlass!"

David repeated, "Cutlass?"

"JESU!"

"Lola, you saw cutlass live?!"

"With my two naked eyes!"

Even Ogundare looked shocked. "Where was security?"

"Sir, security was the one that told me to 'just give the agbero something small' so he wouldn't break the door!"

I clutched my desk. "Ah. God forbid."

Lola wasn't done.

"Sir, I had to fight for my life every day! One woman came to do a transfer, but she didn't have her account number. I asked her to provide it, and she said...*"

She paused, her eyes wild.

"She said, 'Madam, you should know it by now.'"

The entire office collapsed into laughter.

David was coughing from laughing too hard.

Ogundare sighed deeply. "Lola, you have two options. You either go back or tender your resignation."

She gasped. "Sir, you want me to go back to the valley of the shadow of death?"

"Then resign," he said, folding his arms.

Lola opened her mouth. Closed it. Opened it again.

And then...

She collapsed into her chair dramatically.

"I need to pray," she whispered.

"Take all the time you need," Ogundare replied dryly, walking back to his office.

The moment his door shut, chaos erupted.

David, James, Aunty Agnes, Oyinkan and I started laughing and talking among ourselves.

"Guys, I am collecting offering for her return," said James.

"We should take her to a spa. The trauma is too much," added David.

Lola ignored us.

She was staring blankly at her cleared desk, probably seeing visions of Idumota traders throwing naira notes at her feet. Eventually, she got up and dragged herself out of the bank.

Later that afternoon, a new email notification popped up.

"Dear all, please be informed that our colleague, Lola, has submitted her resignation, effective immediately. We wish her all the best."

The office exploded into silent celebration. People were sending memes. Someone ordered small chops.

I turned to Oyinkan. "Lola has left the building."

She smirked. "And Prestige Capital Bank is a better place for it."

19. Surprise Offer

One Monday morning, I was buried in a ton of paperwork when Ogundare and the Operations Manager, Mrs Asiogu, appeared at my desk.

"Ms. Eferogho, do you have a moment?"

My stomach dropped. Had they discovered my side business? I followed them to a small meeting room, my mind racing.

"Take a seat," Ogundare said.

"Your work during the audit was exemplary," Mrs Asiogu began. "Particularly your handling of the examiners' questions."

I blinked. "Thank you, ma."

"And also, the way you have been handling the customers in the banking hall," she added.

"We have an opportunity we'd like to discuss," Ogundare said.

I braced myself.

"Our Premium Banking unit needs an additional Customer Relationship Officer. It would mean a promotion and salary increase." Mrs Asiogu said.

My jaw nearly dropped.

"Premium Banking?" I repeated.

"You'd be handling our high-net-worth clients," she explained. "It's demanding work but offers significant career advancement."

"And commission," Ogundare added.

Commission? My Master's fund could grow faster than expected.

I swallowed. "When would this start?"

"In about six weeks. You'll need additional training, of course."

"I'd definitely be interested."

Ogundare smiled, a rare sight.

"Good. We'll formalise the offer next week. You've impressed us, Ms. Eferogho. Don't let it go to your head."

"Thank you sir, thank you ma", I said, trying to stay calm on the surface.

Later, I practically ran to Oyinkan's desk with the news.

"Premium Banking? After only a year?" she exclaimed. "What did you do, save Ogundare's firstborn child?"

"Apparently, I'm good with difficult clients."

"Well, your jewellery clients are preparing you for that," she teased.

"What do you mean?"

She grinned. "Rich people are difficult everywhere, not just in banking."

Before I could respond, my phone buzzed.

Deji: *Heard about Premium Banking. Congratulations! I may have put in a good word. Dinner to celebrate?*

I stared at the message. Had Deji influenced my promotion? And if so, what did he expect in return?

As if reading my thoughts, another message followed: *No strings attached. Just proud of your accomplishments.*

I exhaled. Maybe, just maybe...he was genuinely happy for me.

The next Tuesday evening, I arrived at Mrs Coker's impressive Victoria Island home, displaying my jewellery collection to eight wealthy women who represented exactly the clientele I had dreamed of.

"You have a remarkable eye," one woman said, admiring a necklace. "Where did you study design?"

"My grandmother taught me about beads. For the others, I'm self-taught ma," I admitted.

"Banking?" Another woman looked surprised. "With this talent?"

By the end of the evening, I had sold eleven pieces, received five new commissions and earned more in one night than in a month of banking.

Mrs Coker pulled me aside.

"You have a gift, Onome. And connections in banking could serve your business well."

"Actually, I've just been offered a position in Premium Banking."

"Perfect! You'll meet even more potential clients." She smiled knowingly. "Just be careful balancing both worlds. Banks can be traditional about employees with side businesses."

"Thank you Ma," I said. I understood exactly what she meant.

Later, as my taxi navigated the late-night traffic, my phone buzzed.

Deji: *How was the showcase?*

I hesitated, then replied: *Incredibly successful. Thank you for the introduction.*

Deji: *My pleasure. About that dinner...?*

I stared at the message.

A relationship with a superior was risky. But he had helped my career and my business.

I carefully typed: *Friday, 7.00 pm. But just as colleagues.*

His response came immediately: *Looking forward to it.*

By Friday evening, I'd convinced myself at least six times that I should cancel. Dinner with Deji? At a restaurant with white tablecloths and candles? This was exactly how *things* started. The kind of things that got discussed in hushed tones at the back of the bank's HR department.

But I still showed up. Of course I did. And Oyinkan had warned me that she must hear every detail.

The restaurant was tucked away in a quiet corner of Ikoyi - subtle, elegant, and expensive. Deji was already there, in a navy-blue shirt and that signature calm expression that was beginning to unsettle me more than I liked to admit.

"You came," he said with a smile that could melt ice.

"I said I would," I replied, sliding into the seat opposite him.

We ordered, and for a while we talked about safe topics, how crazy the quarter had been, the drama in the Retail Bank, and Ogundare's permanent scowl.

Then, midway through my grilled fish, he said, "I wasn't supposed to say anything. But I meant what I texted. Your promotion was well-earned. I only nudged what was already obvious."

I met his eyes. "Thank you. That means a lot."

"You're very welcome," he said with a mock bow.

412

I laughed, more relaxed than I expected to be.

He leaned forward. "You've got something, Onome. Clients respond to you. You listen. You don't try to dazzle with banking jargon. You make them feel seen. Use that."

I blinked. "That sounded like a mini-TED talk."

"Then consider me your fan club president."

We left around 9.30 pm. He walked me to my ride, but didn't linger. No awkward hug. No romantic suggestion.

Just: "Thanks for coming. See you Monday, Ms. Premium."

I smiled all the way home.

Premium Banking training started the following Monday, with intensive sessions on product knowledge, regulatory frameworks, and handling "sensitive personalities", which was code for rich people with attitude problems.

By Thursday, Mrs Asiogu decided I was ready to observe a live client meeting.

"You'll sit in with Mr Bode-Lawal," she said. "Be attentive but silent."

Mr Bode-Lawal, a real estate tycoon with more properties than I had handbags, swept into the private meeting room like he owned the entire bank. Which, technically, wasn't far from the truth. His balances probably out-earned most of the staff combined.

"Morning," he said, glancing briefly at me, then turned to Deji, who gave me a subtle nod to begin the account review. My hands didn't shake, but I adjusted my blazer four times in five minutes.

I summarised his portfolio performance, recommended switching part of his idle balance into a fixed income opportunity and paused.

He leaned back, studying me.

"You're new," he said finally.

"Yes, sir."

"But not nervous."

I smiled. "Maybe just well-trained, sir."

He chuckled. "Hmm. And what's your own personal investment strategy?"

"Diversified. A bit of risk, but with clear goals in mind."

"And your goal?"

"A master's in finance. And one day my own wealth advisory firm."

His eyes sparkled. "Ambitious. I like that."

After he left, Deji turned to me. "You just made a great first impression on a top-tier client."

"Is that a good thing or a terrifying thing?"

He grinned. "Both."

That night, I got a text from Mrs Asiogu: *Mr Bode-Lawal said you were sharp. Well done. Keep it up.*

I stared at the message for a long time.

Then I picked up my sketchpad and began drawing the first design for Mrs Coker's order.

Premium Banking, designing jewellery, dinners with Deji. Hmmm. Somehow, I was juggling it all. For now.

20. The Difficult Colleague

"**H**e's done it again," Lanre said, dropping a fat stack of client files on my desk like they personally offended him.

I looked up from my screen. "Please don't say it's Chidi."

"It's Chidi," he confirmed, crossing his arms. "Three premium client reviews. Incomplete."

I sighed and stared at the files like they might sprout legs and walk away. It had been two months since I got moved to Premium Banking, and honestly, I loved the work. The clients were demanding, the expectations were high, and the commissions were generous. But there was one fly in my pepper soup: Chidi Okonkwo.

"Let me guess," I said. "He told Mrs Asiogu that he's waiting on client feedback?"

"Close," Lanre said. "He claimed the reviews were pending 'essential client information'. I checked, and he never even called them. Nothing. Not even an email."

I rubbed my temples. As the baby of the Premium Banking team, I often found myself cleaning up his mess to avoid the whole team getting dragged in. It was becoming *my* full-time job.

Lanre nudged the files closer to me. "The management review is at 2.00 pm. You're faster on the system. Please, Onome. I've already got three of my own to finish."

Of course. I stared at my neatly organised to-do list and mentally tore it in half.

"This can't continue," I muttered, dragging the files towards me. "We're enabling him, you know."

Lanre shrugged. "What choice do we have? If Premium looks bad, everyone pays."

He wasn't wrong. Premium Banking was the bank's crown jewel. These clients were the high-net-worth darlings who got exclusive products, marble-floored lobbies, and actual fruit in their waiting areas. Our performance determined our quarterly bonuses, performance reviews, and our futures, essentially.

And yet, here I was, fixing Chidi's incomplete reviews while he probably scrolled through Instagram.

As I started the first one, my phone buzzed. Oyinkan, of course.

Oyinkan: *Lunch? I need gossip update on Banker Bachelor Dinner.*

I smiled, despite my irritation.

Me: *Can't. Cleaning up Chidi's mess again. Rain check?*

Oyinkan: *Again? Please report him jare!*

Me: *Working on it. Tomorrow lunch, promise.*

I put my phone away and focused. Each premium client review needed a full portfolio analysis and a customised investment recommendation. By 1.45 pm, I'd miraculously finished the key ones. My own reports would have to wait until the night shift I didn't sign up for.

At the 2.00 pm review, I sat next to Lanre and across from Chidi, who was smiling like someone who actually did his job. Mrs Asiogu was leading the meeting, with Mr Ogundare and Deji also present.

When Chidi started presenting "his" client portfolio updates (my client portfolio updates) I nearly bit through my pen. He even quoted a product recommendation I'd drafted myself.

Across the table, Deji caught my eye and raised an eyebrow. After the meeting, I tried to escape back to my desk, but Deji caught up with me in the corridor.

"You look like you're plotting murder," he said.

"Would I get bail if I'm caught?"

He gave me that soft smile. "Chidi again?"

I hesitated. It felt unprofessional to rant about a colleague to a senior manager, even one who'd once held my hand under the table at a Chinese restaurant.

"It's nothing I can't handle."

"Hmm. That wasn't a denial." He lowered his voice. "Document everything. It's not just for you. The whole team is carrying him."

"Isn't his uncle…on the board?"

"Yeah," Deji said. "But even board members don't like people making them look bad."

Before I could reply, the devil himself appeared.

"Onome!" Chidi beamed. "Just the person I wanted to thank. Those client reviews? Lifesavers."

I blinked. "Chidi, I didn't help with them. I did them. All of them."

He laughed, unbothered. "Teamwork makes the dream work! Actually, I have a small favour to ask. I have this family thing tonight, very important. Could you call my overdue clients for their account updates? I'll totally make it up to you."

I stared at him. "No."

He paused, clearly not used to hearing that word. "Sorry?"

"I said no. I have my own clients, and my sister's school event this evening. You need to do your own work."

Deji, who had been pretending not to listen, turned slightly. I could see the corners of his mouth twitching.

Chidi tried again. "I've been here two years, you know. Premium was running smoothly before you joined with all this...enthusiasm."

"You mean it was running on other people's backs."

Deji stepped in.

"Chidi, those client calls need to happen today. We're submitting final numbers to the board this week."

Chidi swallowed. "Of course. I'll handle it immediately."

As he walked off, Deji turned to me. "That was satisfying."

"That was probably a mistake. His uncle won't like this."

Deji smiled. "Trust me, the board knows who does the real work."

He glanced at his watch. "Still on for dinner Friday?"

I couldn't help smiling. "Wouldn't miss it."

Back at my desk, I saw three missed calls from Mrs Coker. My jewellery business had blown up since the last showcase. My pieces were now appearing on the necks of Lagos elites at an alarming speed. She wanted five custom sets for an exclusive party next week.

"The event is on Friday," she said when I called her back, "but the committee needs to see samples by Wednesday."

"That's very tight," I said, already calculating my calendar. "I have a major client presentation that week."

"If it's too much, I understand," she said sweetly. "I can reach out to that other designer, the one who did the coral pieces for the governor's wife."

That name lit a competitive fire in my chest. "No, ma. I'll make it work. Can we meet to go over the sketches tomorrow evening?"

After the call, I stared at my calendar and sighed. Three long nights ahead. Between Premium Banking and jewellery, my Masters fund was growing fast.

Unfortunately, so was my sleep deprivation.

21. Risk and Reward

The next Chidi crisis occurred at 3.12 pm on the following Tuesday, disguised as a premium client's angry phone call.

"I don't understand," the woman snapped. "Your colleague promised me access to a dollar-denominated savings product, and now he's ignoring my emails?"

I didn't need to guess who the colleague was.

"Mrs. Olatunji, I'm so sorry," I said, trying to soothe her irritation. "Let me look into it and get back to you within the hour."

One hour, two back-and-forths, and three frantic phone calls later, I found a workaround, updated her file, and sent a detailed product brief she *should* have received a week ago. I ended the call with a tight smile and a headache knocking behind my left eye.

I'd had enough.

Deji was right. This wasn't just about me covering for Chidi's laziness, it was about the team, the clients and the unit's reputation. And if I didn't document it now, I'd have no one but myself to blame when the fallout came.

I was halfway through drafting an email to Mrs Asiogu when Chidi materialised at my desk.

"We need to talk."

I looked up, surprised. No grin, no flippant energy. Just a flat seriousness that was both new and suspicious.

"I'm listening."

"Not here." He gestured towards the small glass-walled meeting room.

Intrigued, I followed. He shut the door and turned to face me like someone preparing to make a confession.

"Look, I know what you think of me," he said. "Lazy, entitled and riding on my uncle's connections."

"You said it, not me."

"Fair enough. But..." He exhaled. "The truth is, I'm under pressure."

I folded my arms, unconvinced.

"My uncle, the board member - is basically threatening to cut me off. He says I have three months to show 'real performance or face real consequences.' His words."

I didn't respond. I wasn't sure where this was going.

"I'm not asking for pity," he added quickly. "I just...I need help catching up. I want to learn."

I blinked. "You want me to mentor you?"

"Guide me," he said. "Not do the work for me. And in return…I could help your jewellery business."

My stomach flipped.

"What?"

"I know about it," he said casually. "Everyone does. You're not exactly low-key, Onome. Those necklaces Mrs. Taiwo wore to the bank dinner? People recognised your style."

I swallowed. "That's a dangerous rumour to spread."

"Relax. I'm not here to report you. I'm here to offer you clients. Real ones. Quiet ones. People who like your pieces but want to deal discreetly."

I stared at him, mind racing. Helping Chidi could backfire spectacularly. But if he truly improved, I'd get some breathing room. And more jewellery clients meant more money in my Masters fund.

"I'll consider it," I said slowly. "But there are conditions."

"Name them."

"You do your own work. I guide; but I don't clean up. You stop claiming credit for what's not yours. And you never, ever mention my jewellery business inside this bank again."

"Deal." He offered his hand. I didn't take it.

"Training starts tomorrow. 7.00 am. Bring your full client portfolio."

When he left, I sat alone in the tiny glass box, unsure whether I'd just made a power move or signed myself up for unnecessary stress.

That evening, I was back in my bedroom, which now doubled as a jewellery studio, tweezers and beads in hand. On my desk, were files and client reports.

My dad knocked and poked his head in.

"Another late night?" he asked.

"Banking and beads," I said with a weak smile.

He came in, picked up one of my coral necklace sketches. "Your mother's worried you're overworking yourself."

"I'm fine. Just...investing in the future."

"Sometimes the present matters too," he said gently. "This design is beautiful. Your grandmother would be proud."

I swallowed. "It's temporary. I need to build up the Masters fund."

"Masters in Canada. And after that?" he asked. "Then what?"

I paused. I didn't have an answer.

"Whatever you do," he said, standing up, "make sure it's something you love. Not just something that pays for what's next."

His words lingered long after he left.

The next morning, I arrived at 6.50 am, expecting to wait for Chidi.

He was already there. With coffee.

"Two sugars, no cream," he said, handing it to me.

I narrowed my eyes. "How did you know how I take my coffee?"

"I pay attention," he said, with that familiar smug glint.

To my surprise, the session went well. He asked smart questions, took notes and actually seemed interested. There was a real banker hidden under all that bravado.

"Why pretend to be terrible?" I asked as we reviewed his portfolio.

He shrugged. "Low expectations are easier to exceed."

Hmm. Maybe, but not sustainable.

By 10.00 am, we had plans in place for all six of his major clients. I started to think I might not regret this after all.

That feeling lasted until lunch, when Oyinkan cornered me at my desk.

"We need to talk," she said.

We ducked into the staff break room. Her expression was serious.

"People are talking, Onome."

"Talking about what?"

"You and Chidi. Yesterday in the meeting room. This morning before hours. People think something's going on."

I nearly choked on my water. "What?!"

"I know it's not like that. But perception matters, babes. Especially in this place."

I sighed. "He asked for help, and I agreed. That's it."

"Just... be careful. Chidi's reputation isn't just about laziness."

Before I could ask more, my phone buzzed. Mrs Asiogu. She wanted to see me.

My stomach dropped. Jewellery business? Or the Chidi situation?

In her office, she motioned for me to sit, then removed her glasses.

"Your performance has been impressive," she began. "Client satisfaction, product application, initiative. You're on track for real leadership."

"Thank you, ma," I said, cautiously.

"That's why I'm concerned about your association with Mr. Okonkwo."

Of course.

"He's asked for my help with client strategy," I explained. "To improve his performance."

"Are you aware of the complaints tied to him? Taking credit for others' work. Emotional manipulation."

My heart pounded. "No, ma. I didn't know."

"Be careful, Ms. Eferogho. Document everything – meetings, tasks, outcomes."

"Yes, ma."

She nodded. "Your future is bright. Don't let anyone, colleague, superior, or otherwise, dim that."

I left her office shaken but strangely grateful. Someone was watching my back, even if it came with a warning.

By Friday, I was tired, but I was looking forward to seeing Deji.

We met at our usual dinner spot, off the radar. As I sipped my drink, I filled him in on Chidi's proposal.

Deji listened in silence, then reached for my hand.

"You're too nice," he said. "That's what I like about you, but you need to be careful."

"It's strategic," I replied. "If he shapes up, I get to sleep more than four hours a night. And he knows about my business. He offered client referrals."

That made Deji pause.

"So now he knows too."

"Apparently everyone does," I muttered.

His thumb traced lazy circles on my palm.

"You need to be careful. Mixing banking and personal business...it's risky."

"Says the man who introduced me to Mrs Coker."

"That was different. I'm not trying to trade favours."

That stung a little.

"I can handle Chidi."

"I don't doubt it. I just don't want you getting caught in office politics. Or worse - used."

He hesitated, then dropped the real news.

"I've been offered a new role. Deputy Director, Corporate Development."

My eyes widened. "That's huge. Congratulations!"

"It means moving to Abuja," he added.

Suddenly, my heart was doing strange things.

"When?"

"Next month."

"Are you accepting?"

"That depends." His eyes didn't leave mine. "These dinners, this...us. It matters to me."

"It matters to me too."

He exhaled. "I could turn it down. Stay in Lagos."

"You can't. It's an amazing opportunity."

"There'll be others."

I shook my head. "Take it. If this thing between us is real, we'll figure it out."

He looked at me like he was seeing me properly for the first time.

"You're always so practical."

"Not always," I said with a soft smile. "Sometimes I make boring jewellery until 2.00 am and ignore my alarms."

"They're beautiful," he said. "Like their creator."

I rolled my eyes, but inside, I melted.

As we ate, I thought about everything: Chidi, Mrs Asiogu's warning, Deji's new offer, my side hustle turning into a real business.

Banking, I was learning, was never just about balance sheets and client portfolios. It was about people. Politics. Risk and reward.

One thing was certain: I was in deep now. And I wasn't backing out.

MORE ADVENTURES OF A LAGOS WEDDING PLANNER

A Collection of Flash Fiction Stories

MEET BISI AGAIN

It's me again! You already know I'm not your average wedding planner. Some people call me a miracle worker, others call me a magician, but I prefer to be called "the fixer."

I've been planning weddings for over nine years, and let me tell you, weddings in Lagos are not just events, they're productions, complete with feuding families, over-the-top mothers-in-law, dramatic exes, and surprise disasters. I've planned everything from luxury beachside ceremonies to backyard traditional engagements, and no two weddings are ever the same.

I've stopped fights over aso-ebi, saved brides from wardrobe malfunctions, and even handled a cake that caught on fire. My job isn't just to make sure the flowers look perfect or that the DJ plays the right songs. It's also to make sure that no one notices the chaos happening behind the scenes.

Weddings are like war zones disguised as fairy tales, but with me in charge, the bride always gets her happy ending. Let me show you how I turn wedding nightmares into dream days.

1. The Uncle and the Mic

Lagos weddings are unpredictable. No matter how much planning goes into them, there's always someone or something waiting to throw a curveball. Today, that curveball had a name: Chief Ajayi.

Chief Ajayi was no ordinary guest, he was the bride's uncle, and a prominent family member with a booming voice, a taste for fine wine, and a reputation for long-winded speeches. I was warned about him during the planning meetings.

"Make sure he doesn't talk for too long," the bride said at the second planning meeting, rolling her eyes. "Last year, he hijacked my cousin's wedding with a 45-minute speech about Nigeria's economy."

I smiled confidently. "Don't worry. I'll handle him."

Now the wedding day had arrived and everything was going smoothly. The ceremony was beautiful, the couple's entrance was flawless and energetic, and guests were now happily eating from the buffet spread when the MC announced that it was time for the family to give their speeches. The groom's father spoke first, delivering a short and heartfelt message. Then it was Chief Ajayi's turn.

I felt a pang of anxiety the moment he stepped up to the mic. His agbada billowed dramatically as he cleared his throat, he was clearly a man ready for a performance.

"Ladies and gentlemen," he began, smiling broadly. "Today is a day of joy, but also a day of reflection."

I groaned. *Reflection* was never a good sign.

He continued by recounting a charming story about how he used to carry the bride on his shoulders as a child. The guests laughed. Even the bride relaxed in her seat and smiled at her husband. But then, as expected, the speech veered off course.

"Let me take you back to 1968," Chief Ajayi said, hands gripping the mic. "Back then, yams were cheap, petrol was abundant, and Nigeria was on the path to greatness."

I signalled the DJ. On cue, he started playing soft background music. It was time for Chief Ajayi to wrap things up. But Chief Ajayi wasn't taking hints. He waved his free hand in the air as if he were conducting an invisible orchestra and ignored the murmurs from the restless guests.

"I remember when men knew their responsibilities," he continued. "Not like today's youth who spend their time scrolling on Instagram and taking selfies."

Several groomsmen exchanged nervous glances. One of them mouthed to me, "Do something."

I approached the stage, maintaining my polite wedding-planner smile. "Thank you, Chief," I smiled tightly. "Perhaps we can conclude with a toast to the couple?"

With a quick flick of his wrist, he waved me off like I was a fly buzzing in his ear. "Not yet. There's more to say," he said firmly.

I saw the groom bury his face in his hands, while the bride looked like she was considering murder.

I had to act fast. I went up to the DJ and whispered in his ear. "Play something loud. Cut him off," I hissed.

The DJ nodded and cranked up Davido's *Unavailable*. The speakers blasted the opening beats, and the crowd erupted in cheers. Some stood up to dance, while the others stayed seated but tapped their feet and moved their hands to the rhythm of the music. Chief Ajayi paused, momentarily stunned by the noise and movements. I seized the opportunity.

"Thank you, Chief!" I said into a backup mic, clapping enthusiastically. "What a beautiful speech! Let's give him a big round of applause."

The guests applauded loudly as I gently pried the mic from his hand. "Let's continue with the celebration, shall we?" I added, motioning for the servers to start distributing more drinks as the DJ switched back to a softer tempo.

Chief Ajayi grumbled but allowed himself to be escorted back to his seat, where he was promptly handed another glass of wine. I made a mental note to keep him occupied for the rest of the evening.

When it was time for the newlyweds' first dance, the bride found me near the stage. "You're a lifesaver, Bisi," she said, delighted that I had saved her and her guests from Chief Ajayi and his speech.

"All part of the job," I replied.

Secretly, I was still praying that Chief Ajayi wouldn't try to steal the mic again. Thankfully, he stayed seated, happily sipping wine and clapping along to the music. The rest of the night went off without a hitch, and by the time the couple took the stage to cut their cake, the drama had been all but forgotten by everyone.

Later that night, after the last guest had left and I was packing up my things, I breathed a huge sigh of relief and made a mental note: *Never give an open mic to an uncle with stories from 1968.*

2. The Guest List Incident

Weddings are like ticking time bombs. You can plan every detail down to the napkin folds, but one spark can send everything exploding.

It was 45 minutes to showtime, and I was already drenched in sweat from running around the grand event centre on Victoria Island. The heat wasn't helping, but it also wasn't the source of my stress. No, that honour went to the growing mob of uninvited guests who were gathered outside the venue's entrance, arguing loudly with the security guards.

Nigerian weddings have a way of becoming open markets where random strangers, including long-lost cousins, uncles, and that "family friend" who once gave your dad directions, try to find their way in. When we met to go over her wedding day plans, I warned Tomi, the bride, to be strict with her guest list for this very reason. But she obviously hadn't listened. And now, here we were.

I marched toward the entrance, narrowly avoiding a server carrying a tray of puff-puff and other small chops. The sound of the DJ testing the speakers boomed across the venue as I approached the head of security, a tall, burly man with dark sunglasses.

"What's going on here?" I asked, trying to sound calmer than I felt.

"They're claiming they're invited, Ma," he replied, gesturing toward a group of well-dressed aunties and uncles waving invitation cards like protest signs.

One of the women stepped forward, her gele tilted slightly, as though the stress of arguing had caused it to slide. "We have the invitation!" she shouted, thrusting an envelope into my hands.

I inspected it, and my stomach sank when I saw the gold-trimmed design and the bride and groom's names embossed in glitter. The invitation was genuine.

"How did this happen?" I muttered to myself, flipping through my mental checklist. We'd double-checked the seating chart.

Before I could fully process the situation, Tomi's mother arrived in a flurry of pearls and silk. Her gele sparkled under the sunlight, and her eyes were as sharp as daggers.

"Bisi, what's the meaning of this?" she demanded, her voice loud enough to turn heads. "My sister's friends are outside, and they can't get in!"

"Madam, we're over capacity," I explained, "We have no more seats in the main hall."

She glared at me with the kind of look that could melt steel beams.

"Do you know who my husband is?" she hissed. "We cannot embarrass ourselves today. Let them in, or I will call him right now."

I swallowed hard. Nigerian mothers can be scarier than any bridezilla.

"Give me five minutes," I said, holding up my hands.

I dashed back inside, my mind racing. I spotted the caterer near the bar, arranging bottles of wine, and I got an idea.

There was a secondary room near the main hall. We had secured it for our vendors and for staff to use during their breaks. It wasn't ideal, but it had a large TV, and with a little rearranging, we could make it work as a viewing area. I quickly ran back to the caterer.

"I need trays of drinks and small chops set up in the side room immediately. Champagne, suya, puff-puff, stick meat, whatever you can manage in ten minutes."

He blinked but nodded, already barking instructions to his staff.

Once the room was prepped, I returned to the entrance. "Follow me," I told the aunties and uncles, who looked sceptical but hopeful.

I led them to the secondary room where the TV was showing a live stream of the ceremony, and servers were walking around with trays of small chops and drinks. The guests settled in, sipping champagne and chatting excitedly. One

439

of the aunties grinned as she took a bite of suya. "This is even better than sitting in the hall," she said, laughing.

I exhaled, relief washing over me. Crisis averted. Another day in the life of a Lagos wedding planner.

3. The Runaway Bride

The day had started smoothly for once. The sun was shining, the decor was flawless, and the hall at the luxurious hotel overlooking the Lekki Lagoon was filling up with beautifully dressed guests.

I was mentally checking off my tasks as the clock ticked closer to the ceremony. The musicians were rehearsing, and even the printer of the ceremony's programmes had delivered them on time, a small miracle in Lagos traffic. For once, I thought I'd get through the day without any major disasters.

Then a bridesmaid came barrelling toward me, panic written all over her face.

"Aunty Bisi! We can't find the bride!" she panted.

I blinked, my brain refusing to process her words. "What do you mean, you can't find the bride?"

"She was in the suite getting her hair done. I left to get her shoes, and when I came back, she was gone, and her phone is switched off."

I felt my stomach tighten. A missing bride was a new level of chaos, even for me. "Did you check the bathroom?" I asked, already moving toward the bridal suite.

"Everywhere," the bridesmaid replied, trailing behind me. "She's really gone."

I burst into the suite, hoping that by some miracle the bride would be back in her chair getting her hair done, but the room was empty. The makeup artist sat on the couch, scrolling through her phone. She looked relaxed when she glanced up, shrugged, and said, "She said she needed some air."

"When was this?" I asked her, trying to stay calm.

"About thirty minutes ago."

Thirty minutes was an eternity in wedding time. I tried calling Kemi's phone, but it went straight to voicemail. Panic gripped me as I paced the room and mentally ran through every possible scenario. Where would she go? Then it hit me; the hotel had a small garden with a quiet spot overlooking the water. Maybe she had gone there to gather her thoughts.

I ran outside, scanning the area frantically. Finally, I spotted her. She was sitting on a bench under a large tree, a figure in a white gown, her head buried in her hands, her veil tossed to the side like it was an afterthought.

I jogged over and sat beside her. "Kemi."

Kemi sniffled. Then, wiping her tears on the sleeve of her dress, she looked up at me and said, "I can't do it, Aunty Bisi."

My heart sank. "What do you mean?"

She looked up, her makeup smudged but still beautiful. "I don't love him."

I exhaled slowly, choosing my words carefully. "Does anyone else know how you feel?"

"No," she whispered, her voice cracking. "Everyone thinks this is my dream wedding, but it's not. My parents paid for everything. Guests flew in from London, how do I tell them it was all for nothing?"

I felt the weight of her words. Nigerian weddings weren't just about the couple, they were family events, social statements, and expensive productions. But none of that mattered if the bride was miserable.

"It's not too late," I said softly. "If you want to leave, you can. But you have to decide now."

Her breath hitched, and she clutched my arm like a drowning woman holding onto a lifeline. "Will you help me?"

I hesitated. I had signed up to plan her wedding, not stage a dramatic exit. But as much as I wanted everything to go perfectly, I couldn't force her to stay.

"I'll call you a cab," I said. "Where do you want to go?"

She wiped her eyes and whispered, "Anywhere but here."

I pulled out my phone and booked a ride, giving the driver instructions to meet us discreetly near the side entrance. While we waited, I helped her fix her veil and handed her a bottle of water. She was still wearing her wedding gown, but there wasn't time to change.

The cab pulled up a few minutes later. I opened the door for her. "Are you sure about this?" I asked her one last time.

She nodded. Her eyes were filled with tears but also something else, possibly relief.

"Good luck," I said, closing the door after she slipped inside. She nodded again. Then the cab sped off and disappeared into the chaos of Lagos traffic. I stood there for a moment, letting the reality sink in. I had just helped a bride run away from her wedding.

I sighed. I had no idea how I was going to explain this to the guests or the bride's furious parents. But that was a problem for the next few minutes.

For now, I had a runaway bride to cover up and bad news to deliver. Just another day in the life of a wedding planner.

4. The Torn Dress

The makeup artist had just finished her finishing touches on the bride's glowing skin, and the photographer was busy capturing every magical moment. The bridal suite smelled like fresh roses and hair spray; everything was going smoothly until the scream pierced the air.

I froze.

The bride, Chioma, was standing in front of the full-length mirror with her hands covering her mouth and a look of horror on her face.

"What happened?" I asked her, rushing to her side.

"My dress!" she wailed, pointing to the floor-length lace gown that now had a gaping tear running down the side seam. "It ripped when I bent down to fix my shoes!"

The stylist and makeup artist exchanged worried glances. I crouched down to examine the damage. The fabric along her hip had torn clean through, exposing part of her thigh. It was too large to hide and too complicated to fix without professional help.

Chioma's mother barged into the room, her gele wobbling precariously. "What's going on? Chioma, what happened?"

The bride sobbed harder.

I stood up and took a deep breath. "Don't worry. I'll fix it."

My brain went into overdrive. The tailor was supposed to be on standby, but she had texted me earlier to say she was stuck in Third Mainland Bridge traffic. I glanced at my assistant. "Quick, grab the emergency sewing kit from the car."

She nodded and sprinted out of the suite.

I turned to Chioma. "Take a deep breath. We'll have you ready in no time. Think of this as a funny story to tell your future kids," I said, trying to calm her down.

"I don't find this funny," she muttered, dabbing her tears.

Five minutes later, my assistant returned, breathless, with the kit in hand. I quickly threaded a needle and got to work. The bridesmaids gathered around, whispering prayers as if my stitching abilities depended on divine intervention.

The clock was ticking. We had exactly twenty minutes before the ceremony.

"I don't want anyone to know this happened," Chioma whispered.

I smiled, tying the final knot. "They won't. You'll look perfect."

Once done, I stood back and admired my work. The lace wasn't perfectly aligned, but I had covered the tear well enough that no one would notice unless they were looking for it.

Chioma sniffed, touched her dress, and nodded. "Thank you."

"Let's get you to the church," I said, ushering her toward the door.

As she stepped outside, I felt my phone buzz. It was the DJ asking about last-minute song changes for the reception. I sighed, knowing that my job was far from being over.

5. The Flight Delay

The couple had flown in from the U.S. just three days before their high-society Lagos wedding. Everything was going according to plan until it wasn't.

"Madam, the best man missed his flight," my assistant said to me, whispering, her eyes wide with panic.

"What?" I nearly dropped my tablet. "How? He was supposed to arrive an hour ago!"

"He said there was bad weather in New York, and the next available flight won't get him here until tomorrow."

Tomorrow was useless. The wedding was this afternoon.

I took a deep breath, mentally shuffling through possible solutions, as I ran upstairs to speak to the couple.

The groom wasn't helping matters, he was already in meltdown mode, pacing the suite and muttering about "disasters."

"It's Kunle! My best friend! How can we get married without him?" His voice was rising, and I could sense a full-blown panic attack on the horizon.

"Relax," I said, placing a hand on his shoulder. "There's always a solution. Give me thirty minutes."

I paced the room, phone glued to my ear.

"We need someone confident, who can give a toast and be in the photos," I said to the bride.

She hesitated, and then her face lit up.

"My cousin Olamide! She's a lawyer. She's funny and photogenic, she wasn't able to join as a bridesmaid, so she owes me a favour."

That solution turned out to be perfect. The cousin went home to change and arrived within the hour, hair impeccably done, dressed in a sleek black gown. By the time the ceremony began, she was standing proudly beside the groom, playing her role as if it had been planned all along. Even the photos looked flawless.

Later, at the reception, I saw Olamide laughing and sharing champagne with one of the groomsmen.

I smiled to myself. Kunle may have missed the wedding, but a new connection was forming. Sometimes, chaos has a silver lining.

6. The Groom's Away Match

O ne thing I've learned in my years as a wedding planner is this: the bigger the wedding, the bigger the secrets.

Today's wedding was one of those high-society affairs where the family names alone could open bank vaults. The bride, Sade, was the only daughter of a billionaire oil magnate, whose groom, Jide, came from a respected political dynasty. It was a perfect match on paper. Two powerful families preparing to unite in a grand, televised celebration. Everything was going smoothly until…

I was overseeing the final touches on the floral arch when my assistant, Mary, rushed toward me, her face a mask of urgency.

"Aunty Bisi, there's a problem," she whispered, her eyes darting toward the entrance.

I sighed. "Mary, we always have problems. Be specific."

She swallowed hard. "There's a woman at the gate causing a scene. She says she's carrying the groom's baby."

I froze mid-step. "Excuse me?"

"She's shouting that she's pregnant for Jide and won't let this wedding hold."

Of course.

I smoothed down my dress, straightened my shoulders, and made my way toward the entrance. The security team had already formed a barrier around the woman, but I could hear her voice clear as day.

"I'm not leaving until Jide comes out here! He promised me marriage before this yeye engagement!"

I sized her up. She was stunning, her long curly weave falling over an expensive-looking dress. Definitely not a random troublemaker. No, this one had receipts.

I motioned for security to ease up and walked toward her with my best professional smile.

"Madam, please calm down. This is not the time or place..."

She turned to me sharply. "Who are you?"

"The wedding planner."

She scoffed. "Then go and get your groom. He has unfinished business."

I inhaled deeply and glanced at the security team. "Escort her to a private lounge," I instructed them, "Give her water. No cameras, no social media."

They nodded and led her away. As soon as they were out of earshot, I grabbed my phone and dialled the groom's best man, Tunde. He picked up on the first ring.

"Tunde, where is your guy?" I asked, keeping my voice steady.

"Ah, Bisi, we're just about to leave the hotel."

"You need to come here alone first," I said. "We have an issue."

"Kilode?"

"Your boy's side chick is here. And she's claiming pregnancy."

Silence.

Then, "Ah."

"Ah is not a solution, Tunde."

"Okay, okay. I'm on my way."

Fifteen minutes later, Tunde arrived, sweating despite the air conditioning being on full blast. I led him to the private lounge where the woman was seated, arms folded, her expression a mix of rage and heartbreak.

"Jide has been with me for three years," she snapped as soon as she saw Tunde. "We were together last weekend!"

Tunde ran a hand over his face. "Ah, Cynthia, this is not the time."

"No, this is exactly the time!" she shot back. "He wants to marry another woman while I'm carrying his child?"

Mary, who had been standing quietly in the corner, whispered to me, "This wedding fit scatter."

She wasn't wrong.

I leaned in and spoke to Cynthia gently. "What do you want?"

She hesitated. "I want him to own up. If he wants to marry her, fine. But he will not deny me or this baby."

Tunde quickly texted Jide, and within minutes, the groom arrived. He walked in looking condemned and ashamed.

"Cynthia," he said, breathing hard.

"Don't Cynthia me," she snapped. "Tell the truth."

Jide swallowed hard. "Babe, I..."

I cleared my throat and spoke calmly. "Jide, let's be practical here. Your wedding starts in an hour. What do you want to do?"

He looked at me, then at Cynthia. "Please, just let me handle this after today."

Cynthia smirked. "Oh no, my dear. I want you to handle it now."

Just then, the door opened, and we all turned to see who it was.

It was Sade. The bride.

She stood there, calm, regal, and utterly unreadable. "Cynthia," she said smoothly. "How far along are you?"

Cynthia blinked. "What?"

"How pregnant are you?"

"Four months."

Sade nodded. "And you're sure it's Jide's?"

Cynthia scoffed. "You think I'd be here embarrassing myself if it wasn't?"

Another pause.

Sade smiled.

"Then congratulations," she said, walking over and taking Cynthia's hand. "You should be resting, not causing a scene."

Cynthia's bravado faltered. "I...what?"

Sade turned to Jide. "You will take responsibility for her and the baby. But we are still getting married today."

Jide's jaw dropped.

Tunde coughed.

Even I was speechless.

Sade turned to me. "Bisi, please make sure she's taken care of. And get my father's lawyers on standby."

And just like that, she walked out, head held high.

Cynthia slumped into her chair, stunned. "Did I just lose?"

Mary exhaled beside me. "Omo, this bride get sense."

I turned to Cynthia. "Would you like another bottle of water?"

She shook her head.

"Then I suggest you go home and rest."

Cynthia left. The wedding went on.

And Jide? Well, let's just say I wouldn't be surprised if he started sleeping with one eye open.

7. The Sugar Daddy Surprise

The bridal party was lining up just outside the church hall. They were waiting for the signal from one of the ushers to let them know the processional hymn was about to start. The maid of honour went to the door to pick up copies of the programme and handed them to everyone.

I was adjusting the bride's veil, when she looked up from the programme and whispered, "Aunty Bisi, this officiating minister used to be my sugar daddy."

"What did you just say?"

Her face crumpled with guilt.

"It was before I met Daniel! I didn't know he'd be the minister until just this morning."

A knot of panic twisted in my stomach. "Will he recognize you?"

"I don't know," she whispered, glancing anxiously towards the entrance. "But what if he does?"

This was not the kind of drama I needed on a day when the mother of the groom was already micromanaging me to death. I had only a few minutes to fix this or, at the very least, contain it.

"Stay calm," I told her. "Let me handle this."

I peeked into the hall where the minister was sitting. He looked calm as he flipped through the programme. His face didn't betray anything. No smirks, no sly glances. Maybe he hadn't recognized her name, or maybe he was better at hiding it than she was.

The ceremony began, and the bride marched down the aisle. I watched the minister's face as she approached.

Nothing.

His voice was steady as he welcomed everyone and led the couple through the vows. When the bride said, "I do," I saw it. The brief flicker of recognition in his eyes. But he didn't flinch, didn't miss a word. The ceremony continued smoothly, and after the couple signed the register, I let out the breath I had been holding in.

"You knew," I said, discreetly approaching him after the service.

He smiled faintly. "Of course. But God forgives. Even me."

I watched as he left, his back straight, no sign of regret.

The reception that followed was spectacular, no one else was any the wiser. The bride danced happily with her new husband, and I busied myself with making sure the rest of the event went smoothly.

However, I promised myself one thing: next time, I'd vet all ministers more thoroughly. After all, Lagos weddings have a way of digging up secrets when you least expect them.

8. The Hungry Guests

I knew something was wrong when my phone buzzed for the fourth time in ten minutes. I glanced at the screen; it was a text message from my assistant: *Caterers are late.*

It was the nightmare every wedding planner dreads. The ceremony had gone off without a hitch, and guests were now pouring into the reception venue, chatting and dancing. But without food, I knew that their good mood wouldn't last.

I made a beeline for the head of catering. He was pacing the empty serving area. "Where are the trucks?" I demanded.

"Traffic on the Third Mainland Bridge," he muttered, avoiding my eyes.

"How long until they arrive?"

"Maybe an hour."

I could already see the signs of impending chaos: guests waving waiters over, asking when the food would be served; children growing restless; the groom's father glancing at his watch. I had to think fast.

"Call the hotel restaurant," I said to my assistant. "Order as many small chops and appetizers as they can prepare within 30 minutes. Have them send everything up to the ballroom."

Then I quickly ran to the DJ. "Start playing the upbeat music and crank up the volume," I said to him, shouting over the music and voices in the ballroom.

He nodded, gave me a thumbs-up, and then cranked up the music. I prayed that would work as I made my way toward the hotel restaurant.

It worked. Within 20 minutes, there were trays of spring rolls, puff-puff, and chicken wings circulating through the hall. I spotted guests munching contentedly, the tension beginning to ease.

The younger guests danced and live-streamed their dancing challenge between the groomsmen and the bridesmaids.

An hour later, the catering trucks arrived, and the main courses were served.

"You saved the day," the bride's father said, approaching me and patting me on my shoulder.

I smiled. Inside, I knew I would be having nightmares about this for weeks.

9. Fire on the Dance Floor

The party was in full swing when it happened.

The couple had just finished their first dance, and the DJ had just transitioned to a high-energy afrobeats song. The dance floor was packed with guests, heels clacking, agbadas swinging, and gele-wearing aunties shaking their shoulders. The lights above pulsed in sync with the beat.

Then the lights flickered. Once. Twice.

And then the room was plunged into darkness.

Turning on my cell phone's flashlight, I rushed toward the venue manager who was already on his walkie-talkie. "What's going on?" I demanded to know.

"Power surge," he said. "We're switching to the backup generator."

Just then I smelled smoke, and then a shout from the back of the hall confirmed my worst fear: the fabric-covered decorations near the stage had caught fire, likely from faulty wiring.

"Get everyone out, now!" I yelled to my assistant, who quickly scurried off.

The next few minutes were chaotic: The backup generator powered up, and the lights flickered back on just as guests scrambled toward the exits, women held onto their gele-covered heads, and men grabbed plates of jollof as if they couldn't bear to leave without their food. My team worked with the hotel staff to douse the fire using extinguishers before it could spread.

Once the fire was out, the smell of smoke lingered, but we quickly aired out the space.

My team and I surveyed the damage and called an electrician to fix the problem with the wires.

The bride, Funmi, her makeup smudged but her spirits intact, walked up to me and said, "Can we still have our party?"

I looked around. The DJ was ready, the caterers were serving desserts, and the guests were already trickling back in.

"Yes," I said. "Let's dance."

10. The Secret Dutch Husband

The ceremony had just started, and everything was going well. The bride's father had led her to the altar and the priest was just beginning to say the opening prayer when the doors violently swung open. Heads turned. In Lagos, we are used to uninvited guests, but this man didn't look like a "party-crasher." He had the energy of someone who was there on a mission.

"I need to speak to the bride," he demanded, striding down the aisle, his voice echoing through the church.

The priest paused mid-prayer, confused. Murmurs started among the congregation.

I quickly bolted from where I was sitting and rushed forward to block him before things spiralled out of control. My assistant followed close behind, panicked.

"Sir, you can't interrupt the ceremony like this," I hissed under my breath. "Security..."

But before I could finish, he stepped past me and turned to the crowd. "I'm Dimeji, and this wedding can't go on. The bride is already my wife."

A collective gasp rippled through the church. The groom looked as if someone had punched him in the stomach. The bride? Her face went pale, and she swayed slightly.

462

"W-what are you talking about?" she whispered.

"You know what I'm talking about, Tiwa. We got married in Amsterdam three years ago. Don't pretend you've forgotten."

I have handled my share of drama. Missing rings, feuding families, and even a drunk father of the bride, but this? An ex-husband-turned-wedding-crasher? This was new territory.

The priest cleared his throat. "Young man, this is highly inappropriate…"

"No, Father, what's inappropriate is pretending this woman isn't already spoken for."

I signalled my assistant to bring in the church's security guards while I led the bride and groom toward a side room. The priest told the congregation to remain calm and seated while we tended to the matter privately.

The groom was shaking with rage, his jaw clenched. "Is this true, Tiwa? Were you married to him?"

Tiwa burst into tears. "It was a civil marriage. We lived together in the Netherlands, but it wasn't real to me."

"Well, it's real enough for him to show up here," the groom snapped.

Meanwhile, I was on my phone calling my legal contact.

"What happens if a previous marriage isn't annulled?" I asked.

"Wedding's legally invalid," came the reply. Great.

When I returned to the room, Tiwa was begging the groom for forgiveness.

She was still begging when the groom's mother entered the room, her face like thunder. "What kind of nonsense is this? We told you not to marry someone who's lived abroad!"

After some negotiations, Tiwa agreed to sign annulment papers immediately and postpone the wedding. Dimeji left, smugly satisfied.

As for me? I rescheduled the wedding, this time with a new checklist item: *verify marital status at the first meeting.*

11. Aso-Ebi Disaster

Anyone who knows Lagos weddings understands that *aso-ebi*, the matching fabric chosen by the couple's families, can either bring harmony or absolute chaos. Today, it was chaos.

I knew it the moment I saw the three women arguing in the parking lot. Their voices were raised, their hand gestures frantic, and their vibrant blue *aso-ebi* fabric clashed in a way that hurt my eyes.

"You think you're the only one who can slay in this style, eh Funmi?" one of them snapped, flipping her braided hair. "You copied me!"

"Abeg, shut up," Funmi shot back. "Your tailor didn't even do a good job. That slit is too high."

The third woman laughed. "You look like you're selling pepper at Balogun Market."

I groaned and approached them. "Ladies, please. What's the issue?"

The problem was simple and ridiculous. All three women had the same fabric but had tailored their outfits similarly: plunging necklines, thigh-high slits, and dramatic puffed sleeves. Now, they were accusing each other of "stealing" ideas, and neither one of them wanted to feel overshadowed.

"Listen," I said, using my best authoritative tone. "This is a wedding, not a fashion show. If you can't settle this quietly, I'll have security escort you out."

Funmi scoffed but lowered her voice. "Fine but tell her to stop throwing shade."

I called my assistant and asked her to seat the women at separate tables at opposite ends of the reception hall. Even then, I still kept one eye on them throughout the wedding. Sure enough, as soon as it was time to dance, they started competing for attention on the dance floor.

By the time the party was over, one of them had ripped her dress from twerking too hard. I made a mental note: *next time, assign someone to manage aso-ebi disputes*.

12. Bride in Labour

The couple was making their grand entrance to the reception room. Applause filled the room, the lights dimmed, and the DJ started playing the first notes of their chosen song. The double doors opened slightly, and I got ready to clear the crowd of photographers from their path.

And that's when it happened.

"Bisi!" the bride gasped, clutching her belly. "I think my water just broke."

I was like, "What, now?"

My assistant, wide-eyed, whispered, "Ma, what do we do?"

"What do you mean what do we do? Let's get her to the hospital!" I snapped, my mind racing.

It was not the grand entrance the guests were expecting. The groom was in shock, and his bride was doubled over with her white gown soaked at the hem, and a small puddle of water at her feet.

Very quickly, the bridesmaids surrounded the bride and guided her outside to a waiting vehicle which rushed her to a nearby hospital. Meanwhile, word spread and the guests began to murmur. Without the bride and groom, we still kept the reception going.

Later, I received a text which read: *Baby boy arrived safely even though he was four weeks early! We'll continue the reception after the naming ceremony.*

Only in Lagos.

13. Love at First Dance

I always say that weddings are magical because you never know what can happen. On this particular day, the magic worked overtime.

The couple, Tunde and Amaka, had spared no expense. From the cascading floral arches to the imported champagne, everything was designed to be perfect. I had just finished supervising the last-minute touches to the five-tier cake when the bride's sister rushed over.

"Bisi, there's a guy sitting at the wrong table," she said to me. "He's supposed to be on the groom's side, but he's sitting with my cousin Chika on the bride's side."

I brushed off her concerns. A few misplaced seats weren't unusual, and at least they weren't causing any chaos. But my interest was piqued when I glanced over and saw the man in question. He was a tall, clean-cut gentleman in a tailored suit, and Chika was leaning into him and giggling like a schoolgirl. I made a mental note to keep an eye on them.

Which I did. Throughout the meal, I saw them talking. I even noticed when they exchanged numbers, and I also saw when he escorted her outside to get something from the car. By the time dessert was served, they were inseparable.

The next hint I got that something special was happening came when guests were on the dance floor. The DJ transitioned from slow music to afrobeats and the dance floor became a whirl of brightly coloured aso-ebi, gele, groomsmen in suits and older men in agbada. Chika and her mystery man were dancing so closely you would have thought they were the ones getting married.

Then I was distracted for a brief second and they were gone. "Madam, they've left the reception hall together," my assistant whispered to me.

I chuckled. "Let's hope they're not getting into any trouble."

Months later, I got an email from Chika which read:

"Dear Bisi,

You probably remember me as the cousin who disappeared with a man at Amaka and Tunde's wedding. His name is Dapo, and we're getting married next year, on the exact date of my cousin's wedding. Can you plan it for us?"

And that's how one magical dance stemming from a seating mix-up became a new love story.

14. The Sabotaged Buffet

The reception was going well. I should have known something was about to go wrong. The guests were dancing, some clinking glasses, others helping themselves to the lavish buffet which featured everything from asun and peppered snail to smoked salmon canapés. I was just about to check on the cake table when my assistant rushed over, her face pale.

"Madam, guests are complaining of tummy upset."

My stomach dropped. "What do you mean?"

"Some are already in the restroom. Others are calling for antacids. It's the food, Aunty Bisi. Something's wrong."

I grabbed my phone and called the head caterer who was just as shocked as I was.

"Our food is fresh! Everything was prepared under strict conditions," he protested.

But the complaints kept coming, and panic was setting in. One of the groom's uncles was doubled over and clutching his stomach near the drinks table. I called my assistant and asked her to discreetly hand out bottled water and painkillers while I tried to control the chaos.

Then the whispers started: "It's the groom's ex. I saw her earlier, near the buffet."

My heart raced as I scanned the crowd for any sign of her. The bride had once confided in me that the groom's ex, Kike, had a vindictive streak. She hadn't taken the breakup well, and the bride was worried she'd show up uninvited.

"Find her," I told my assistant. "Now."

Twenty minutes later, she came back shaking her head. "I can't find her. But one of the servers said a woman matching her description was seen near the serving area before the reception."

I knew I needed proof, and fast, so I pulled the hotel's security manager aside and demanded that they check the surveillance footage. An hour later, we had it: a woman in a green dress and red high heels, slipping something into the trays of jollof rice.

By then, most of the sick guests had either left or been treated, so we quietly disposed of the contaminated food and ensured the unaffected dishes were properly served.

Later, I heard that Kike had fled the scene once she realized that people were getting sick. When I told the bride what happened, she cried, but she was also grateful that the attempted sabotage hadn't ruined everything.

"I knew she was petty," she whispered. "But this?"

I patted her on her shoulder and said, "The most important thing is that you and your husband are fine. I will report this to the police and have her arrested for causing harm. She will be banned from your life permanently."

I learnt my lesson that day. I now instruct caterers and serving staff to *never* leave any food unattended.

15. Souvenir Scramble

I always say souvenirs can make or break a Lagos wedding. If they're too cheap, people complain. Too luxurious, and chaos ensues. This time, it was the latter.

The bride's mother, a woman known for her love of extravagance, had insisted on importing customised souvenirs from Dubai. Guests were to receive crystal vases, silk scarves, and expensive perfumes. I had warned her to prepare for extra, but she brushed me off.

"Only close family and VIPs will get them. The others can take regular gifts."

Big mistake.

The distribution started smoothly. My assistant and I ensured that the VIP tables received their premium souvenirs first. But once word got out about the crystal vases, things took a turn. Guests from the "regular" tables started swarming the distribution area, demanding luxury items.

"This is unfair! Why should I get a keychain while they get vases?" one woman shouted, trying to snatch a box from my assistant's hands.

Another man shoved past the queue, yelling, "I'm the groom's cousin! Give me the good stuff!"

Within minutes, the area had become a battlefield. Guests tugged at boxes and fought over silk scarves. One elderly woman slapped a younger guest who tried to take two vases.

I knew I had to act fast, so I grabbed the microphone.

"Attention, please!" I said, "Due to the overwhelming demand, we will be distributing the remaining souvenirs tomorrow at the family house."

The mention of the family house worked like magic. No one wanted to show up and cause trouble under the bride's parents' watch. The fighting subsided, and the crowd dispersed, grumbling but compliant.

As I packed up the leftover boxes, the bride's mother came over, sighing.

"I didn't think it would get this bad."

I chuckled. "Next time, madam, let's stick to one type of souvenir."

She laughed. "Or maybe next time, you'll manage me better."

"Deal," I replied with a wink.

16. The Groom's Daughter

Yinka, the bride, was glowing in her custom-made gown as she prepared to dance into the reception hall. The morning had gone smoothly with no drama and no delays. I was already patting myself on the back when I noticed the groom's six-year-old daughter, Dara, darting through the hall with her white flower girl dress swishing behind her.

"Dara, be careful," I said gently, but she giggled and kept running, weaving between tables and narrowly missing the DJ's setup.

"Bisi, what's happening?" Yinka whispered, noticing the commotion.

I quickly reassured her that everything was fine and signalled for my assistant to take Dara back to her seat.

The grand entrance began. Yinka and her new husband danced into the venue accompanied by confetti. But no sooner had they taken their seats than Dara reappeared, this time on the stage.

She clutched the microphone the DJ had carelessly left unattended and shouted, "Daddy! Daddy, come dance with me!"

The crowd burst into laughter, but Yinka's smile faltered. The groom, Kunle, tried to coax Dara down, but she wasn't having any of it.

"Dara, sweetheart, let's sit down, okay?" he whispered.

"No! Dance with me!"

So, to avoid a scene, Kunle obliged. He lifted her into his arms and twirled her around to the delight of the guests. The applause was deafening, and cameras flashed as father and daughter stole the spotlight.

When they finished, Dara curtsied dramatically, earning another round of applause. But as Kunle carried her offstage, I could see the tension brewing in Yinka's face.

Backstage, Yinka grabbed my arm.

"This is supposed to be *my* day," she hissed. "I didn't plan this wedding for a six-year-old to be the centre of attention."

I sighed. Weddings are full of unexpected moments, but this one hit differently.

"I understand, but she's just a little girl. The guests will remember you, Yinka. You're the bride. No one's taking that from you."

She exhaled, her shoulders relaxing slightly. "Just… make sure she doesn't do anything else."

I nodded and stationed my assistant next to Dara's seat for the rest of the night. The drama didn't completely disappear, but by the end of the reception, Yinka was smiling again, especially when the photographer showed her a picture of her and Kunle dancing, with Dara clapping joyfully in the background.

17. The Aisle Tussle

It was barely 8.00 am and the bride's suite was already a war zone. I was helping Feyi adjust her veil when shouting erupted outside the door to the suite.

"What's happening?" she asked, panic creeping into her voice.

I opened the door. The bride's stepfather and biological father were right outside the door facing off. Feyi's stepfather, dressed in a perfectly tailored agbada, had one hand on the doorframe. Her biological father, his face set in a scowl, was gripping his *fila* cap tightly.

"I'm her father," the biological father spat. "I should be the one to walk her down the aisle."

The stepfather scoffed. "Where were you when she was growing up? I raised her."

The argument was getting louder and drawing the attention of the bridesmaids and hotel staff. I needed to diffuse this, fast.

"Gentlemen," I said, firmly, stepping between them. "This is Feyi's wedding day, not a battleground. Let's talk privately."

I led them into a side room and closed the door. "Feyi should decide who walks her down the aisle," I said.

Her stepfather looked smug, sure of his victory, but her biological father wasn't giving in.

"She won't even be here if not for me!" he said.

"We can compromise," I suggested. "Maybe both of you can walk her down the aisle together."

They stared at each other and looked at me as if I had lost my mind.

I quickly came up with another idea.

"Okay, how about this? You sir –" I said to Feyi's biological father, "– walk her from the car to the church entrance. And you sir –" I said to her step-father, "– walk her from the entrance of the church to the altar."

They both eyed each other and then reluctantly agreed.

An hour later, Feyi entered the church flanked by her biological father, who walked her partway and handed her over to her stepfather.

She beamed with happiness as her step-father handed her over to the groom. I breathed a sigh of relief.

The morning's chaos was buried under smiles and camera flashes. Another day, another victory.

18. The Ex Name Slip

The reception was running like a dream. The chandeliers sparkled, dinner was being served, the band was playing soft highlife music, and seated guests were tapping their feet to the sound. I had just checked on the cake table when the groom, Bode, took the microphone to give his speech.

"Ladies and gentlemen," he began to speak, grinning ear to ear. "I'm the luckiest man alive today, and I'd like to say a few words about my wonderful wife."

The bride beamed at him, her eyes glistening with emotion. Even /felt the warmth as I adjusted a centrepiece near their table. Bode seemed relaxed, confident, and completely in love. What could possibly go wrong?

"I knew from the moment I met you, Tola, that you were the one for me."

Loud gasps rippled across the hall. The groom froze and chuckled nervously. The bride's smile, once wide and beaming, had vanished. In its place was a look of confusion, horror, and what looked like embarrassment. My own heart dropped into my stomach.

Did he just call her *Tola*?

I rushed toward the table, hoping the moment would pass quickly, but it was too late. The bride's older sister was already whispering something furiously to her mother, and the groom's friends had their hands covering their mouths, some trying to stifle what seemed like laughter.

"I-I mean Adesuwa," Bode stammered. He cleared his throat and tried to continue, but the damage had already been done. Adesuwa's face was now a storm cloud of rage. She pushed her chair back and stormed off toward the bridal suite, leaving her plate half-finished. I followed her, my heart pounding in my chest.

Inside the suite, Adesuwa paced back and forth. Then she yanked off her veil. "I knew it! I knew he wasn't over her!"

"Adesuwa, it was a mistake," I said gently. "He's nervous, that's all."

She stopped and glared at me. "He called me *Tola* in front of everyone!"

I took a deep breath, trying to channel all my experience in wedding disasters. "You love him, right? And he loves you. Don't let this be the memory you take away from today."

A knock on the door interrupted my speech. It was Bode. He looked like a man ready to beg for forgiveness. "Can I come in?" he asked, sticking his head through the door.

I nodded. He stepped into the room, and I quietly slipped out.

Ten minutes later, they returned to the reception hand in hand. The DJ quickly played a love song to lighten the mood, and by the end of the night, Adesuwa was laughing and dancing again.

But when they cut the cake, she made sure to whisper something in Bode's ear. I couldn't hear what she said, but the look of fear on his face suggested he wouldn't be forgetting her name again anytime soon.

19. The After-Party Dress Disaster

The wedding was a masterpiece. From the grand floral arrangements to the live saxophonist serenading the couple, everything had gone exactly as planned. Now it was time for the after-party where the bride, Ireti, planned to change into a stunning sequined mini dress for a night of dancing.

"I'll be ready in ten minutes," Ireti said confidently as we entered the bridal suite. Her makeup was still flawless, and she was glowing with post-wedding excitement.

The dress lay on the bed, shimmering under the soft light. It was custom-made, flown in from Paris. Ireti was excited to slip it on, and when she did, disaster struck.

"It's too tight!" she said. I could hear the panic in her voice as she struggled to pull up the zipper.

I rushed over to help, but it was clear that the dress wasn't going to budge. "Did you try it on after your final fitting?" I asked her.

She groaned. "No! I didn't think I needed to. I haven't gained weight!"

I tried everything. I adjusted the fabric, loosened the seams, and even suggested that she wear it half-zipped and drape a shawl over it, but nothing worked. Ireti sat on the bed, close to tears. "What am I supposed to do now?"

I had to think of something fast.

"One of the bridesmaids," I said. "They're about your size. Let me see who's available."

I sprinted out of the suite and found the perfect candidate. Shola, a bridesmaid had planned to change into a simple yet elegant cocktail dress that could easily pass as a second bridal look. She didn't hesitate to lend it out, and within ten minutes, Ireti was standing in front of the mirror, spinning in her borrowed dress.

"It's not what I planned, but it works," she said, dabbing at her eyes. "Thank you, Shola."

"You look amazing," I assured her.

And she did. No one at the party guessed that her Parisian dress was stuck in a heap back in the suite. They only saw a radiant bride dancing the night away.

20. Surprise Afrobeats Superstar

I had just finished checking the dessert table when the lights dimmed, and a hush fell over the crowd. My heart skipped a beat. This wasn't part of the plan.

"What's happening?" I asked, whispering to the DJ, but he just smiled and nodded toward the entrance.

The doors swung open, and in walked none other than Kizz Daniel, flanked by security and wearing his signature shades. The guests erupted into cheers and scrambled to pull out their phones. The bride, Tope, was frozen in shock, her mouth hanging open as Kizz Daniel approached the stage.

"Is this real?" she whispered to the groom, who was grinning like a mischievous schoolboy.

"It's real," he said, pulling her into a hug. "My dad made it happen."

Apparently, the groom's father, an oil magnate with deep pockets, had secretly arranged for the Afrobeats superstar to perform at the reception as a surprise. I watched as Tope wiped tears from her eyes, overwhelmed by the gesture.

Kizz Daniel launched into his hit song *Cough (Odo)*, and the crowd went wild. Even the bride's elderly relatives were on their feet, dancing and taking tons of photos on their phones. The energy was electric, and I knew this would be the highlight of the night.

Later, as the couple shared a private moment backstage, Tope hugged me.

"Thank you for keeping everything together," she said.

I smiled. "You're welcome. But you should be thanking your new father-in-law."

"Oh, I will," she laughed. "Right after I dance my heart out."

ABOUT THE AUTHOR

Tolulope Popoola was born in Lagos, Nigeria and has lived most of her adult life in the UK. She started her career as an Accountant, but discovered blogging in 2006, which rekindled her love for writing and telling stories. She took a few writing classes and then co-wrote an online fiction series which was well received. In 2012 Tolulope quit her Accounting career to focus on writing and publishing. She has published a novel and six collections of flash fiction stories, earning her the nickname of Africa's Flash Fiction queen. She is also a writing coach and consultant for aspiring authors. When she is not writing, teaching or coaching, she can be found reading, eating and listening to Afrobeats.

Other Titles by Tolulope Popoola

Nothing Comes Close – A Novel
Fertile Imagination – Flash Fiction Stories
Looking for Something – Flash Fiction Stories

Lagos Flash Fiction Series

Memoirs of a Lagos Wedding Planner

Memoirs of a Lagos Taxi Driver

Memoirs of a Lagos Junior Banker

More Adventures of a Lagos Wedding Planner

Memoirs of a Serial Best Man

Memoirs of a Lagos Baker

Come and chat about the Lagos Flash Fiction Series on Facebook!

A NOTE FROM THE PUBLISHER

Thank you for buying this book. If you enjoyed reading it, you can help spread the word and support independent publishing by doing the following:

Review it. Leave a review online on the retailer or other sites. It's easy to rate and leave reviews on Goodreads and many other great book websites.

Recommend it. Suggest this book to your family, friends, to your book club or reader groups.

Talk about it. Mention it on TikTok, Instagram, Facebook, or Twitter. Create a conversation about it. You can talk about it on your blog or podcast. You can share excerpts and post the cover image on your social media handles.

We love good stories as much as you do! Thank you for helping us to spread the word.

Accomplish Press

www.accomplishpress.com